FRAYED ANGELS

by

Vicky Tunaley

TABLE OF CONTENTS

Acknowledgements

My sincerest thanks go first and foremost to Eirian Houpe, without whose encouragement and support I would not have continued to write.

Also, thanks to all those who helped through the editing process, giving me valuable feedback and opinion, even when I didn't agree!

These are, in alphabetical order: Lisa Bates, Dawn Brooks, Michael Govers, Peter Hill, Julie Noble and Heather Pierson.

Further thanks to author M P Wright, with whom I studied creative writing many moons ago, for his advice and guidance in the area of publishing my works.

Thank you to pagan author Anna Franklin for believing in me years ago and telling me, "just write".

I would like to thank Suzanne Bond for offering me advice in relation to the nursing environment Further thanks to Heather Pierson for her advice in connection with Trusts.

It has been a lifetime ambition of mine to write a novel – and I'm finally pleased to say, "I did it".

Dedicated to my children, from whom I learned

at least as much as I taught.

Danielle, Kane, Schuyler and Savannah

CHAPTER 1

"Fake friends are like shadows: always near you at your brightest moments, but nowhere to be seen at your darkest hour.
True friends are like stars, you don't always see them but they are always there."

— HABEEB AKANDE

"They're doing it again!" My little sister Amy tugged on the sleeve of my jacket annoyingly. Her interruptions were irritating and I pulled my arm sharply away, opened my eyes and yanked my ear buds out.

"What now? You're ruining my chill time."

"But that's when it happens Luna."

"What happened this time?" I looked around, everything looked pretty ordinary to me.

"It was the birds again. I don't know, they just started acting funny."

"Funny how?"

"It was like they were all looking at you."

"That's stupid. Why would birds be looking at me?"

"I dunno." Amy shrugged her little shoulders, warm brown eyes looking up into my icy blue ones. "I've told you before, they always do it when you're not looking."

"You're a pudding." I said, planting a kiss on top of her head and looking around the Town Hall Square where we were lounging about on the grass. There were plenty of pigeons around, pecking the ground for leftovers, and a few smaller birds too, but I couldn't notice anything strange about them. I intensified my stare, watching a pigeon that was pecking very close to the sign that asked people not to feed them. I thought it was bloody unfair that everyone considered them to be disease-riddled pests. Doves never got a bad rap, even though they were exactly the same type of bird.

I turned my attention back to Amy, who'd started digging into the ground with a piece of broken twig.

"We have to go home soon, mum will be back from work." The remains of our random picnic littered the grass next to us and I slowly started collecting the crumpled wrappers together, bits of melted chocolate sticking to my fingers as I did so. Today had been a special treat, a welcome diversion from over-thinking.

"I miss dad," Amy spoke with a tremble in her voice, looking across to the central fountain where a circle of winged lions spewed water into the surrounding font.

"Me too," I smiled down at her sadly. "But it's been six months now and it's going to start feeling better soon." I wished I believed that, but the truth was that it still felt like I had a brick lodged in my chest, where my heart used to be. Not a day went by that I didn't think about how he'd slipped away from us, first into agony and then into oblivion.

Until dad got cancer, life had seemed pretty normal and the word death was something that belonged to other people – it had nothing to do with my life at all. Its black shadow hadn't crossed my sunshine face or poured itself into my trusting, open heart.

Somewhere in the middle of all the drama Amy and I had been relegated to the side-lines, watching from a distance while the grown-ups ran around making all the decisions and sorting everything out. I'd been confused by this, thinking there was still time for goodbye, time to claw him back from the brink of non-existence. His body was still there wasn't it? His heart was still beating, his hands still warm. But it was only later, when I sat quietly at his bedside, that I realised that I'd left it too late. His mind, and the unique part of him that made him my dad, had already migrated to that twilight world where my words couldn't reach him.

Now my every thought was tinged with this peculiar shade of sadness and regret, feeling cheated out of those precious last moments. Not just that, but I'd realised that the rest of my life could never be the same again. It was this thought that made everything seem so pointless, including the crazy stories my sister came up with.

Amy clung to my arm as we walked towards the bins where I diligently threw our rubbish. Would a bad person be so well behaved? I thought not, but these feelings inside me fuelled a flurry of petty rebellions that had become more and more normal for me. I was a pigeon in a world full of doves, it seemed, and one with ruffled feathers, at that.

Amy clung tighter.

"You'll never leave me, will you?" The way she said that stabbed at me, prickling my conscience. I would leave her one day, of course I would, after all I didn't plan to stay in Leicester my whole life. I gave a sigh and crossed my fingers as I told another white lie.

"No pudding, you're stuck with me." Amy smiled up at me, still tightening her grip. She was so clingy now, terrified of being left all alone, and sometimes she suffocated me with the tendrils of her anxiety. I tried to understand how she felt but it was a real pain in the backside, because I was the one who'd been lumbered with all the babysitting duties while mum kept working through the holidays. That was just another reason to feel so miserable – didn't mum understand I had my own life to live too and that my friends didn't want a nine-year old baby tagging along all the time and, at almost sixteen, neither did I.

It was later that night after Amy had gone to bed that I managed to convince mum to let me go out for a bit.

"Home for nine Luna, I mean it. And make sure you keep your phone on, I can never get hold of you when I want you."

"For God's sake mum, stop nagging. Isn't it enough that I'm your unpaid childminder and housekeeper, without going on all the time?"

"You want clothes and food, don't you?" Mum retaliated as she always did, "there's only one wage now and we all have to make sacrifices."

"Whatever," I'd replied, pushing past her and out the back door. I didn't look back, knowing that if I did, I'd see her face pulled into a frown that would sit on my shoulder, clicking with disapproval as I walked.

I made my way down the street and past the post box that stood like a lone sentinel on the corner. There were no houses on this side, only very tall dark fencing that hid the local cricket ground from the prying eyes of passers-by. My friend Tara lived about half way down the hill in an average looking semi with a slightly overgrown privet hedge at the front. She was already waiting outside, looking up the street at me as I approached.

"Hey," Tara screwed her eyes up as she gave me the once over. "Is that a new top?"

"Nope. I dug it out from the bottom of the ironing pile. It's been festering there for months."

"Fucking Goth, when you gonna stop wearing black?"

"Maybe when you stop asking me the same old dumb questions. You know black's my thing... besides, it's how I feel."

"If you say so, but I reckon it's time you stopped looking so fucking miserable all the time."

"Easy for you to say, you're a fucking bubblehead," We'd somehow fallen into the habit of hurling a verbal volley of insults at each other and although it used to be fun, now it seemed to erode our friendship. I sometimes wondered whether we were even real friends anymore or whether we just hung out together because it was the convenient thing to do.

"Three weeks till we go back to school and I've decided that this year I'm going to do IT." Tara started talking about her favourite subject, in particular about which guys she fancied and who she would lose her virginity to. I'd heard it all a hundred times before. 'Troy this, and Troy that,' as if he was the be all and end all of everything. Well, maybe he was... but she didn't have to go on about him all the time. As far as legendary fifteen-year olds go, Troy was as close as you could get. Great at football, lead singer in an amateur band, popular, gorgeous as F-U-C-K and everyone wanted a little piece of him. If I was honest with myself, I admired him as much as anyone but I knew he'd never look at me in a million years. I was the weird one, the one that nobody in their right mind would ever want to date even though I knew I looked reasonably okay underneath the layers of make-up that I piled on. It was easier to hide my real self in this way, standing out from the crowd for different reasons. One thing I'd learned is that most people just do everything they can to blend in with everybody else, because that feels safe and makes them feel like part of the group. I'd stood against that and had gone out on a limb to be different, simply because I felt different on the inside and I thought life had treated me differently too – in fact, more unkindly than anyone else.

As she rambled on, I found myself drifting away, tuning out her conversation and focusing more on my internal world. My brain felt like it was ticking.

"Are you even listening to me?" Tara shook my shoulder and I jumped, "fucking hell, don't do that, you freaked me out."

"You dizzy bitch, don't you ever listen to a single thing I say?"

"What?"

"I was saying how weird it was, all those birds on the telephone wire, they looked like little statues a minute ago. Could have sworn none of them were moving."

"You're the dizzy bitch," I said, feeling somewhat

troubled. Twice in one day something odd had happened around birds. Was it a coincidence that weird things were happening around me and seemed to be occurring more and more frequently? Maybe it was a sign from my dad. Would he have come back as a bird to give me a message? I somehow thought not. He wasn't really chaffinch material.

"Do you ever wonder what it's all for?" I suddenly felt compelled to voice what was on my mind.

"What what's all for?" Tara looked at me with a blank expression on her face.

"What's the point of being alive?" I wached Tara's face drop. I knew she hated it when I became too serious.

"The point of being alive is to get together with someone like Troy, have great sex and make babies of course."

"But then what? There must be more?"

"Nope. I reckon that's it. Think about your dad, he met your mum, had kids and then died. All the rest of it is just commercial bullshit."

"God, that's so fucking depressing."

"Yeah, well that's how it feels, hanging around with you."

"If you say so."

"Yeah I do. You know your problem, you need to move on with your life."

"What do you mean, 'move on'?"

"Well, it's been ages. I thought by now you'd get back to normal."

"I am normal."

"Fuck off! You're not one bit normal. You don't even act like yourself anymore – and it's not just me who thinks that, everyone says so. You used to be fun, now you don't join in conversations and half the time you're not even listening."

"You don't understand... I just can't okay? I don't feel like

15

it."

"Yeah, well, that's my point. When your dad first died, everyone felt sorry for you, but now... well, it's kind of boring, you know?"

This was a conversation I'd been expecting. I'd felt its presence in each unspoken word, the things that had no voice, left hanging in the air between us. I wore my sadness like a darkness around me, unable to shake it off, and those people I counted as my friends found it more and more uncomfortable to be with me.

"You know we're friends, right?" Tara said and I shrugged, not really feeling the vibe of friendship between us at that moment.

"And I didn't want to be the one to tell you this but... well, next weekend Cam is having a party..."

"So?"

"So... well, she kind of... she asked me not to tell you about it. She doesn't want you there."

And that was it. The moment when even the people I had considered to be my friends were closing ranks against me, pushing me out.

I nodded, "That's fine. I don't want to go to Cam's fucking party anyway."

The conversation ended abruptly, with neither of us knowing quite what to say next. As we continued to walk down the street, Tara offered me a cigarette, something she wouldn't normally do.

"No, I don't want one, thanks." I hated the smell of it, even though Tara still thought it was cool to smoke. To me, it was death in a stick. It reminded me of dad's cancer too, and that was what I was trying so hard not to think about. It was ironic, I thought, that she was the one giving me lectures about life.

It was ten thirty before I got home. All the downstairs lights were still on and when I opened the door mum rushed at me, her face tight and pale.

"What time do you call this? I told you nine o'clock. When are you going to start doing as you're told?"

"I forgot the time," I said, not wanting to be bothered with another one of her sermons.

"I tried to call you a dozen times. Do you know what you're doing to me?" There was a hint of hysteria in her voice and although part of me knew I shouldn't feel how I did about my mum I just couldn't help it. I knew she was suffering too, that it was her husband who had died, not just my dad, but instead of dad's death bringing us closer, it seemed to push us apart. I hated being around her these days and, worst of all, the more alienated I felt out there, the more I took my feelings out on mum, the one person who had some understanding about what I was going through.

"Well as soon as I can, I'm leaving home, then you won't need to worry about me at all." I shouted and stormed off into my bedroom, leaving her standing at the bottom of the stairs, hands on hips, and anything she might have wanted to say in reply withering on her lips.

CHAPTER 2

"Love thy neighbour, but don't pull down your hedge."

- BENJAMIN FRANKLIN

I t was Saturday morning and Mrs Clarke, the woman from number 48, was sipping tea with my mum.

"She's quite adorable, isn't she? Oh, what a little love, and look at that face." As I listened to her stupid comments I couldn't help but feel annoyed. I hated the way she talked but my curiosity was roused and I couldn't resist the urge to glance up quickly. I already knew that she wouldn't be referring to me, because whenever we met she usually made some snidey remark about my heavy use of black eyeliner and hair dye. What's more, I was pretty sure nobody in their right mind would ever have called me adorable in a zillion years.

As it was, my mum was showing photographs of the new puppy again – the puppy that we were supposed to be collecting in five days' time.

"Are you getting excited, Luna dear?" Mrs Clarke looked over her glasses at me, fixing me with a sharp green-eyed stare that always made me feel uncomfortable.

I shrugged, "it's just a dog."

"You could show a bit more gratitude to your mum," she scolded as I put my head down and continued to play with my phone.

"Dumb ass" was the word that sprung to mind, although I locked it down inside.

I don't know why she thought she had the right to have a go at me in my own house when she was just the visitor. Of course, I was excited about the dog, who wouldn't be? I knew it would probably eat my clothes, chew my shoes, pee and crap everywhere and generally be a big nuisance, but being so fluffy and cute, none of that would matter, of course.

I'd fallen over myself in happiness at the kennels when we were introduced to the puppies and actually, for a short time, I'd even forgotten to be miserable.

The little bundle had looked shy and alone at the back of the pen and my heart had opened up to it.

"Hello, little fella," I'd whispered, coaxing it to me with my fingers. They called it the runt, but it didn't matter to me, that was the one I wanted, a beautiful smooth haired Golden Retriever – a good family pet, they said.

"My, you have got a knack with animals," the seller had said, as I gave the little puppy a gentle rub around the back of his ears.

"He's never so much as took one step towards anyone else before." My mum gave a weak smile and I knew she was thinking that was all a load of baloney sales pitch.

"Are you sure you want that one?" Mum had asked three times, as she checked out the way it wobbled over to me as if one of its back legs wasn't quite working properly. Sensing a potential no-sale, the seller had upped his efforts.

"I'll make a deal, if you take that one, I'll give you fifty quid discount right now, how's that?" It was an offer too good to refuse and mum made the deal there and then.

My mood had quickly changed back to miserable when we were part way home and I'd remembered to stop smiling. They didn't need to know how happy having a dog of my own would make me... after all, what was the point of being a Goth if I didn't do my best to look miserable all the time?

My mind came back to the present and I became aware of a sudden awkwardness in the room which had descended like an oppressive cloud as mum hurriedly changed the subject. I knew she'd recently been trying to avoid criticising me and would probably have asked Mrs Clarke to be gentle with me too, not that she'd be one to listen. Mum's efforts had fluctuated between falling over herself backwards trying to make things alright and then being absolutely horrible, angry and out of control. It was all pointless. Didn't she know that nothing would make things right ever again?

I couldn't stand being in the house any longer, half listening to their conversation and half engaged with what was happening on Facebook.

"I'm going out mum."

"Make sure you're back in time for dinner. We're having spaghetti bolognaise, it won't keep."

I rolled my eyes and did the non-committal grunt thing that teenagers are apparently so good at. Amy was playing with her dolls in the corner. She didn't even look up as I left the room – probably a good thing because it meant I didn't have to take her with me again. We'd really done enough bonding lately and I needed some space from all of them.

I slipped quietly out of the room, hating the way I was behaving but not seeming to have any control over it.

As I closed the door behind me I could hear Mrs Clarke's voice, "really Helen, you've got the patience of a saint with that girl. If she was mine, I'd have given her a good hiding well before now."

"I can hear you!" I shouted through the thin wooden veneer that shielded me from their scowling faces, before heading out and slamming the front door behind me.

What Tara had said about me was true, I never used to be so difficult and unhappy. It wasn't all about dad either, because on top of that, my bloody hormones had kicked in. That's what my form teacher, Mrs Jefferson, had said anyway. She'd sat me down for a chat after class one day, no doubt feeling sorry for the reject kid with the dysfunctional home and bad attitude.

"You're at that age when your hormones are causing lots of

changes inside, so it's hardly surprising you're feeling so rebellious." Blaming the hormones did make me feel a bit better, after all hormones didn't single anyone out, did they? They were a normal part of every teenager's life, not like death.

I know Mrs Jefferson was trying to be kind and after her chat I felt absolved from some of the responsibility of my actions... it didn't last long, and it didn't stop her from giving me detention for setting fire to the waste paper bin in my history lesson last term either, or for painting graffiti tags on the wall behind the bike sheds. I guess her talk didn't quite have the desired effect on me.

I continued walking towards Tara's house, thinking about the state of our friendship as I went. I realised I hadn't been big on effort lately and I begrudgingly thought that maybe I could work at getting some of my old mojo back. I remembered how things were before dad died, the fun we used to have back then and I missed the person I used to be. These thoughts were going through my mind as I stood on her doorstep and rang the bell. I could show Tara and all the others that I didn't have to be so miserable all the time. Even in the midst of my misery I knew there was another part of me too, that old part that still needed to go on living. And it was that part of me that finally admitted that it was damned hard work being so depressed all the time.

Standing there on the precipice of change I felt an enormous surge of new hope but, as fate would have it, it was only a short-lived moment. There was no answer at the door and as I looked around I realised no car in the drive either, which probably meant her stupidly happy parents had dragged her off for another expensive shopping trip or something. My hope deflated like a popped balloon right there on the doorstep.

I texted a message, with the slim hope that she might be somewhere local.

"Hey, save me from boredom, where are you?

I kept checking my phone but there was no reply. Tara and her family were probably at a Designer Village somewhere which was one of the things they did regularly, like a full-on daytrip. She was lucky enough to be a spoiled brat of a child. Her wardrobes heaved with chavvy designer wear, half of which she never even wore. It made me thankful that my style was so different to hers. I didn't want to be in line for her cast-off clothing.

Thinking what I could do to kill some time I decided not to return home just yet. I hated that Mrs Clarke would probably still be there, wearing her unspoken disapproval of me like a great big overcoat. I glanced at the time. It wouldn't be dark for ages, which meant I could go for a walk along the towpath near the canal. Just a little walk, some fresh air to clear the stress inside my head and give me chance to think some more.

I unzipped my jacket, feeling a little too warm, and carried on walking towards the main road, loving the feeling of summer on my skin. It wasn't a long walk, maybe only fifteen minutes before I reached the leafy lane near the canal. The feeling of walking away from all the irritations of my day and into nature lifted my spirits. Every few feet the roadside trees formed a canopy of green, dappling the ground with shade, but it was the creamy petals of a magnolia tree in the garden of one of the houses that caught my attention the most. I'd noticed it seemed to bloom all year round and I had no idea how. It was super weird but it made me think that when I was older and had a house of my own, I would have a magnolia tree too and a garden full of wild flowers, butterflies and ladybirds to laze about in.

As I walked by, the net curtain twitched a little and I felt the slightly curious unease of being watched. It seemed to me that whoever lived in that house must stand at the window all day, silently watching the comings and goings of everyone passing by. I scowled at the window, picked up my pace and returned my attention to the lane in front of me. I wasn't going to let a nosey parker spook me. "Fucking paedo, get a life." I swore under my breath.

It only took a few minutes to reach the packhorse bridge with its ancient moss-covered stonework and then down and round onto the canal path itself. Careful not to stumble on the uneven slope, I slowed my pace and settled my mind as I walked past the sprawling mass of hedgerow plants and wild-flowers that grew at the side of the path. Often there were ducks and swans that splashed around or glided towards me, hoping for food, and sometimes barges, either moored up at the banks or navigating through the waterways.

It seemed like a different world here, a quieter, slower world, far away from the hustle and bustle that was going on in the streets and houses just a short distance away.

I swiped at the gnats that were fizzing around my head as I walked and smelled the aroma of freshly cut grass which must have been from the sports fields beyond. This was my very special place where I felt I could let go of my problems and be myself for a while. The adults in my life thought they had the answers for everything, saying that teenagers my age didn't have anything to feel stressed about at all, that we should count our blessings because we didn't have to work for a liv-ing, pay bills or bring up our own bratty teenagers. The way I saw it though, they were the ones who screwed everything up, including the planet.

My thoughts drifted back to last weekend when I'd delib-erately stayed up late waiting for mum to come home from a night out because, despite her doing my head in, I needed to know that she was alright. Clearly she wasn't. She'd come home drunk, crashing into the hallway with ladders down her tights and make-up smeared around her mouth, like she'd been snogging the face off someone. It had been a shock to see her in such a state but as I connected a few random things together, I'd started to build a picture in my mind. Twice the week before she'd asked me to keep an eye on Amy while she 'popped out' as she called it, and then I'd noticed a few empty wine bottles in the recycling bin too. I'd felt suspicious that she might be drinking too much, but I never saw her do it and that made it tricky.

There was something else troubling me too, and that was the thought that she might be out there looking for a replacement dad for us. That really upset me. He couldn't be replaced, our dad. He had been just perfect.

I'm sure what I thought of her at that precise moment was etched all over my face – disgust, contempt, embarrassment, mixed with that 'vomit-into-my-own-mouth' kind of feeling - but she was the one doing the vomiting, lurching desperately towards the downstairs toilet to hack up her insides.

"You'll understand when you're older Lu", she'd said as she re-emerged at last, wiping her mouth with the back of her hand.

"I'll never understand," I'd replied, feeling totally miserable, standing there like a shadow in the darkness. I'd turned away then, before she could see that I was crying. My one wish was that my dad could have been there, because I felt sure he'd

have known what to do. But that was futile, stupid wishful thinking on my part, because he would never be there, ever again.

I turned my attention back to the path and tried half-heartedly to avoid the muddy bits, but not bothering overmuch. It was only mud after all and, let's face it, washing dirty clothes was mum's job. That would give her something more important to do than going out getting drunk with stupid people.

The birds were twittering to themselves and the weather

was warm with a bit of a breeze blowing around my face and I started to feel a small sense of contentment in my own company. It was just a short distance to the bench up from the Lock House, where I planned to sit down and think about the imminent arrival of Alfie the puppy, and whether the book I'd ordered on dog training would arrive before he did.

This place had been here since forever, such a familiar landmark that it was almost invisible to me. Many years ago, the Lock Keeper had lived in this cottage, but it was well before my time, back in the days when canals had been used as trade routes. We even did a study about it in our social studies lesson as a place of local interest and I'd found myself absorbed in the rich tales about the area, totally against my better judgement and sense of rebellion. Nowadays, it was just a little tea room that opened for a few hours a day.

I can't understand exactly what happened next, because it seemed to me as if it was straight out of the pages of a science fiction book. My mind had wandered... drifted, as it often did, much to the annoyance of my teachers during classes, and when I brought my attention back to the moment, I was standing very close to the bench where I'd planned to sit. Everything around me felt kind of different and I had an overwhelming urge to look around me to see what was making me feel so weird. I'd walked these canal paths hundreds of times in the past but I'd never experienced anything quite like this before.

The first sign of something not being quite right was that the birds had stopped singing. They'd been chirping merrily away only moments before, but now there was no sound at all, no breeze and no rustle of leaves in the trees. Even the canal was flat and motionless, like a long ribbon of dirty grey glass etched into the banks of the surrounding countryside. I couldn't even hear the sound of the water rushing through the lock, which I'd passed only moments before. It was almost as if I was the only thing that could move against a backdrop of total inertia.

Following this, there was a sudden drop in temperature, to the point where I felt myself hunch over a little bit, my thin jacket not really protecting me from the coldness that began to penetrate through my clothing. I'd been too warm only seconds ago, but now I started to shiver. Just last week I had been reading a book that had described 'a cold icicle of fear' and although this book had been about a zombie apocalypse, that was exactly how it felt to me now, as if ice was running from the base of my skull all the way down through my spine.

I shivered and hurried quickly back to the front door of the tea rooms. The lights were off and the door was locked and bolted. I knocked loudly anyway, just in case, scraping my knuckles against the hard wood of the door. "Hello, is anyone there? Hello?" Nothing stirred, no movement, no sound, except for my own heartbeat which I could feel thudding against my rib cage as if it was trying to break free of my body.

A tide of rising panic welled up inside me as I looked around. I couldn't see anybody… that should have felt like a good thing, right? I mean, I couldn't see a weirdo waiting to hack me to death or anyone crouching in the bushes with a dirty raincoat on exhibiting his floppy bits. I cursed my own mind for putting such ideas into my head at a time like this. I wished my dad was with me, he'd have known what to do. He had been strong and brave and so full of life, and he had a certain wisdom too, a way of seeing things that could put everything into perspective. It was easy to imagine what he'd have said to me if he'd been with me.

"Lu, we always have a choice about what we think about. Bad thoughts lead to bad feelings, it's as simple as that. Your mind doesn't know the difference between what's real and what's imagination, so if you're going to imagine anything, make sure it's something nice, love. Make your thoughts good and you'll never go far wrong."

I hadn't been taking his advice for quite a long time now,

but faced with this feeling of fear that had suddenly over-whelmed me, I tried to follow his teachings now.

I would just think good thoughts... I wasn't too far away from the bridge and just over the bridge was the little lane that meandered into the village and then people, houses, the pub... safety. If I could have just walked back towards that safety maybe things would have turned out differently but as it was, I found myself walking further away from the Lock House and the village and towards a patch of tow path that gave me a panoramic view of the sky above me. And that's when it happened - the sky shifted. I know that doesn't make sense but truly it's the only way I could explain it. The sky moved just like someone had shook it or slid it – something strange, something unexplainable.

It was one of those defining moments when I knew nothing would ever be the same again. Some things change our per-spective, they challenge everything that we think of as real, true and solid. This was one of those moments. I categoric-ally knew the sky could not move – not in the way that I had just witnessed. Sure, the earth could move, earthquakes and tremors were real, and clouds could move, but the sky? No, the sky could not move. I knew it to the very core of me. A thousand thoughts cascaded through my brain but not a single one of them made sense.

The first thing that crossed my mind was whether I was having some kind of brain failure, like an hallucination or per-haps I had developed a tumour that had affected my vision, or maybe I was just going plain old stir-crazy? There were more global worries too... what if it was the end of the world? Or some super dominant world power had been released to deci-mate humanity? I shook my head, trying to stop the train of negativity that was crashing through my mind.

"Think good thoughts, only good thoughts. It's not hap-pening, you're just imagining things again..." The conversation I was having with myself was occurring at the same time as a steely tipped large shape emerged, hovering in the sky directly above me.

I felt the blood drain from my face, and my knees buckled beneath me. Had the bench not been right there to the side of me I know I would have just fallen onto the path, regardless of the dirty patches on the ground, bruises or broken bones.

The shape manifested slowly, appearing from nowhere as it materialised into solid form, exposing its huge presence in the sky. It wasn't like it had just flown there, I hadn't even seen it moving. More like it had maybe been there all the time but somehow cloaked and invisible to me, waiting to reveal itself at just the right moment.

The craft was oval with two sharp, pointy-looking protrusions at each end of the ellipse, and it was shining really brightly, like the sea does when the sunlight hits the water. Later I would describe it as a shimmering, hazy glow but at that precise moment, coherent thoughts failed me. I knew I was going to faint about ten seconds before I actually did. A far away, detachment descended over me and my vision started to fade as I blacked out.

CHAPTER 3

"You can't plan for the future, because some guy's going to land in a spaceship with three heads and a big beak and take over everything."

- PAUL KANTNER

When I came around my head felt groggy and heavy, as if I'd just been woken up from a very deep or drugged sleep. I became aware that I was in a darkened room and that I wasn't alone. There were hushed whispers all around me that seemed to come from a distance away and although I thought the voices sounded English, I couldn't make out what they were saying. Closer by, I could hear a steady bleeping noise which reminded me of the electrical equipment in hospitals, except I knew I wasn't in a hospital. I was lying on my back on a hard platform and felt as if I couldn't move, even though no physical straps bound me. The intense cold I had felt at the side of the canal had diminished and I was now comfortably warm. I kept my eyes shut for a few moments as I tried to gauge what was going on around me, my ears pricking to distinguish any words I might hear.

"Are you sure we've got the right girl?" A doubtful sounding voice carried from the other side of the room.

"She's nothing like we expected."

"Yes, this is the one."

"But she's... she's so... common looking."

"It's a style some humans project in order to hide emotional turmoil. It can also be seen as a statement to reject normal society."

"Thank you for clarifying, well she's certainly not what we expected."

"Styles have changed in the last hundred years Jeqon. If you had paid any attention or at least graced us with your presence more often, you would know this."

"I have no interest..." the voice trailed off and I was left to wonder what was happening around me, until the commentary resumed again.

"Her bone structure is very sound, facial features well balanced and proportional... her hair has been stained black by unnatural products... she has a healthy and strong constitution, although slightly underweight." They were talking about me as if I was some kind of commodity and I prickled with a sense of indignity, although hardly in a position to answer back.

As I lay there trying to take it all in I felt the presence of someone very close to me and my eyes jolted open, immediately shocked to find myself looking directly into another pair of very blue eyes, almost the same colour as my own, with a hint of turquoise or aquamarine... just like mine. He was leaning in very close and I felt vulnerable and exposed under his watchful stare. His skin emitted a dimly golden glow that flowed around him like an aura, and for a moment I felt mesmerised by the strangeness of him. Paralysed with fear, my breathing rapid and shallow, I thought I might experience a heart attack at any moment.

"Blue eyes," he commented, relaying the information back to the others in the room before abruptly stepping away from me.

Another voice from further away began to speak, but I was almost oblivious, unable to turn my head to see where it was coming from. What should I do? I couldn't think straight, nothing in life could have prepared me for an encounter like this. My head and heart were racing and, for a moment, it felt like I couldn't take a breath. A more urgent sense of fear grabbed me, fuelled by the most dreadful of thoughts that I could no longer shut out.

"We need to sedate her, she's going into shock."

"I will handle this," the blue-eyed man placed a large hand on my shoulder. I automatically flinched, screwing my eyes tightly closed and willing myself to be still. A few seconds passed where I could feel the warmth of his hand pulsing through my clothing and then, from beneath the fear, I started to feel other, more private emotions, and realised that I was becoming increasingly receptive to a chemistry that was flowing between us.

I called him a man, but he wasn't, because even from my prone position he appeared as a giant towering over me. In only a matter of moments my breathing started to settle and I was surprised by a ripple of calmness that spread down my spine and into the pit of my belly. Slowly I opened my eyes, scrutinising him as he had done me earlier. He was so close that I could even see the pores on his skin... pores or scales? I couldn't be sure, as the reflection of light upon his skin seemed to change the surface of it. His hair was mid-length, a strange white-gold colour, and he was dressed in a cloak of dark blue feathers, reminding me of olden day kings from fairy stories. I couldn't put an age to him, certainly not young but almost timeless looking, with an aura of ancient knowledge surrounding him, allowing me to believe that I could just slip into enlightenment merely by being so close to him. I recognised that he was beautiful, not in a human way, but possessed of an alien beauty that was beyond my imagination, and even though I sensed he was so much older than me, at that moment nothing mattered.

I felt my mind calming, as I drifted down into a quiet place inside myself. I didn't understand what strange technique he was using on me, but his hand flowed with an energy that circulated in my body and I felt an electrifying connection to him.

From fear, to calm, to a slow sensual arousal, I pulsed with emotions that I previously had little understanding or experience of. This strange being was still looking at me with that intense gaze, and it made me feel flushed with an embarrassing warmth.

"Stupid Luna," I said to myself, cringing at the way I was feeling. I had no idea where I was, taken against my will, held as a hostage or something worse, and there was no telling whether I might be murdered, probed, or some other disgusting or horrifying thing. Why then was his gaze and the close proximity of his body the only thoughts surfacing in the pool of my mind? No one had ever looked at me like that before, not ever. It was intense and I could feel myself beginning to blush all the way up to the roots of my hair. By comparison to this being, the image of Troy from school faded into a meaningless blur.

During those moments of connection with him my fear diminished and I felt a safe sense of contentment, as if I belonged in this place, and an almost religious feeling too, like I could connect to a higher part of myself that I had never known existed. I wasn't religious, never had been, but since dad's death I'd started to become increasingly interested in ghosts and the afterlife, wanting to believe that he could still be with me in some way. But aliens? I'd never even contemplated they were more than just make believe.

"Your feelings, they are quite normal." The blue-eyed being spoke directly to me for the first time, and I was surprised to find myself answering him without any thought of the consequences.

"Oh my God, I'm on a fucking space ship or something and you're talking about what's normal." The figure didn't acknowledge what I said but continued to stare into my eyes, almost as if he could read my very soul.

"I am Isayel. You are my guest here and, as such, you will be treated with respect and have everything you need. In a little while you will be moved to an Adaptation Pod and, once there, your emotions will start to settle."

"You can't keep me here, I need to go home," I said, my

bottom lip beginning to tremble as the full weight of my situation dawned on me, even through the veil of calm that he had drawn around me.

I watched the pulse at the base of his throat pound like a small hammer as he scrutinised me further but quickly averted my gaze when I realised he was watching me watching him. I felt out of my depths and out of control.

"My mum will be worried about me, I need to go home now."

"That is not possible."

"But my dinner will be ruined... and... and... you must have made a mistake... I heard you talking... I'm nobody... you can't need me for anything..."

My ramble was cut short when Isayel placed his finger over my mouth in a shushing motion.

"None of this is of importance right now."

The touch of his finger against my mouth felt too intimate and I burned with the sudden urge to taste his skin with my tongue. I resisted the temptation – I was not *that* girl, and as soon as he withdrew his finger I started to beg for release.

"Please let me go. I promise I won't tell anyone... don't hurt me... I haven't done anything wrong... you've got the wrong girl..."

I don't know what they did to me but it was a while later that I regained consciousness somewhere else, which I guessed to be the Adaptation Pod they were talking about earlier. The walls were lit with iridescent colours from floor to ceiling, cubes of colour that flashed with some unknown purpose, bathing the room in a soft rainbow light. In any other circumstance I would have found it incredibly pretty.

I raised myself to sitting and held my hands out in front of me, examining the fronts and backs of them. The odd lighting cast its shadows, changing the colour of my skin and spellbinding me for a moment as I watched the patterns of light play upon their surface. I didn't think I'd been hurt in any way but stood slowly, just in case, stretching myself out before walking around the room. It was comfortable in size but the only visible furniture was the bed that I'd been resting on, nothing more. In the middle was just a large space, which seemed wasted. I circled the oval, for that's all it was really, very similar in shape to the exterior of the ship.

Now that the terror had subsided I felt restless, feeling like a prisoner, a specimen of humanity enclosed in a room that to all intents and purposes was no different to a prison cell. It felt like a long time since anyone had checked on me and I didn't know what to do with myself. There was nothing in the room that could hold my attention and I wasn't used to just doing nothing.

I'd watched films about alien abductions, but they were Hollywood spectaculars, full of special effects and not based on reality at all. The heroes were all special in some way, gorgeous or handsome with gritty nerves and daring person-alities, whereas I was just the very ordinary Luna May Mason, who day-dreamed half her life away and had been a total screwed-up headace since her dad had become ill and died.

I couldn't think of any reason why a bunch of aliens would particularly pick me to abduct over anyone else on the planet. I was scrawny, hardly even possessing a pair of tits yet, and my dirty blonde hair was now a scruffy jet black, to match my clothes. A late developer, my mum said, but my friend Tara said it was because I was abnormal and retarded. What a bitch.

I sat down again, hugging my knees close to me, trying to think about what I should be doing, but instead my head was filled with images of my dad, because he'd been the real super-hero in my life and had always guided and supported me whenever I'd needed help. I wondered what he would have done if he'd been here. He would stay calm, I could almost guarantee it, and maybe he would have had something in his pocket, like a special screwdriver or piece of equipment which he could use to prise open the doors and escape out into the night. I imagined him doing just that.

He would tell me to think smart too, to be one step ahead of the enemy. But I didn't even know if they were enemies. I didn't think they'd hurt me so far, unless they'd erased memories from my mind, that is. I shuddered. What if they'd transplanted me and I was no longer me? Perhaps they'd cloned me… I'd seen films about that too. Maybe they were going to suck my brains out. I didn't like the turn of my thoughts… my imagination was my downfall, everyone said so.

It wasn't long before I started thinking about Amy too and wondered whether she was okay. Every morning the first thing she'd do when she woke up was to come to my bedroom and climb into bed next to me for a few minutes of snuggle time. I could picture her in my mind, wearing her baggy flannel pyjamas with pictures of bouncy sheep or little cats on them and the way she'd curl up next to me, sleepily telling me about her dreams, which were always so weirdly absurd I was convinced she made them up just to impress me. I'd groan and tell her to stop talking and go back to sleep so that we could enjoy another few minutes of dozing before the alarm went off. Funny how those gentle, tender moments are disregarded at the time, but how valuable they become when they're no longer possible. What would Amy do in the morning, seeing a cold, empty bed with no big sister to cuddle up to? My insides churned with the thought of that, because I knew that since dad died I was the one she looked up to, the one who made her feel safe and without me by her side, her little life would crumple into bits and she'd blow away in the wind.

Then there was mum. She was probably going mad already, wondering why I was home late but just expecting that I was being my regular rebellious self. I wondered how long it would be before she realised I wasn't coming back and called the police but, even if she did that, there was little chance that they'd find me in the sky on a spaceship. After all, they couldn't even find missing people still on the planet.

I knew mum wouldn't cope, she'd hardly been managing before, because I'd pushed and pushed at the boundaries of her sanity, the belligerent, uncooperative teenager who didn't give a damn. How would she manage to console Amy after this?

As my thoughts spiralled out of control I became vaguely aware of a keening noise in the room, not yet conscious of the fact that it was myself who was making the sound, bundled up into a huddle of skin and bone, pining for a life that I'd never appreciated until it'd been snatched away from me. To my own ears I sounded like a wild animal who'd just discovered the slaughtered remains of its family.

It was some time during this onslaught of twisted emotion that a soft music began to play in the background. It was an unearthly melody that seeped into the spaces inside me, lacing me back up again, forcing a bending of my will so that, despite myself, I started to feel a little better. I wanted the pain, wanted to remember my family and what they meant to me, but as the harmonies wove their dreamy magic over me, I stopped thinking about the people I loved and had left back at home. A vague acceptance formed itself around me as my mind wandered in a different direction, led like a bull from the nose, to new pastures.

"Deep breath", I said to myself, and took a nice long intake of air, allowing it to work its way through my body. A few minutes later, I really started to feel more like my old self and as my thoughts settled down I suddenly remembered my phone. Feeling like an idiot because I hadn't thought about it before, I quickly delved into the pocket of my jacket and was relieved to feel its familiar contours in the palm of my hand.

I brought it into view and examined the screen – it still had battery life, that in itself was a minor miracle. Maybe that meant I hadn't been away too long, although I had no real idea of the time. I didn't even consider phoning my mum first, as her and Amy's memories settled somewhere outside my conscious mind. Instead I keyed in the shortcut to Tara's number, holding my breath in anticipation of being able to contact someone. Maybe I could be rescued.

My heart was in my mouth as I waited for the connection, and I could actually feel my hand shaking. What would I say?

"Hi, it's only me, aliens are holding me captive on their spaceship over the canal. Can you bring a helicopter and a rope ladder please?" I cringed at the thought. There was no way she would believe me, she'd think I'd gone nuts. Beyond all belief, the phone connected and I listened to the ring tone on the other end of the line, once… twice… three times… answer the phone, answer the phone… I was screaming inside with frustration… nerves strung out like piano wires. I wouldn't get this chance again - my battery would die and it's not like I could just ask a friendly alien to plug it in for me. On the fourth ring the line went dead. Not in any normal way, it just stopped ringing and there was silence on the line. Those familiar tears were biting at the back of my eyes again as I looked at the screen. It was still bright… it should have worked.

"Damn it!" I swore and kicked out at the walls, lashing out. Why did everything always have to go wrong?

"Let me out you fucking bastards" I screamed at the top of my voice and started banging my fists against the walls. I wasn't going to adapt in their stupid adaptation pods. I would fight it every step of the way.

CHAPTER 4

"Angels are like diamonds. They can't be made, you have to find them. Each one is unique."

-    JACLYN SMITH

I ntroductions are not necessary, but as a form of courtesy I will acknowledge my presence in these writings. I am Isayel. Some will refer to me as a Watcher, one of the Grigori, or even as an Irin Lord. I have been called many things over many thousands of years, during which I have watched over countless of your species.

Your race is cruel and not unlike animals, you hunt and kill for pleasure, but some of you may also exhibit a dignity and grace that shows a more elevated spiritual nature.

We know that life on earth will ultimately come to an end and, despite our past endeavours, the evil and chaos that penetrates into the heart of man will eventually cause calamity and destruction. The sins of humanity show us that the knowledge we generously shared with humankind in the past was abused in countless unprecedented ways.

We mostly keep our distance now and have strict, self-enforced codes about involvement with humans. There are, however, certain circumstances that require our intervention.

By way of explanation, it is necessary to speak of experiences from the far distant past when our two species lay together in love and subsequently gave birth to a terrifying race of giants, known as The Nephilim. These monstrous beings caused destruction and carnage wherever they went and it fell upon us to hunt them down, destroying our own offspring, until they became extinct from the face of the earth.

The unfolding of these events stimulated a great deal of interest in hybrid technology and instigated a genesis project that was created for the purpose of ensuring the evolution of mankind over a thousand years. Our aim was to manufacture a different type of species by utilising advanced and detailed research and experimentation. Our trials were eventually successful and a new race of beings now exist, known simply as Zarns.

Zarns are superior to humans in every way, a peace loving, gentle people who show higher cerebral function and greater emotional capacity. They are the next step in the evolutionary chain and are a vital component to ensuring human DNA survives.

We became aware during our biological research that there are certain human females who emit a particular energy frequency that is a necessary prerequisite for our programme. Humans cannot detect it as the spectrum is outside their capabilities, but we see it as a harmonic light and sound vibration, sometimes sensed by other animals and birds.

When one of these female children are born we step in and intervene in their development because these are the ones who will grow to maturity and eventually become the mothers of this new race. Our mission is to mine these children, as one would a rare jewel. They are precious beyond all and as such their safety and survival is of paramount importance to us.

Luna was the first child born in seventy-seven years with the frequency that we require for our project and we have therefore monitored her progress since the time of her birth. Her specific DNA and energy matrix will provide much needed input into the genetic pool, helping to sustain this hybrid species that currently inhabit a planet far outside the earth's solar system.

Luna will not yet be aware of this great honour that is to be bestowed upon her and the expectation is that the news may not be entirely welcome.

The girl had looked at me with alarm and fear on that first day, reminiscent of a wild animal caught in a trap. I could empathise with her position, knowing that dislocation can be a traumatic experience and takes a great deal of adjustment in order for the emotions to settle. I could also feel her frequency running through me, which I may describe as the echoed response of a tuning fork that vibrates in unison with its struck counterpart. I knew Luna would not yet understand what that strong connection was, and it is likely she will mistake it for physical attraction. But I am an Irin Lord and I will hold myself beyond the temptations of human flesh, at least for the present.

CHAPTER 5

"A gentleman holds my hand.
A man pulls my hair.
A soulmate will do both."

— ALESSANDRA TORRE

I found out that kicking walls is a pretty energetic occupation and that there's only so much time you can spend doing it before either stubbing your toe or collapsing into a heap of spent frustration. I'd gotten to the stage where I'd given up on being heard or listened to and was now sitting numbly back on the bed. On the bright side, the effect Isayel had had on me was becoming less vivid in my mind, to the point where I thought I might even have imagined it. He hadn't spoken to me or seen me since I'd been put in the pod and I was partly pleased – I didn't like the thought of anyone having that kind of control over me. It was bad enough that my mother thought she could rule my life, without a strange guy coming along and pushing all my buttons.

At certain times of the day the lights in the wall would flicker, transforming into something like a huge cinema screen. News from earth was broadcast, followed by shoddy entertainment shows from the 1970's, much to my dismay. I expected my kidnappers, which is how I now thought of them, would know that I hated these dated programmes. I was quite certain mind reading was amongst their many skills and had they taken the trouble to listen to what my mind was telling them they would have swapped for something more modern or at least given me a remote so I could pick my own Netflix channels. Bastards.

Before dad got ill, me, Amy and dad regularly used to watch nature programmes together. I loved learning about the amazing abilities of the animals and how the natural world worked. We'd share family bags of crisps, chocolate and coke, and I'd feel cosy, warm and safe. Mum would be off doing her thing, whatever that was, probably enjoying the break from us kids. So, these moments became our special times, mine, Amy's and dad's. My shoulders dropped slightly as a big sigh wrenched itself from my body. Those days had gone and thinking about them only made me feel overwhelmed with sadness. Back then I hadn't been hostile or angry. Before dad died I could hold a decent conversation with people and be as polite as anything. I hadn't needed to swear and be vicious because life had been absolutely okay. My mind drifted back to mum and Amy frequently, pouring over the things we used to do together and the urge to try to escape tugged at my mind. I felt incompetent and stupid because I had no idea how I could even try to get away. Was sitting around waiting good enough? I thought maybe it wasn't but didn't know what else I could do, and each time I became too immersed in my grief or fear that music would trickle into the room and work its way into the inner recesses of my mind. I wasn't sure if I was being brainwashed by the melodies but I began to welcome the gentle balm of forgetfulness that flowed through me at those times.

I could only imagine the extent of technology on board this craft, it seemed so much more advanced than on earth. At some point I realised I needed the bathroom, and a feeling of panic started to surface because there wasn't so much as even a bucket to piss in, but no sooner had the thought entered my mind than a cubicle materialised in the middle of the room, just like a real bathroom. I now knew what all that empty space was for. It shimmered into place and then became a solid three-dimensional room, which I could just step into. It was amazing, reminding me of Dr Who's Tardis, without the naff retro music. I could bathe, brush my teeth, get changed and relieve myself, all in privacy. There was a toilet, sink and huge bath, made from an oyster pink material that was soft and silky to touch. It was a slice of heaven and I managed to linger in that bath tub for hours on end, luxuriating in the strange coloured oils that shimmered on top of the water. I can't even say it was water like on earth, it had more of a slippery quality to it, if such a thing is possible. Slippery water... maybe it was the oils, or just the colours, but when I immersed myself into the depths of the tub it looked like I was stepping into a rainbow. And when I came out my skin radiated with a soft aura too.

Whilst bathing, my clothes and possessions had been removed, including my phone. I hadn't heard anyone enter the room and wasn't sure how it was done but in place of my clothes I was left with a selection of dresses, all of similar style but in different colours. They were shapeless, ugly things and it looked like someone had just sewed up a rectangle and cut out a space for my arms and head to poke through. I hated them but the alternative was to go naked and, hell, that wasn't going to happen.

Days went by and my life settled into this very solitary routine. Nobody came to see me but the entertainment on the screens had become a little more interesting. Interspersed with what I considered to be normal television, there were videos of strange places, planets that weren't earth and lots of nebulae that wafted around in the darkest regions of space. I didn't know it then, but these weren't videos at all, but were actually real-life footage of our journey through the universe. Call me dumb, but I couldn't even tell the spaceship was moving, as I hadn't felt any turbulence or motion of any kind. Had I known, I would probably have totally freaked out because, in my head, we were still parked just a little way from the canal. And that felt safe to me.

I had no idea what day of the week it was, and time had stopped existing forever ago, so I was caught off guard when the door to my chamber opened and Isayel loomed in the entranceway. I'd gotten so used to being on my own that his appearance made me jump. Immediately, that feeling of connection was there again and I felt the urge to run over and throw my arms around his neck.

"Oh fuck, not again," was the first thought in my mind. It was enough to subdue me a little and I cocked my head to the side, waiting for him to speak. He didn't disappoint me.

"Good day Luna, I hope you feel a little more settled than at our last meeting?"

"Settled? How can I be settled when I've just been fucking kidnapped and then dumped here to rot?"

"A necessary step for your own benefit as part of your re-alignment."

"My what??"

"Today we start your realignment training."

"Realignment training? You've got to be fucking kidding. What is this, alien school for dumb kids or something?"

"Enough!" His voice held such authority that I held my tongue, just for a moment. I wasn't used to people being so direct.

"Your manner is uncouth, you swear and curse and behave in a way that is totally inappropriate. At present you are not a fit specimen but by the end of your training your attitude will have improved sufficiently for purpose. This training is not optional."

He sounded severe and serious. His blue eyes bore down into mine and I had to lift my head a little higher just to see him properly, such was his height. I guessed he was over 7ft, maybe even 8ft or more. It seemed to me that, however tall he was, his presence filled so much more space than even his physical form.

"This is so not funny anymore. I want to go home right now, you've no right to keep me here as a prisoner. I don't think you realise, I'm just a fucking kid. I'm fifteen, okay? I know I try to act older but really, I only do it so people take me more seriously and I'm damned well not a fucking specimen, as you call it."

"Luna, I think we both know that you are no longer a child. You will soon be sixteen, a landmark age on earth. Everyone you meet on board this vessel will be taking you very seriously because, whether you believe it or not, your existence is very important to us."

"I don't get it. What are you planning to do with me?"

"Right now, that is not your concern, but when the time comes, you will understand a great deal more and even be pleased with your involvement. This is why you need to be trained."

"You make me sound like a fucking dog."

"There are some similarities."

I was shocked then, that he could say such a thing. I looked into his face and saw a smirk of humour. He was deliberately provoking me.

"I'm no dog and I don't need training." I thought of Alfie. He was probably already at home now, settling in without even knowing I existed. I wondered if the police were looking for me and whether there was any possibility I could run away to safety.

"Your petulance will not save you. Follow me."

The concealed doorway opened silently and I knew that if I walked through it, I would be able to question Isayel some more about my reasons for being here, and also learn more about Isayel himself. Not only that, I would be able to explore more of the ship and leave this soulless confinement for a while.

I watched Isayel's retreating back as he went through the doorway. I think he'd gone about three or four steps down the corridor before he realised that I wasn't following him. My insides were bursting with a suppressed giggle, which seemed so out of place but it felt just too good to defy him. Sure, he'd like me to just follow him around and do everything he asked but I wasn't going to. I had decided that I would make it inconvenient and annoying every step of the way. Even if I had to spite myself in order to do so.

When Isayel appeared in the doorway moments later, he was no longer smiling.

"Whether you like it or not, you will start your training today, even if I have to carry you over to the teaching area myself."

"Yeah right." I answered. There was no way I wanted him to get any closer to me. As it was, I was already fighting my emotions around him and I couldn't chance a closer proximity. He didn't seem to be having any such difficulties with his own emotions though and I watched as he looked me up and down like I was some kind of insect to be squashed.

"At present, you are a spoiled brattish girl child. You think you are funny but you are not. You think you are original, but you are not. Greater people than you have tried to defy orders and have come up against the full force of my anger. In time you will come to realise that it is pointless to try to resist a process that is ultimately for your own good. What's more, I expect to be obeyed. Do I make myself clear?"

"Are you on fucking drugs or something? If not, you should be... your medieval way of doing things isn't how things work on my planet. I'm not some kind of slave girl who you can just pick up and expect to do your bidding. If you're so clever you would know this."

"I know all I need to know about planet Earth. You creatures are destroying it and seem completely ignorant to the complexity of its systems. The greed and ruthlessness of mankind has caused famine, wars and untold suffering. And, may I remind you, that we are not on your planet now. This craft is named The Omicron and whilst aboard you will conduct yourself according to the rules of this vessel."

He left me speechless. His tone was arrogant and unforgiving and I was only half listening because he'd called me a creature. Is that what he really thought about humans? About me?

I had no time to argue because in an instant he swept me into a strong grasp and carried me through the doors and away. He strode purposefully through the passageways whilst I kicked against him, living up to the 'creature' label.

"I don't want to be trained, I want to go home. Put me down. You're a fucking ass-hole."

He was silent to my pleas, and carried me as if I weighed nothing at all. I felt the muscles of his arms pressing around my waist and imagined what it would be like to be held properly by him, like a lover. I knew I'd made a terrible first impression, that he thought I was nothing, an inferior kind of being. I wanted to rebel but I also wanted to prove him wrong.

Begrudgingly, I had to admit that he was right about the world that I inhabited. I loved nature and the beauty of my planet and at school we were taught all about deforestation, fracking and other scary processes, but school kids didn't have much clout when it came to changing the world.

I'd stopped kicking part way towards our destination, becoming limp in the arms of my captor, like a rag doll against his side. Isayel relaxed his grip on me and then slowly allowed me to slide to my feet, steadying me and supporting me against his body as he did so. My heart was racing and I felt the colour rising up my neck and flushing my cheeks. Surreptitiously I threw him a quick glance to see if my closeness was having the same effect on him, but his face was inscrutable. His mouth had tightened into a thin line and he was looking straight ahead. If anything, he looked kind of angry with me. I wished I knew what to do with my feelings for him as I felt betrayed by my own longings – after all, if it wasn't for him, I doubted I would have been taken prisoner in the first place. I felt sure he'd been instrumental in my capture and it seemed I was his sole responsibility.

It was only a few moments until we arrived at a room that flickered with the soft orange glow of candlelight and the aromatic scent of crushed herbs, which were smouldering in a large, centrally placed, brazier. It was worlds apart from the typical classroom set-up I'd been expecting. An older looking lady came forward to greet me, holding out both hands and smiling broadly. Immediately I felt as if she was someone I could trust, and she looked human, which felt absolutely fucking amazing.

"Luna, I'm so pleased to meet you. I can't tell you how much I've looked forward to today." Blimey, she made me feel like royalty. I took her hands, which felt soft and papery in mine. They were fragile and belied an age I hadn't noticed so drastically in her face. There again, she had one of those profiles that was timeless, perfect bone structure, high cheek bones and her hair swept up in a silvery bun. She looked every bit like a classical ballet teacher, but instead of leotard and ballet shoes she was wearing a flowing purple robe tied with a thick sash around her waist and with deep trailing sleeves.

"My name is Elisia and we will be spending quite a bit of time together. I smiled as Elisia gestured for me to sit on one of the deep, soft cushions that were scattered around the floor. Isayel gave a discreet nod to Elisia and then turned to me.

"Behave," he said, before exiting and leaving me to the first part of my training.

CHAPTER 6

"The teacher who is indeed wise does not bid you to enter the house of his wisdom but rather leads you to the threshold of your mind."

- KHALIL GIBRAN

In my wildest dreams I could not have imagined a place like this existed on board The Omicron. It evoked all the feelings of being outside in the evening time, even though that was physically impossible.

The ceiling was transparent, and the indigo darkness beyond merged with the coils of fragrant smoke that drifted upwards from the smouldering herbs. Countless stars glistened like distant diamonds on a bed of velvet. It was a breath-taking vision of loveliness and, at that moment, I became small, a miniscule part of such a wondrous and perfect visage that everything I thought I was, and all the concerns in my head faded into insignificance.

From my sitting position I hugged my knees close to my chest and looked around the room. Tree-like roots burgeoned through the floor and there were tangled vines that clung to the walls in certain sections, creeping and growing just like ivy or clematis might at home. Twisted branches grew upwards through delicate leaves and foliage, and everything I saw suggested we were outside in nature. Being here felt absolutely amazing, like I was in a theme park setting or something, and I couldn't help but notice the way my whole body had suddenly started to relax. I'm sure I looked as amazed as I felt, maybe drooling at the mouth or something, because when I looked back to Elisia she was smiling broadly.

"You can get up and walk about if you want to." She gestured a full sweep of her arm, turning gracefully to encompass the whole room. "Explore with all your senses, not just your eyes. That way you get a much more complete knowing."

"Knowing? What do I need to know?"

"Well, take this plant, for instance." Elisia wandered over

to a shrubby growth that seemed to be rooted close to the left-hand wall.

"If I just look at it, I can say that it's green. The leaves are slightly heart shaped and appear bristly. I can add more visual details, such as pigmentation and shade, variegation, size, overall appearance and so on, but that's where my knowing will end. However, if I touch a leaf, I can feel how soft it is. It feels velvety beneath my fingertips, but there's more. When I touched it, it quivered. I now know that it's aware of me – in other words, this plant is a sentient being."

"But it's a plant." I was mystified. Maybe plants on other planets were different because back on earth I was pretty sure no plant responded like that.

"Yes, it is a plant, but they still have feelings, personalities, if you will. And, although you may not know it, they are very tuned into the way you are feeling. They can pick up emotional discharges, such as anger, joy, love or fear. What's more, they can even acknowledge and react. It's our job to learn to interpret what they can tell us, just like we might learn a foreign language. And, trust me, after you learn to communicate with plant life, nothing will ever feel the same again."

Throughout the afternoon Elisia went on to teach me what I can only describe as 'plant etiquette', aka, how to behave when a plant is present and what to definitely not think about or do. For example, she told me that if I thought hateful, nasty thoughts around a plant it would show fear and it seemed so far-fetched that I couldn't help but wonder whether she was winding me up.

I felt self-conscious and clumsy around Elisia too, she was so calm, graceful and peaceful, and it made me shamefully aware of my own lack of manners. Wanting to please, I made a determined effort not to swear in front of her.

AS the afternoon wore on, I became more and more absorbed in the teachings. This was nothing like science lessons at school, where we only studied stuff like photosynthesis and stamens. My mind drifted back to my science teacher, fondly named Bilbo on account of his big feet. A couple of terms ago he had foolishly brought a Venus Fly Trap into class for us to study. One of the lads in my class, Ethan Knight, had tried to force feed it a McDonalds burger and a chip. The whole class was in an uproar, it had been so funny. Bilbo didn't think so though. That got the lot of us detention every Tuesday lunch-time for a month. I couldn't help but smile at the thought. We were a disrespectful, bad bunch of kids.

"Over here" Elisia's voice snapped me from my reverie and diverted my mind from the unfortunate Venus Fly Trap. On Elisia's instruction I placed my hand on a leaf, waiting expect-antly to feel the quiver.

"Nothing's happening," I commented.

"You're wrong. A lot is happening. You just cannot per-ceive it yet."

"Did it quiver?"

"Yes, greatly so. There are many things that this plant is communicating right now. To start with, it's uncertain of you, somewhat afraid too."

"A good judge of character then, eh?" I laughed, a little ner-vously. I could hardly believe the things Elisia was telling me, but she seemed so nice and I felt more and more certain she was human. It shouldn't have mattered, but in my eyes that made her more trustworthy than anyone else aboard this ship.

It crossed my mind that she might be crazy but decided I liked her anyway and wouldn't hold it against her. Perhaps she was that way because they'd tortured her or something. If she was going to be one of those weirdos though, like a hippy or something, I'd be better off not letting her influence me too much. Dad always said he never felt comfortable around that hippy vibe, whatever that meant, and I believed he was a pretty good judge of character.

"Why can't I feel it?"

"No one would expect you too yet. This is part of your training. At the moment your energy is low. You haven't used your extra senses in a proper way yet."

"I didn't know I had any extra senses. Do you mean like a sixth sense?"

"You can call it that if you want to. We call it the Pranamios sense. Prana is breath. You need to breathe to survive but you're not just breathing in oxygen. There are numerous elements to air composition, and on earth the most common part of air is not oxygen but nitrogen. Nitrogen for humans is not necessary and it doesn't actually react with anything in the body. You breathe it in and then breathe it out. That's not the whole story, though, because we also inhale molecules of carbon dioxide, methane, helium, many different gases, together with spores from plants and water, dust, microbes... minute particles that we never even consider. We are breathing these random particles all the time, exchanging parts of ourselves with parts of the universe. These tiny elements are recycled over and over again, which means that through the breath you are connected with a vast proportion of your universe. You breathe the same air now as your ancient ancestors did thousands of years ago." I listened intently. Nobody had ever explained simple breathing like that to me before and she made it sound amazing.

"The training you are commencing will enable you to know more than you ever thought possible. You will see connections where before there were none. You, my dear, will become gifted in extraordinary ways. You will know beyond any doubt that you are part of this great cosmic web of life."

She sounded convincing and her scientific theories combined with the mysterious in a way that made her argument fantastically conceivable to my immature brain. I felt a little more comfortable with the concepts she was sharing with me. Who was I to stand in the way of becoming extraordinary? Imagine what I could do if I developed these special powers. I imagined Troy back at school. Maybe if I breathed in some of his molecules and he breathed in some of mine I could get him to ask me out on a date. The possibilities could be endless.

"What a wonderful imagination you have". Elisia commented, and I became fully aware at that moment that she could read my mind too. Maybe she wasn't human after all. Her eyes twinkled with unexpressed humour, no doubt highly amused at my childish thoughts.

"Your imagination will come in very handy later, but for now, we need to use our minds for another purpose".

Elisia went on to instruct me in the art of meditation and mindfulness. I had to still my mind and find the centre of myself, where peace resided. It was a lot harder than those simple instructions would suggest and throughout the rest of the time that day she had to keep drawing my wandering mind back to my breath, the mighty Pranamic vehicle through which all knowledge was possible.

By the time Isayel returned to take me back to my quarters I felt exhausted in body and mind. I never realised a practice like meditation could be so tiring. I looked up as he entered the room, so handsome and yet so unlike anyone I'd ever encountered before. I wondered why I liked him as much as I did.

"Wait by the door Luna," he instructed and I slowly did as he told me. Now didn't seem like a good time to argue.

"Same time tomorrow," Elisia called out, before turning her attention to Isayel.

I watched intently as they whispered together, their heads

almost touching, both smiling and looking truly animated in each other's company. He must have said something funny because she laughed, a rich, throaty laugh.

I swallowed back the lump in my throat. I felt like I was eavesdropping, witnessing an intimate private moment between the pair of them. The earthy environment they were ensconced in seemed to pulse with life and I wondered if the plants were having any thoughts about their behaviour.

In a touching moment, Isayel brought his hand up to the side of Elisia's face and gently stroked her temple with his thumb. As soon as he did so, I felt an immense feeling of jealousy run through me. It was such a stupid, unwarranted feeling and I hated it. My previously positive thoughts about Elisia suddenly shifted, as I looked at her through the cruel lens of jealousy that tainted my perception. I found myself thinking that she looked so much older than him and I couldn't believe that he would find her attractive. I wondered whether they were in a relationship and, if so, how she managed to keep him interested in her. Nasty, cruel thoughts pierced my mind and challenged my rational brain. Elisia didn't deserve my censure because she'd been a truly lovely and inspiring teacher, dedicating her time to help me learn so many new and wonderful things.

I realised there was so much I didn't know about the people on board this ship. Sighing deeply, I tried to blank my mind. The last thing I wanted was for either of them to know the turn of my thoughts right now. Worst of all, I wanted Isayel to look at me like that and felt a sudden craving for affection. Maybe I just missed having a male influence in my life and wanted someone to take notice of me, but whatever the reason for my sudden feelings, I just wasn't prepared for them.

When he leaned in to kiss her gently on the lips I had to turn away. My heart was being squeezed by these traitorous emotions and I couldn't get my head around the way I felt betrayed by him. Fucking hell, how insanely stupid was that?

I turned away to face the door but it stayed resolutely closed. I obviously wasn't to be trusted and I didn't even know how these mechanisms operated anyway. There were no keys or locks, no handles or protuberances, and when we had entered earlier it just seemed to open on our approach without any particular action from Isayel. Maybe it was mind power.

"Door open" I said in my mind. It didn't. I tried again.

"Open door". Still nothing. "Fucking open and let me out of here, you stupid bastard retarded good-for-nothing piece of shit door." The door swiftly opened and I experienced a split second of triumphant shock until I realised that Isayel was standing next to me, looking at me with a puzzled expression on his face. I couldn't bear it and strode ahead of him in silence, stomping along the corridor, feeling stupid and ridiculously insignificant.

"Want to talk about it?" he ventured when we finally entered my room.

"No, I don't," I pouted, feeling petulant and unfriendly.

I sat down heavily on the bed and distracted myself from his presence by fumbling with the laces on my boots. Sodding hell, they'd tangled into a mess of knots and it seemed that the more my clumsy fingers tried to tug them apart, the worse a mess I made.

Isayel gently moved my hands away. "Here, let me." I sat obediently while he moved with dexterity and grace, allowing the laces to unfurl in his hands. Not content with his success, he went on to slowly loosen each lace and helped my leg and foot become free. I loved my knee-length leather boots and even though they suited my jeans better than the dresses I'd been given to wear, I didn't feel like swapping them for the clompy shoes they'd provided.

As Isayel removed each boot, his hand smoothed down the sides of my calves, sending little rockets of desire deep inside me. Leisurely he cupped one of my feet in his hands. His touch was gentle and light and the rockets intensified.

"You're tense," he said. No kidding, Sherlock. Every muscle in my body felt coiled, waiting for this moment between us to unfold into something extra special. His hands rubbed my feet, his thumbs kneading into the arches and along the soles. It felt nicely pleasant and... oh... I didn't want to think about where this might lead. His head was bent into the task and he seemed oblivious to the desire that was mounting inside me, like a little time bomb waiting to explode. I wanted him with a physical urge that felt more powerful than anything I'd ever felt before. And here I was, a virgin, just a few weeks shy of my sixteenth birthday. I'd always said I was going to save myself until I loved someone like Elizabeth Barrett Browning described in her famous poem – I was so different to Tara in that respect, who couldn't wait to get laid. Could I love an alien being, I wondered, and thought that yes, maybe I could.

"Your feet are very important Luna, you must take care of them while you are young. There are exercises that you can do to stretch and strengthen your toes and plantar fascia."

I ignored his commonsense statement, that was the last thing I was thinking about. Surely he had more on his mind than the condition of my feet?

"Do you love her?" I asked suddenly, saying the words out loud before I was even aware that I was thinking them.

"Who?"

"Elisia of course. I saw the way you two looked together. Do you love her?"

"Yes" he said. "I love her very much, she is a beautiful soul." My heart crashed back from its romantic foolishness.

"Oh" was all I could think of saying, before I drew my feet quickly up underneath me and away from his hands, literally tugging them away from his gentle grasp.

"Please go now." I wanted, no... needed... to cry really badly. I felt the lump rise in my throat and a colour flush my cheeks as I cringed with embarrassment about the nature of my thoughts. How could I have imagined that he liked me in that way? I was so immature and stupid, stupid, stupid.

"I will explain, if it will make you feel better." His gorgeous eyes searched my face, concern etched into his beautiful face.

"I don't need you to explain anything to me. I'm not your keeper, am I? It's nothing to do with me."

"Yes, but I feel your confusion, your sadness. My explanation might help take your pain away, might help you to understand your feelings more."

"No. I don't want to hear anything you have to say. Please leave me alone. I want to be by myself." Part of me wanted him to persist, to insist on staying with me despite my telling him to leave. I did want to hear an explanation that would make everything feel better, but, conceding to my wishes, he silently retreated from the room and I was left with more unanswered questions and a heavy heart.

CHAPTER 7

"You took me to Heaven and put me through Hell. And I'd go back and do it all again."

— KATE MCGAHAN

I do not suffer fools. I have no time for nonsense and for the games that humans play. They are full of conflicting emotions, just like the ones I see in Luna. She is infuriating, so immature in countless ways, and yet she is trying valiantly to understand her evolving womanhood and pubescent feelings.

I knew she desired me but I would not lead her into an inappropriate romance. When we mate, as we undoubtedly will, it will not be for love, but for creation. The human female has a sensuality that is not present amongst the angelic realms, there is a sweetness about them and a smell that is like a unique signature. We know to our cost that human emotion can be crippling to us. She could not know the effect she had on me, how much I wanted to know her better. I would not have her know.

When with humans it is sometimes useful to scan their thoughts. It can be a strategic opportunity to progress in negotiations and understanding. However, it can also be critically inappropriate and damaging. The range of human emotion swells like an orchestrated piece of music, throbbing with angst, violence, hatred, joy and passion... a limitless outpouring of feelings that can quickly overcome the mind of the observer. It is useful and necessary that we can turn off these abilities. I had already decided I would not plunder Luna's mind. I knew how important those secret thoughts would be for her. It was not in my interest to know more than I already did.

What of my secret thoughts? To know me is to understand my burdens. I have existed since before time itself. I have no age but will continue into infinity unless God in his wisdom decides to alleviate those like me from the yoke of our suffering. That, I believe, is not likely. We are outcasts, eternally being punished for our sins. But even in this sorry state we are more powerful and more accomplished than the whole of humanity put together.

When we first came to earth there was confusion. Mankind worshipped us and we enjoyed that adulation. We were curious too. These humans were different from all the other species that roamed the earth. We found delight in the way they could be taught new things. Over time, we encouraged their language and speech capabilities, enabling them to become sophisticated communicators. Some learned woodcraft or building. Others became scribes, artists or musicians. It seemed that the humans could flourish when given the opportunity to do so. Foolishly, we became inflated with our own worth and self-importance.

The women, in particular, craved us. We were physically strong, superior to their males. When darkness fell the women of the tribes of men would seek us out. They lay with us, curled into our chests, finding comfort in our warmth and our compassion. We loved unconditionally as the asexual beings that we were, but now other feelings began to stir. This was new to us and we didn't fully understand.

It is important to realise that in Heaven there is purity. We were born fully formed and not through the act of procreation. The process of mating was but a system that God designed in order to automate the succession of the species. We did not have the sexual organs that are prerequisite in the act of mating. Of course, we could give and receive certain pleasures, and we often did so, but we could not experience the full act of copulation.

Over time, this aggrieved us greatly. We watched from the shadows as men and women performed their sex acts and we hungered for this ability for ourselves. We felt lust, a burning longing that we could not fulfil.

In desperation we created a sacred rite, a magical act of self-transformation that could be performed, and which would make us whole. For the three nights while the moon was in the fullness of her glory, we hid in mountainous caverns, away from the eyes of men. We charged ourselves with power from the elements themselves – air, fire, water and earth. The building blocks of creation, together with the fifth element of spirit. This was archaic, dark magic, which cast us further from our Lord. Even knowing this, we continued with our quest.

The physical transformation was excruciatingly painful. Our sexual organs were nestled inside our bodies, fully complete but sealed within, and this rite was, in effect, a spiritual surgery, where our organs were exposed to great trauma. Our stomachs became distended, swollen and distressed. At the junction between our lower limbs, in order for our sex to drop into place, we were ripped apart by a spiritual fire so profound that no words can ever describe the harrowing pain of that transformation.

Our screams echoed throughout the worlds, and we broke our backs in the agony of this self-inflicted metamorphosis. We writhed in the blood that flowed from us, tearing at our own flesh and begging for the wretchedness to end. We longed for release, for death, because the torment was unprecedented and unrelenting.

Long into the nights we howled in our misery, blind to ourselves and each other. God had truly turned away from us, for we had become abominations in his eyes. Only on the third day, when dawn broke above the tops of the mountains, did our bodies repair and we became like men.

Was it worth it? Yes, my friend. It was worth every torturous moment of agony for now we had the ability to truly know the physical love of a woman.

It had always been my pleasure to raise a woman up, to allow her to go beyond her dreams and her expectations so that she could flourish and reach her potential. In my life I have had involvement with countless women, but there are only a handful that have truly touched my soul and for whom I would yearn for through time. I already knew that Luna would be one of those.

Unlacing her boots earlier was an accident, meant purely as an act of kindness. She had sat on the bed, half reclined, looking at me with those startling eyes of hers. She was mad with me, I knew it. In truth, her anger excited me. I liked to push her just a little bit, to see what she was capable of emotionally.

I remembered the weight of her foot in my hands, the delicate bones, the soft arch of her sole, so sensory, aching to be touched. I had no choice but to stroke that skin that still glowed from her earlier bathing. Her beauty shone all around her and yet she seemed oblivious to it. She was like a light in a dark room, radiating out and penetrating everything she touched. I was basking in that glow and our frequencies had just begun to harmonise when she'd asked that question.

The intensity of her jealousy had caught me unawares. It had not been my intention to hurt her feelings at all and yet her perceived ownership of me sent a thrill through me. Luna wanted me to be hers. She did not know how close she was to getting her wish, nor what she would need to sacrifice in order to be mine.

CHAPTER 8

"Someday they would discover that the stars were not sacred, but made from the same material as their bodies. They would learn it was the stars that created their worlds, that worlds created their minds, that minds created tools, and tools could create stars."

-    JAKE VANDER ARK

T he day started like any other day. I awoke at an unknown time, assuming it was morning, but because the lighting was artificially generated I really had no idea. I had queried this. Why was space so black, when it should have been filled with the light of a thousand stars and suns?

"That's a very complicated question," Elisia had answered. "On Earth you would be directed to study Olber's Paradox to find theories that might give you an answer."

"But we're not on Earth. Surely you know more than Earth people do?"

"Of course, but there are still unanswerable questions that may seem simple in the asking, but in truth are only known in the Mind of God."

"I don't believe in God." The blasphemous words tumbled out of my mouth without thought, but were heartfelt nonetheless. I had never believed in God or any other higher power. It seemed a ridiculous concept to me. I was surprised to see the emotion expressed on Elisia's face. Was she angry with me, or disappointed? Judging from the look that quickly flitted across her features, those words should have lacerated my mouth like barbed razors as I spoke.

"Why, child, you live in darkness if you don't believe in God." She sat me down in the centre of the room, where I had first sat so many months ago. Her hand laced with mine and I felt her warmth and gentleness penetrating through my skin, allowing a glow of relaxation to pour though me. "I'm not sure if it's my place to instruct you further, but as one of your teachers, it's perhaps appropriate for me to let you know more about the inhabitants of this ship." I was curious, this was definitely something I would like to have learned more about. I'd noticed that Isayel had kept his distance, allowing me to escort myself to and from the training room in recent weeks. I think he was purposefully avoiding me, only seeing me at times when others were present. I could hardly blame him, I still cringed when I thought of the way I'd acted during our last moments together.

I'd become aware of several of the ship's inhabitants, although most kept their distance from me, as if I was contaminated or off-limits. I didn't understand this lack of socialisation, but thought maybe they'd been ordered to keep away.

There were also those onboard who looked similar to Isayel in height and size, men like giants, robed in vivid feathered cloaks, and I was curious about them. They were different, exuding an air of power that wasn't there in the ones who looked more human. I'd tried smiling and looking friendly, and whilst some of the human-looking ones gave a quick smile back, the giants looked through me as if I was invisible or somehow below their radar. It was disconcerting.

"Let me shed some light." Elisia took a deep breath.

"We come from a planet that is known as Zarnett-9. It is 199 AU from Earth. Each Astronomical Unit is 93 million miles, so you can imagine how far away that is."

I nodded, but could not comprehend the distance at all.

"Zarnett-9 is outside your Earth's solar system but in many ways is very similar to Earth. It has mountains and lakes, fields and deserts. The gravitational pull is slightly less, but in all other respects, Zarnett-9 is almost a replica for Earth. It was chosen specifically for this reason. It can support carbon life."

Carbon life. Is that what it all boiled down to? Was life just the sum of molecules and particles whizzing around in a state of constant flux? What about feelings, memories and histories?

What about me? What about my history and the millions of small, insignificant moments that I carried with me, not just inside my mind but within my heart too? I thought about the street where I grew up and the countless memories I had of my life there. I remembered watching the raindrops race down the window panes when stuck inside on bleak wintery days, and the outline of the chimney pots that had always made me think of Mary Poppins floating to the ground with her big umbrella. I missed the rain and all the countless things that I'd taken from granted around my hometown. Then there were the people I cared about, the relationships that meant something to me. My sweet Amy, memories of dad, mum, Tara, even Mrs Clarke from up the street with her annoying little habits. I missed everyone and everything more keenly now that I was away from everyone than I ever had when I was there. A million memories and thoughts flooded my mind, all of a place and time I might never see again.

What really terrified me was that those memories had started to seem less and less real to me. In the early days here, I kept imagining I would wake up and it would all be a silly dream that faded away when I rubbed the sleep from my eyes. But as each day went by, life here became more and more solid and it was my old life that began to feel like the dream. That was the scariest thing of all. I realised that I wasn't even thinking about my dad as much as I used to either.

During those first few weeks I'd begun to rely on Elisia as a true mother figure and she'd held me in her arms as I'd wept for my lost family. She'd stroked my hair and told me about her own family, so far away, and how she'd managed to adjust to life away from them. I was comforted to think she'd experienced similar feelings, even if it was a long time ago. She'd told me that I carried my family with me, in my heart, and in this way they would always be close to me. I hoped it was true.

Elisia's words penetrated my mind's wanderings. "Although Zarnett-9 has come to be thought of as our home, it's not Isayel's place of origin. I know you think of him as an alien, and in the true sense of the word that's what he is, but it's far more complex than that. Isayel, and the others like him, they're not aliens Luna... they're angels."

"What do you mean?" I couldn't comprehend what Elisia had just uttered. Ironically, I'd gotten used to thinking of him as an alien. It felt totally normal that he was different but an angel? That was one stop beyond where aliens left off. To start with, everyone knew that angels were fluffy, gentle beings with harps and halos, who spent their days balancing on clouds – none of which could ever describe Isayel. Also, as I didn't believe in God, this meant by default that I didn't believe in angels either.

"Isayel is an Angelic Being, created by the Will of God as one of his Holy Messengers."

"I'm sorry Elisia, but I can't believe in angels..." I defended my position, whilst internally questioning, what if there was the slimmest, remotest possible chance that what Elisia was saying was true, and if Isayel truly was an angel, it would definitely explain why he was avoiding me. He would have seen the wicked thoughts in my mind and the betrayal of my body when he'd stroked my feet. I was the worst sinner ever. The worst.

"Oh, rest assured, they are real enough." Elisia went on to describe the Great War and how the renegade angels fell to earth to begin a new life amongst mortals.

"Isayel was cast from the Fifth Heaven thousands of years ago, which is why those like him are sometimes referred to as Fallen Angels. We call them The Watchers, because throughout the history of humanity they have watched and, when necessary, they have intervened. They work mostly for the good but sometimes, just as with men, their passions dictate their purpose and they can become selfish and wicked."

"I thought angels were meant to be good all the time?"

"That is a heavenly rule, yes. But these angels disobeyed that rule. They no longer reside in heaven and can make their own rules now, just like men."

"I don't understand why that would be a big problem." I watched Elisia's face grow thoughtful as she considered my statement.

"How can I put this? When angels were created their sole purpose was to perform as instruments of love, peace and guidance and they followed these teachings for thousands of years. They were God's messengers, his mouthpiece if you will, and they could only do his bidding, without ever thinking for themselves. They were vessels of light but had no purpose beyond that which God demanded of them."

"That sounds awful. No wonder they weren't happy." My eyes had become big as saucers as I listened, for once not wandering off into a daydream.

"Yes, it could not have been entirely pleasant, but it all changed after God created mankind - people."

"Didn't the angels like people?"

"At first they were of no consequence to them, but God had also given mankind free will and this is something that the angels had not previously had any concept of. Angels were vastly superior to mankind in intellect and spirituality but they could not act for themselves. They saw how foolish the humans were, how they abused the gift of free will and carried feelings like hatred and anger in their hearts. It felt very wrong to the angels and some of their kind became jealous of humanity, wanting free will for themselves."

Elisia paused for breath, watching my reactions. "The angels petitioned God, but He dismissed them, reminding them that they were beings of Light and Spirit and that free will would never be theirs."

"Sounds mean," I said.

"The angels thought so too. It caused a great war, unlike any that had ever been seen. Two hundred million angels disobeyed the teachings of God, and of that number two hundred fell to earth, where they began to merge more completely with humans."

"What happened to the rest of them?"

"It is said they were entombed until Judgement Day, cast into eternal darkness."

"Wow.. seriously?"

"Yes, very seriously. Locked away for eternity for the sin of coveting free will. As for those that came to earth, they walked amongst your ancient ancestors and encouraged study and knowledge on a vast scale. They taught humanity writing, art, sorcery, astrology, warcraft - so many different skills. The greatest thinkers, inventors and teachers throughout time were blessed by the angels."

"That's crazy. So maybe if it wasn't for the angels we wouldn't know half the stuff we do now?" I was transfixed as Elisia recounted the angels' histories and felt that I could maybe understand Isayel a little better.

"That's right, without angels you would probably still be little more than monkeys walking around hammering coconut shells with clubs. They were the spark and the inspiration that allowed mankind to develop as he did."

Elisia's teachings were fascinating and I begged her to tell me some more but she insisted on a break, nimbly rising to her feet and making us a herbal concoction to drink. "Nettle, mint and red clover, all from earth. Full of minerals and very good for you."

I tasted the bitter brew and shuddered. "It's not like real tea though, is it?"

Elisia tutted at me and rolled her eyes, lightening the mood by chatting with me generally about what I used to do with my time on earth and what I liked best. Just talking to her made me feel calmer. She softened my rough edges and I'd almost stopped swearing altogether. Even my looks were changing as the black hair dye was growing out and the blonde started to show through, softening the contours of my face.

"Sofia will help you with that," Elisia had commented when I'd complained about how I looked like a stripy badger, "she's the artistic one." I hadn't met Sofia yet, but was looking forward to it.

"Tell me some more about the angels," I said at last, having drank as much of the nasty brew that I could.

"Well, let's see… we were talking about free will weren't we? Yes, well, once they had free will they realised it came with its own problems and they became immersed in both the agony and the ecstasy of it. Cast away from God's side, they felt abandoned and quickly fell into sin, lusting after the daughters of men and behaving wickedly. When an angel turns completely bad Luna, he is no longer deserving of the name 'angel'. Instead he becomes a demon."

I gasped sharply and felt my blood run cold at the thought of a demon… but they weren't real either, were they?

"Is Isayel a demon?" I was scared to know the answer, but had to ask the question.

There was a long pause and I waited expectantly as Elisia seemed to consider my words. Finally, she spoke.

"Isayel has been called a demon by some. Not recently, you understand. There were times in the past when he has made some seriously grave mistakes and errors of judgement, but I have known him for many, many years and I can tell you, hand on heart, that I have only ever seen him do good. He fights to atone for his past sins every day and he has spent hundreds of years refining the planet of Zarnett-9 so that it can be safely inhabited by the new race."

"What new race?" I was intrigued. Nobody had spoken about this to me before. Elisia looked uncomfortable.

"Child, your planet is in severe decline. We can see the future of your people... there will be suffering and death. Destruction will come and it will be sudden and fast. Just like the fall of the great dinosaurs and beasts of old, in a heartbeat humanity will be gone, wiped from the face of the earth as if they had never even existed."

I listened glumly. This was hardly good news, but it was the same bad tidings that I'd heard on the television and in the newspapers over and over again as I was growing up.

"The new race is a genesis project overseen by some of the angels. It's been designed to advance humanity."

"I don't understand what you mean."

Before Elisia could speak further on the subject the door opened and Isayel entered the room, his vivid cloak flowing around him as he strode in.

He nodded to Elisia by way of greeting and then advanced towards me.

"How are your studies going Luna?" I flushed, feeling the colour rising up through my face.

"They're going okay, thank you."

"And you're enjoying the subject matter?" He raised an eyebrow, almost as if he knew we'd been talking about him.

"It's... it's... er... it's very interesting."

"Good. Elisia tells me that you are an excellent student."

"Does she?" I looked across at Elisia who nodded and smiled in agreement. I'd never been called even a good student before, never mind an excellent one, and I stood there dumbly, without knowing how to respond.

"I'm pleased you're making progress Luna. I speak from my heart when I say that I want the very best for you."

"Can I ask you something?" I looked up at him and waited for his consent. "Have you known many human people yourself?"

"There has been a long history between humans and my people. In the beginning, the only involvement we had with humanity was as a duty, but later on this became a personal interest. Some formed relationships and attachments and since that time we have been gently guiding mankind, helping to influence the universal direction in which people have been evolving."

"That wasn't my question."

"I'm aware of that, but perhaps you need to consider that you asked the wrong question, not that I gave the wrong answer." He was infuriating. I scowled darkly at him as he gave one of his lazy smiles. He hadn't given a personal answer to my question at all.

"I bid my leave. Goodbye ladies," and with that he swept from the room as abruptly as he arrived.

"Maddening isn't he?" Elisia voiced what I'd been thinking.

"Does he do it on purpose?"

"Oh yes, for sure. He enjoys the sport of it."

"Maybe he is a demon then," I answered, feeling myself prickle. "How come no-one has ever seen an angel on earth?"

"Well, that's an interesting question. Isayel was talking about the guidance they gave to humans, which they gave for hundreds of years, but it was never enough. There were difficulties with mankind, betrayals and untold problems... so the angels simply decided to retreat from having any permanent physical form on the earth. That's why there are fewer and fewer sightings of them in modern history."

"But nobody really believes in angels do they?"

"In modern times, no. They are simply thought of as legends or mythical beings, like unicorns or mermaids. Some of the greatest artists who ever lived painted angels, using their vision to keep alive that which could no longer be seen, but they are now relegated to a dusty religious history and angels far prefer to be anonymous these days."

"Can you tell me some more about the new race?"

"I don't think Isayel would approve of me discussing this further with you."

"But why not? What harm can it do?"

"It's perhaps best if he speaks to you about it himself."

"Please Elisia, please tell me. I feel that I should know, after all I do live on The Omicron now. I'm part of all this, aren't I?"

Elisia looked at me doubtfully but slowly revealed further information. "They are a very new species, only a few hundred years old. We call them Zarns, named after the planet where they reside. Physically they are taller than humans, but not as tall as the Watchers. They are very distinctive because their features are strong and perfectly balanced. There is no way to say it tactfully, but there is no such thing as an ugly Zarn because their gene pool has been carefully monitored since the very beginning. It's not like on earth where anyone can have a baby, only a chosen few are allowed to procreate."

"I can't imagine that, not being able to have a baby if I wanted one."

"It's just the way things are done and because it's always been that way, everyone accepts it. There are three specific types of Zarns, each unmistakable. There are blonde haired, fair skinned and blue eyed Zarns, also dark haired, dark skinned, brown eyed Zarns and lastly red haired, green eyed Zarns with the freckly skin that you would expect. The three different types cannot interbreed."

"So, they've created a master race, like Hitler wanted to?"

"Not at all. All people are loved and respected on Zarnett-9. None is better than the others, none are held in favour. All are equal in every way – equal but different. Everyone in the communities understands the order of things and helps to keep their respective gene pools pure."

"Sounds like a disaster waiting to happen if you ask me. What if the wrong ones fall in love, like Romeo and Juliet did?"

Elisia smiled but didn't answer my question. "You're such a romantic Luna, who would have thought?"

I dismissed her evaluation of me, I didn't feel like a romantic at all. "It must be hard to find humans who want to take part in this project?"

As soon as the words fell out of my mouth my brain had already begun to make the connections, click, click, click... and it all suddenly fell into place. "Oh fuck!" In my wildest dreams, I'd never considered they were planning to use me as a breeding machine.

CHAPTER 9

"Love never dies a natural death. It dies because we don't know how to replenish its source. It dies of blindness and errors and betrayals. It dies of illness and wounds; it dies of weariness, of witherings, of tarnishings."

— ANAIS NIN

I had wandered back to my chambers in a state of numb fear. Why hadn't I realised? I was young and healthy and maybe at that perfect age to start reproducing a sporran of kids. I wiped a singular tear from my eye but as soon as I did so, another swelled up to take its place.

Once again, I wondered how I had ever got myself into this mess. One of the main thoughts that occupied my mind was that of Isayel. I had thought he liked me, at least a little bit, but I was nothing more than a fertility cow in their stupid programme. So far away from everyone I ever knew, isolated and surrounded by people I couldn't really relate to and whom I couldn't really trust, I had absolutely no one to turn to for help or advice. I longed to see my mum again, to watch her bustle around the kitchen at home, making tea or giving me one of her weary smiles. Now, instead of grunting at her, I'd smile back, give her a big hug and tell her how much I loved her. I'd thank her for everything she'd ever done for me and really mean it. I tried to send my thoughts out through space, to let mum and Amy know I was thinking about them and that I missed them with every part of me, but it felt like an impossible task.

I was lying there, drowning in my own misery, when Isayel appeared in the doorway.

"Come," he said and held his hand out to me. "We need to talk."

I took the offered hand without answer, having no fight left in me. He gently guided me away from my room and led me in a direction I'd never been in before. This corridor seemed to run the whole perimeter of the ship and we passed many doorways, all of them sealed.

"Where are we going?" I snivelled, hurrying to keep up with his long stride.

"I want to show you something."

It felt as if we had walked an impossible length and I was wondering just how big this ship was when we finally stopped outside a set of double doors.

"Brace yourself," he said as the doors silently opened.

My jaw must have dropped to the floor. I had never seen such a magnificent landscape. There were trees and rivers, with distant hills and the sound of waterfalls cascading into pools of aquamarine water. This scenery was as bright, golden and open as my training room was dark and mysterious. All my senses told me that I was outside in bright daylight and yet I knew I was still on the ship.

"How are you doing this?" I asked at last.

"It's holographic, three dimensional and totally real while its activated." Isayel answered, as if that explained everything.

"So, if you can make a holographic world, with all this space and dimension, why do you keep me locked in just one boring room?"

Isayel smiled, "because you would run away and we'd never be able to find you again if we gave you this much freedom."

I recognised the truth in that, but still felt sorely treated.

Brightly coloured birds swooped and circled in the clear blue skies and butterflies flitted from flower to flower, seeming to dance with the pleasure of being alive on a beautiful summer's day.

"Let's walk." Isayel encouraged. I didn't need to be asked twice. Hurriedly I untied my boots, kicking them away from me so that I could feel the grass beneath my feet. It felt so soft and real as I curled my toes into the ground that I laughed with the sheer pleasure of it. This place was like a balm, anointing me within a shroud of forgetfulness and I began to feel dreamily absent from all my concerns.

"While you are here, everything will feel better." Isayel promised. It already did. Why had I been so upset? Something scratched at the back of my mind but I couldn't recall what and, what's more, I didn't want to remember.

We walked, our hands laced together, chatting in gentle ways about everything and nothing, and it all felt so natural and normal. My heart was close to bursting in my chest with the simple joy of being here with Isayel in this perfect setting.

The sun warmed my skin, and a rivulet of sweat ran slowly down between the almost non-existent swell of my breasts. We were only a short distance from one of those dazzling pools, the waterfall tumbling down the aged green rocks in a cascade of frothy, lacey water. I was beginning to feel uncomfortably hot and the water looked so refreshing and inviting.

"Will you swim with me?" I'd asked, turning to stare into Isayel's eyes. That connection was there again, stronger than ever, like a pulse rushing through me.

"Would you like me to?"

I bit my bottom lip, recognising the temptation of being in such close quarters to him. "Yes, of course. Come swim with me Isayel."

In this place I was a different version of myself. Without thought or inhibition, I pulled my shapeless dress over my head and dived into the water. If Isayel had caught his breath at the site of my almost naked body, covered as it was only by a thin camisole and pants, it was drowned out by the noise of the foaming waterfall.

As I plunged into the water, the coolness took my breath away and for an instant I grappled with the shock, kicking my legs quickly so that I could rise to the surface.

Isayel was already in the water when I broke through and took a gasp of air. I watched his arms as he swam, pounding the water with strong strokes, causing ripples that cascaded around him. Giggling, I dived below the surface again, exploring the exotic underwater vista, catching rippling glimpses of colourful crystals that formed the structure of the riverbed. Tiny colourful fish darted around me, swimming in unison as if they'd rehearsed this perfectly synchronised dance just for my pleasure.

"This is magical. I feel like a mermaid." I declared, surfacing again and splashing the water around me.

"You look like a mermaid." Isayel smiled and wiped a strand of hair from my eyes, looking deep into the depths of me as he did so. As his hand dropped away from me into the water, I felt it graze my breast, just ever so slightly. I shuddered and instantly felt a jolt of electricity startle my senses. Had that happened by accident or was it intentional? Did he know where he had just touched me?" I didn't know the answer because he had swum quickly away, towards the waterfall. I couldn't help myself, I swam after him.

The nearer I got to the waterfall the icier the water became and I could hear my own heartbeat pounding in my ears. I kept swimming, wanting to reach him. As I swam it became harder and harder and took more and more effort. My breathing was coming in ragged, shallow breaths as the palpitations in my chest increased. I kicked my legs out, pushing forward in a breast stroke movement but my arms suddenly felt weak and useless, the muscles straining to keep going but forced into submission by a heavy ache that pushed through me. I felt weighted down, as if the force of gravity was crushing me. Then, I was totally immersed, the sounds of the water lapping all around me, sloshing over my head and forcing itself up my nostrils and into my ears. I struggled against the pressure, trying desperately to pull myself up, but the more I tried, the deeper I sank. The last thing I remember was flailing wildly, my lungs burning as I fought to keep my mouth closed and not breath in the icy water. Using the very last of my strength, I tried to propel myself upwards, before losing consciousness.

◆ ◆ ◆

When I came to, Isayel was looking at me intently, his eyes full of concern. Goose bumps covered my flesh and he clasped me closer to him, sharing his warmth with me. I cried, right there in his arms, as he gently told me that everything was going to be alright.

"I... I thought I was going to die..." I sobbed noisily, coughing to release some more water from my lungs. My initial panic slowly receded as I realised I was going to be okay.

"I will always keep you safe, my little mermaid." He kissed my eyelids as I clung closer to him. "You were going into shock. The water was too cold for you."

"I didn't think... I saw you... and I just wanted... I wanted..."

"Sshhh... it's okay. I know." I felt his strength and the heat that radiated from him as he lay there beside me, cradling me next to him, his nakedness warming my body.

It was a slow awakening, from fear to sensuality, but as inevitable as night follows day I became ever more aware of his skin touching mine. Without thinking, I slowly wrapped my arms around his neck and pulled his face nearer to mine, kissing him around the sides of his mouth, along the base of his throat, close to his pulse points.

My recent fear and panic fuelled my passion, making me reckless and needy. He had saved my life, and my emotions zig-zagged dangerously out of control as my body responded to the nearness of him. My kisses, butterfly soft, languid, were becoming more and more urgent as I felt him stir beside me, and the moment he claimed my mouth with his own I felt a wave of love wash over me. When his lips released mine, I instinctively found myself arching upwards, wanting him to bury his face into me, to savour me, to taste my skin and know how I yearned for him. His breath was hot, I could feel it through the wetness of my top, so close... so close I felt I wanted to burst with longing, desperate for his touch.

"Yes... yes... do it... do it...." I needed him with a physical pull that was so strong I could no longer control myself. Here I was, acting desperate, begging to find a way to fill this growing ache inside me, harldy understanding the needs of my body.

He pulled my top down then, just a fraction, his fingers scorching my skin, the pressure of his thumb resting on the mound of my chest and his breathing becoming shallow before I felt his tongue grazing my skin. Oh my god, this was sweet torture. "Lower, lower... "my mind screamed as I sucumbed to his explorations. He took his time, slowly skirting around where I really needed him to kiss me. I heard the hiss of his breath through his teeth, as if he was fighting with himself.

"I want you..." I whispered, my voice husky in his ear, my legs now coiled around him. I knew he would be aware of the sticky wetness that pooled between my thighs, pressed up so close to his own. Then, in an instant his mouth was upon me, licking and suckling upon the tender bud of my nipple, creating a whirlpool of emotion inside of me. I surrendered to him as he licked and flicked his tongue over me, teasing and pulling ever so slightly, causing somersaults in my stomach. This is what I wanted. His hand came to cradle my other breast, his thumb and forefinger rubbing me, pulling gently as his mouth came down on the other side. I burned with passion, imagining how it would feel to have him buried deep inside me, his eyes devouring me before he took my virginity, perhaps even tasting my flowering, that forbidden nectar that flowed like a river between my thighs. What it would feel like to welcome him into me, giving myself to him in every way. My mind spun with the prospect of our intimacy.

He lifted his head from me then, and although his eyes had darkened with desire, he shook his head and quickly pulled himself off me.

"No, not like this. What are you doing to me?" He released me suddenly and rolled away, as if he'd been burned by fire. Quickly he created a distance between us.

"This is wrong. It's not how it should be."

"But... I'm sixteen now... we can... it's legal... I want you Isayel, I want you to love me."

"No, no, no." His face was full of torment and all at once I felt like the immature kid that I was when I'd first met him. What had I done wrong?

Isayel robed himself and waited while I did the same and, once we were demurely dressed, he came to sit with me, not touching, but a little further distant.

"Luna, every moment with you is a torture."

"Thanks!" I felt indignant at his choice of words.

He smiled sadly. "A torture for my body and mind. You know very well what I mean." I felt the colour rising up to my cheeks. "Well, if you want your master race you will need to have sex with me, won't you?"

"About that... Elisia told me about your conversation. It was not her place to speak with you, but it's done now."

"I think it was time someone around here told me something, don't you? After all I didn't ask to be here, did I?"

He ignored my question and went on to explain in detail about my frequency and vibration and how it linked us together. He explained that was the only reason I felt so attracted to him. We would eventually mate, but it would be a carefully monitored and calibrated process, nothing more.

"It might feel like love, but it isn't Luna. It's just sex. If your frequency matched one of the other angels, it would be them that you wanted, not me."

"That's brutal.. how can you even say that? What I felt just now was real… more real than anything else I've ever known and I know you felt it too."

"You don't have to believe what I am saying but it is still true. We cannot just mate Luna. Mating has to be an act of procreation and to become the mother of my child there are certain… criteria… that need to be in place. It's not random and it's not like on earth where people do not care with whom they exchange their bodily fluids."

"I wasn't planning to have your baby Isayel, I just wanted us to make love."

"Unfortunately, it cannot be that way."

"Why not? Why can't we just be together and make each other happy?"

"Because when we make love properly it will be a rapture of mind, body and spirit. A pleasure unlike any that you have ever experienced before, but it can only happen whilst creating a child."

I sighed and turned my head away from him. "So, what would be involved?"

"To start with, you will need to be a virgin."

"But I am a virgin."

"Yes, that is true now, but you will need to be a twenty-one year old virgin for the process to work."

"Twenty one? For fuck's sake!" The expletive burst from my mouth without thought. "I can't be a virgin at twenty one. I want you now Isayel, I can't wait five years for you!"

"But you must, and that is why we cannot have a physical

relationship yet. In the next five years you will be trained, not just with Elisia but with the other Mothers too. You will learn so much throughout your time here, so that at the end of five years the process will seem very natural to you."

"The other Mothers? You mean Elisia and you..."

"Yes. She is the mother of one of my children - Tri-ane, my third child."

"How many children do you have?"

"Only seven."

"Jesus Christ. Seven children. And now you want more."

"Each Mother can only have one child. Her first born. Any other offspring from the coupling of an angel and a human creates a monstrous being, called the Nephilim. The women that become the mothers of the Zarn race can only have a physical relationship with their angelic mate up until the first pregnancy is confirmed. After that, it is done with."

"You mean, you use them and then leave them?"

"No. Never that. The Mothers are sacred. Each of them is revered. They stay with their children, true mothers in every sense of the word, and when there is need they become the guardians and teachers of those destined to follow in their footsteps."

"So Elisia is your cast-off lover, relegated to teaching younger versions of herself, like me? I can't believe she would be happy doing that... and from what you're saying, you don't intend to ever let me go home again. I had a family, a life on earth and you took that away from me. Why should I agree to any of this, and why should I wait so long just to have sex?"

"It is decided. It is your destiny and you cannot fight it. On your twenty first birthday there will be a great ritual, a cleansing of your mind, body and soul, purifying you as a vessel for the child to be. You will know your greatest joy and the feelings you experience during the coupling will stay with you for all time."

I shook my head in disbelief at his explanation, unable to comprehend why anyone would submit to pregnancy and childbirth in this way.

"Once every week during your pregnancy we will spend time in isolation together, where we will merge on a frequency level. This imprints the foetus will angelic rays that will further nourish its spiritual development. It will nourish and strengthen you too. When the child is born you will raise it yourself with the assistance of the other Mothers."

"You're not selling this to me. I don't think I want to be a mother to one of your children. I'm not a vessel, as you put it, I'm a real life person with real feelings. I'm not going to let you ruin my whole life just to fulfil your stupid programme. And for your information, I hate kids."

"Luna, you are the first Mother that has been born in the last seventy-seven years. That makes you incredibly special."

"Seventy-seven years? So, your other children... they're not children anymore?"

"No, some have already passed from this life. My youngest child is now fifty-six earth years old."

"Bloody hell. How old are you Isayel?"

"I am old beyond time. I am eternal and will never die. As a Mother, your life span will greatly increase but, sadly, you cannot live forever."

"I don't want to live forever. In fact, I don't want to be part of any of this, it's all totally screwed up. I can't believe your children are older than my mum and you still want to have sex with me. It's so fucking wrong." He'd got me to swearing again, creating such a volatile tension in me that I couldn't help reacting against him.

"My love, there is nothing wrong about it, the spirit is eternal and age is nothing, a manmade concept which is not even considered by angels, except as a measure of past events.

"I'm not your love. You've made that perfectly clear, I'm just part of your stupid project and I'm never going to agree to have your baby, not ever."

Isayel's lips drew into a tight line. "It is a great honour to host the child of an angel and in the fullness of time you will change your mind."

"Never," I said, getting up from my seated position and re-tracing my steps back to my boots and then to the exit. I realised that just because somebody had one head, two eyes, one nose and one mouth, just because they had what I considered to be a human body, it did not mean they were anything like me. His thinking processes were entirely alien to mine and I vowed I would not allow myself to be touched by him again.

CHAPTER 10

"Life would be infinitely happier if we could only be born at the age of eighty and gradually approach eighteen."

-       MARK TWAIN

I sayel made himself scarce around me. It had been weeks and I had only seen him from a distance. Even Elisia avoided my further questions and my frustration led me to think all sorts of nasty things. I missed him but despised him at the same time, how could he remain so aloof and cold towards me?

On the bright side, I'd been given more privileges and I was able to attend in the main dining room for meals. There were planned seating arrangements around me, with Elisia always sitting to my left but often someone I didn't know to my right. On this particular day, I became aware that the person on my right was an angel. He looked at me with the same intensity of gaze that Isayel had used, and whilst his scrutiny initially made me feel uncomfortable, there was definitely no lust and no attraction, for which I was immensely relieved.

"Don't let it get to you, it will get better you know." He finally spoke to me, tearing a bread roll into smaller pieces on the plate in front of him.

"Do you know who I am? Can you see me?" I asked. This was the first time another angel had spoken to me or even properly looked at me. Mostly they looked through me as if I wasn't there.

"Yes, of course I know you. You are to be the next Mother. Let me introduce myself, my name is Cassiel."

I smiled. It was nice not to feel so invisible. "Just to get things straight, I'm not going to be the next Mother, but pleased to meet you anyway. I haven't seen you before, what do you do around here?"

His eyes twinkled, vibrant against the darkness of his skin, "I am a master of time."

"Wow, sounds cool, although I've been told angels don't believe in time." I glanced down the table to where Isayel sat with one of the Mothers, deep in conversation, smiling and talking animatedly. As if he felt my eyes upon him, he looked up then, a frown creasing his brow as Cassiel leaned closer to me, to whisper in my ear.

"A little jealousy won't hurt him." I laughed. So true, I thought, and turned my gaze away from Isayel, intent on enjoying my evening. There were no age restrictions on alcohol here and I held a glass to my lips, savouring the flavour as it slipped down my throat with a smooth readiness. Through the course of the meal I found myself laughing and smiling, warmed from the drink, and becoming firm friends with Cassiel as he entertained me with outlandish stories and funny anecdotes. It was the start of a friendship that I valued above most. He wasn't as serious as Elisia and treated me more like an equal. I appreciated his light-heartedness, it made me feel relaxed in his company, much more so than with anyone else. In the following months he came to visit me regularly, escorting me to different parts of the ship and telling me so much more about angelic life.

"What's it like to be an angel?" I'd asked him, curious to know how it felt.

"Well, it's like being a finely tuned instrument. We allow the music of the universe to flow through us and in so doing, we create the symphonies of the ages. Now we are away from our heavenly home it's different. There is discord. We all feel it, even if we try not to talk about it. Free will can be a difficult burden and there's so much that we know now that we didn't comprehend way back then." I knew he was referring to the exile.

"How long ago was it?" I'd asked.

He flicked his hand to dismiss my question. "Ancient times, we don't count…"

"You must miss it very much."

"We all do, though none would say so to the other. Nobody likes to admit being wrong." He smiled then, a slow sad smile.

"Did you ever create a child with one of the Mothers?" I asked, curious as to how many angels did the mating.

"Me? Oh no... it's not for me... I'm... well, can I just say my interests lie elsewhere?"

"Oh my god, Cassiel, you're gay, aren't you?" I was surprised, but now that I thought about it, it seemed pretty obvious.

"No need to look so surprised, young missy. Angels have free will and preferences, just like humans do."

I looped my arm into his and hugged him briefly to me. "I wouldn't have you any other way. You are my truly special friend and perfect as you are."

My circle of friends was widening. Elisia introduced me to two more of the Mothers, both older women who must have looked stunning in their earlier years. Corinne was blonde and petite like Elisia, but Sofia was dark, and timelessly beautiful in an exotic, bewitching way.

"Corinne will teach you world knowledge. This will be necessary because your earth education has been cut short. Should it ever be needed it will be there for you. You will become more informed and better taught than at any earth school." I groaned inwardly, I hated the subjects I had to study at school.

"Do I have to?" Elisia gave me one of her looks that told me arguing was out of the question.

"What will Sofia teach me?" I'd asked.

"Sofia will teach you the arts. Writing, drawing, all creative endeavours. She will quickly know where your aptitude lies and structure her lessons accordingly."

"Guess I'm going to be super busy then!"

"More than you know, child." Elisia commented as the other two nodded in agreement but Sofia winked as she smiled and I felt she would probably be less rigorous than the others. Elisia was right, after lessons every day I felt exhausted. My brain was reeling from all the new information. I never realised I had it in me to study so intensely and to learn so much.

The Mothers each had their own areas, suited to what they were teaching. Corrine's room was much more what I had expected a school room to look like, with charts and maps on the wall and a desk where I could sit and write. Her lessons were extensive and it seemed she knew just about everything that was on the curriculum at my old school. She saw where I had struggled in the past and explained in ways that I could grasp so much more easily. That was just the start of it though, because Corrine believed that for lessons to be interesting, they should also be alive and full of detail.

On the far side of her classroom there was a door, beside which was a complicated looking keypad. "Today we will see just how things went down in 1066."

As we stepped through the entranceway I felt the late autumn warmth of the day caress my skin.

"Oh, my god…. it's… wow… I don't know what to say." I was speechless. We were standing in the midst of a field, surrounded by horses and mounted men in heavy armour, with many more infantry milling about, seemingly preparing for battle. I felt as if I'd stepped into the middle of a historical action movie.

"Can we get hurt?" I'd asked, as a horse charged down the field at a gallop, seeming to be heading straight at us.

"No, not at all. We can't interact with this world. It's like a recording of events but in 5D, so everything about it feels real."

As we watched Corrine pointed out details. "The Anglo-Saxons have a strong position at the top of that mound, which has come to be known as Battle Hill, and Harold Godwinson will be there with his men. And see over there? I followed the line of sight to where a fortified camp was set up. "William of Normandy and his men are preparing to attack. William will stop at nothing to win the English throne, and only Harold stands in his way."

History came alive in a way that I'd never dreamed possible and by the end of the lesson I felt as if I knew everything I could possibly know about the Battle of Hastings. I'd listened to the bloodcurdling cries and the clash of weaponry as I made my way across the pitted ground of the battlefield. Even the breeze that rippled across my skin seemed to become agitated at the violence, whipping my hair until I had to tie it back from my face.

"That was amazing" I gasped, as we finally made it back unscathed to the classroom. "I feel exhausted just watching all the drama."

"There will be plenty more for you to see." Corinne smiled. "Earth people have a rich and varied history. Wherever you live, whichever world you find yourself in, it's still important that you know and respect your own roots."

I nodded in agreement. This was my history and I felt as if I owned it, more than I ever did in the past. I was proud to belong to the earth.

However much Corrine's lessons captivated me with their detail and interest, nothing could have come close to my time with Sofia. I had always enjoyed art, in fact it had been one of my favourite subjects at school. Dad had teased me that it was because I wasn't clever enough to enjoy my maths lessons, but... well, he was wrong. I loved the act of creating and bringing something to life on the paper so that it felt real, alive and vivid.

When I went through to the holographic world with Sofia, I studied the great masters in all their glory. Rembrandt, Michael Angelo, Leonardo Da Vinci, Vincent Van Gogh... I felt that I knew their personal challenges and the pain they experienced for their art. My favourite, although not so antiquated, was John William Waterhouse and I studied his techniques for hours on end, learning and absorbing just how he created the Lady of Shalott and Circe, the witch, two of my favourite paintings of all time.

As part of our lessons Sofia and I travelled through time, walking the pebbled streets of Rome and other great cities together, absorbing the sights and sounds, reflecting on the lives of the painters we were studying. We walked where they walked, visited the same shops and taverns. Maybe by osmosis I could draw up their skills and accomplishments simply by breathing the same air and strolling down the same hallowed streets. I sat with them and watched as they worked, mesmerised by the detail and the clarity they brought to their art.

"It is a pleasure to teach you" Sofia commented one day as she stood behind me, watching me sketch Isayel from my memory. I worked diligently around the eyes, capturing the look he had when he was deep in thought, and the shape of his nose, noble, strong... his features were perfectly formed... I guessed there was no such thing as an ugly angel. Men and women would truly desire them throughout all of time. As I sketched his lips I imagined how it would feel to have his mouth linger over me, trailing soft kisses upon my skin, perhaps even devouring me with the passion that we'd momentarily shared in the past. I quickly closed my mind against such traitorous daydreams, I didn't want to be contemplating these things anymore. Besides, I was selfish and naive to think he would want plain old me. I was just the fertility programme, not special enough to keep his interest.

"I hope Isayel knows how lucky he is to have found you." Sofia spoke softly and I had to wonder whether I had misheard her as she had already moved away and seemed intent on cleaning parts of the classroom. Lucky! As far as I was concerned, Isayel had forgotten I even existed. Now I needed to learn how to do the same.

I tried really hard not to think about him, truly I did. Sometimes it worked, especially when I had been particularly engrossed in my studies, but usually, as evening approached and I was alone in my chambers I couldn't help but relive those moments we'd spent together in my mind.

On this particular evening I wasn't alone. Cassiel was sitting with me and I'd just dealt the cards in a first round of Rummy.

"Do you know what day it is?" Cassiel had asked, studying his hand.

"Nope. Why?"

"Why? Girl, you've been on board this ship for almost two years... do you know what that means?"

"It means I will never see my real home again." I said abruptly. It never crossed my mind anymore how long I'd been imprisoned. It had actually gone quite quickly. I was treated well, not tortured, had enough to eat, friends, an education... there was nothing I could complain about, except for the gaping hole where my family lodged in my chest. I tried not to think about how their lives would have moved on by now, probably thinking I was dead.

"You've changed a lot in those two years."

"Sure, I was just a kid then."

"My point exactly. You were a foul-mouthed wild thing, but look at you now... blossoming into a beautiful young woman."

"That's a bit rich coming from you, isn't it?" I laid down a Three of Hearts and picked up the Jack of Clubs. "You don't even find females attractive, so I can't take anything you say like that seriously."

"You're talking like a fool. I may be gay, but I'm not blind. Just because I don't sleep with women doesn't mean I can't admire the physical form."

"If you say so." I'd answered tersely.

"Touchy today, aren't we? I know you're feeling down on yourself because of your memories, and because of Isayel."

I looked up at the sound of his name, Cassiel hadn't been one to talk about him much, so this conversation seemed almost off-limits.

"You mustn't pay too much attention to the way he is," Cassiel confided. "It's part of his nature to be intense. I know he avoids you because he doesn't trust himself to behave himself in the proper manner. He would love to spend more time with you, you know."

"It's okay, you don't have to spare my feelings. Isayel has already told me that the mating process is nothing but a chore that has to happen."

"He said that, did he?"

"Well, kind of, yes. I know he has no feelings for me anyway."

"Hmm, I wouldn't be too sure about that, if I were you. I know he's jealous of the time we spend together. He struggles to maintain a platonic relationship with you and that's why we get all the fun!"

"Don't be silly. If he was jealous, he would come and visit me, wouldn't he?

I tried to question Cassiel further about his knowledge of Isayel's feelings for me, but he refused to be pressed on the subject.

"You know what we need, something to cheer you up... an eighteenth birthday party, that's what. Why didn't I think of it before? We will invite everyone and anyone and it will be the most fabulous event of the year." His excitement was infectious, and the more he talked about what we could do, the more I liked the sound of it. Maybe it would be just what I needed to get me out of my morose ways of thinking.

We had three weeks in which to plan my party, which seemed like hardly any time at all.

"First of all, we need to get you looking the part. It's all about the dress." Cassiel commented.

One of the Mothers whom I'd not yet studied with was an amazing seamstress. I'd sketched a flowing dress, made with emerald green silk and asked if she could help me to make it. I'd wanted a crinoline petticoat with hoops and a corseted top, laced at the back and with a sweeping neckline to show that I really did have some curves now.

"It's lovely" Christie had said, "but not very practical. How about we design it so that the hoops and petticoats can be released at some point of the evening and you can be left with a much more comfortable dress to dance in?" It was a clever idea and I liked the sound of what she was describing. Two dresses in one, and maybe three if I fancied getting my legs out too. Christie busied herself and we were left to discuss all the other details.

"We will have it in one of the holographic worlds of course" Cassiel was saying excitedly. "Do you have a preference?"

I thought for a moment, "yes, as it happens, I do."
Cassiel clapped with delight as I described the perfect place I wanted to spend my eighteenth birthday.

"So much to do. I will organise a hairdresser for you, and a beauty therapist... oh girl, it will be magnificent, and you will be magnificent too!"

CHAPTER 11

"What matters is to understand pleasure, not try to get rid of it — that is too stupid. Nobody can get rid of pleasure."

— JIDDU KRISHNAMURTI

So, she was having a party. I fingered the black and silver invitation, tracing the embossed letters that spelled my name, *Isayel*, with the tip of my finger. Cassiel had placed the envelope in my room earlier, along with the dire warning that I had better turn up.

"I will not be going" I had told him, but Cassiel had other plans for me.

"I don't know what you think you will achieve by staying away Isayel." His eyes had glittered with an anger rarely seen. "But, let me tell you something. If you do not attend, I will shift the sands of time, recreating this party over and over again until you do the right thing by that poor girl."

Cassiel had dominion over time, but he very rarely threatened to use his powers unless he meant it. Could he not see the struggle I faced? To stay away from this party was not a selfish act on my part. To the contrary, it was the most decent, selfless thing I could have done. I prickled with the anticipation of sharing time with Luna. Had I not diligently avoided being near her? Was I not a martyr, compelled to sacrifice my own wishes and desires in the name of doing the right thing?

Of course, I'd watched from a distance as she had occupied her days. It is straightforward to do so. As Watchers, we can mutate into the spaces between atoms, existing on an entirely different level, unseen, privately observing all that goes on. It is a dutiful habit that is hard to break. It is our nature and, some would say, our very purpose in being alive. Sadly, we see the underbelly of human suffering as well as the triumphs and successes. By observing without being observed we gain a greater understanding of human nature. We see beneath the many masks and find the truth.

Those times that I took the opportunity to observe Luna my heart had glowed with warmth. She was flourishing into a beautiful young woman, accomplished and talented on so many levels. I had been there too when she had sketched my image in Sofia's classroom. I was surprised by her memorised knowledge of my face, catching my resemblance and the quality of me in ways that greater painters in ages past had failed to do. As she bent over the canvas, intent on perfecting every detail, I was left breathless not just by her loveliness but also by her total disregard of it. She was still wearing those shapeless ugly dresses that she had been issued during her first weeks on board the ship. She could have asked for so much more, but she did not.

"Cassiel, you remember the day we brought her on board The Omicron?"

"Yes, she was a wild thing… we thought her a mistake, if I recall."

"Exactly… she was rebellious and belligerent, rude, opinionated and disrespectful."

Cassiel chuckled at the memory.

"I loved every inch of her then Cassiel, just as I love her now, but do not force me to spend time with her."

"You loved her passion too, did you not? But that is gone now, her emotions are settled and she has more control. Why would you deny her your company on her special day?"

"You know very well that the passion will erupt again if we are brought together. It's my inattention, not her maturity, that has dampened her spirits."

"This party means a lot to her, and if you saw how her eyes sparkle at the thought of it, you would feel joy yourself. You know your problems, Isayel, is that you've forgotten what it is to be youthful and carefree. Everyone deserves to enjoy their youth and remember, she has dealt with major difficulties, losing everyone she ever cared about… losing you…".

"But I cannot afford to jeopardise the Zarnett-9 project. She is needed for the mating and if that chemistry gets triggered too soon.. who knows what will happen?"

"You owe her some time Isayel. If we hadn't intervened, her life would have been entirely different."

"Different, but not better. Her life has improved because of our intervention."

"Her life is better only because of The Mothers and myself, not because of you. When she needed you, it was me who supported her. When she cried for you, I was the one who held her hand. Zarnett-9 can wait. Luna cannot."

I flinched at Cassiel's words, finding it disagreeable that he was fulfilling a role that should have been mine.

Initially I had disapproved of his growing friendship with Luna, becoming jealous of the easy way that they could share their time together. I longed to be able to do that, but that was not the way of things for us. Ours was a different path.

CHAPTER 12

"You're right. You're not a princess -- you're Little Red. and I'm the Big Bad Wolf."

— JULIE JOHNSON

It was hard to believe how much work we had done to prepare for my party. I had Cassiel to thank for most of it, he was a natural organiser and had an amazing flair for the outrageous and the unusual.

I had decided that I wanted my party to be held in a castle, with two sweeping staircases each side of the main entranceway, which led to a main hall.

"You will be Cinderella" Cassiel had said, clapping his hands in excitement.

"Cinderella?" I'd questioned his sanity but he just laughed.

"Oh yes, we will arrange a little sorcery... a pumpkin carriage, mice into footmen, that sort of thing."

"Don't be silly" I'd giggled at the thought of it, but he looked totally serious.

"Wouldn't you like to step into a fairytale like that, on your special day?"

I cast my mind into the daydream of what he was proposing. If I was Cinderella then Isayel would have to be my Prince Charming – maybe he would be compelled to dance with me all night and fall totally and madly in love with me, to the distraction of all else. And those damned ugly sisters would not – could not – make him change his mind. I sighed, it sounded amazing.

"That's settled then."

I smiled, "okay, let's do it."

September 18th arrived in a flurry of activity. As soon as I awoke there was knocking at my door and The Mothers swept in laden with gifts for me. A wonderful exotic looking plant with purple blossoms from Elisia, new pencils and chalks from Sofia and a map of space and the outer systems from Corrine. Then other people I'd slowly come to know arrived and I was treated to flowers and chocolates. Someone handed me a cup of tea and insisted that it wasn't my true birthday unless I had breakfast in bed, and so it was that this troop of friends and acquaintances shared some time with me on this most special of occasions, cooking me up a real English breakfast against the backdrop of morning radio and idle gossip.

It could have been home and my heart swelled with joy and love. Cassiel breezed in just as I was tucking into a crispy piece of fried bacon and insisted I put my fork down and unwrap his present immediately. I did as he asked, his enthusiasm absolutely brimming over. I quickly ripped open the pink and white wrapping paper and squealed with delight – a new pair of amazing knee-high boots in the softest kid leather. I hugged him tightly to me. They were the best.

"This is just the beginning," he said cryptically and gave me one of his huge smiles. The only person missing from my special day so far was Isayel.

The whole day went by in a blur of activity. Cassiel escorted me to the spa rooms, leaving me there to indulge myself while he went off to oversee the final party arrangements. There were jacuzzi pools and hot tubs of all different shapes and sizes, swimming pools, saunas and flotation tanks, and I took my time, wandering around leisurely, ensuring that I tested each and every one. Water fizzed and bubbled all around me, pulsing from jet streams that pummelled into my body, relieving aches that I never even knew I had. In the steam room I felt as if my whole body and all the tensions and stresses just melted away from me as I breathed in the calming aromas of neroli and lavender essential oils. I was pampered and spoiled in such a complete and wonderful way, I felt that I never wanted the day to end. There were more treats in store too and as soon as I stepped out of the steam room I was directed towards the steaming mud baths, where the warm mud bubbled up like some weird chocolate soup.

"This is amazing for the skin." the attendant had informed me, when I had paused at the edge of the pool, slightly worried by the fact that I couldn't see the bottom.

"Well, I guess I should try it then," I replied and, taking my life in my hands, jumped in. As the mud swirled around my body, I couldn't help but laugh out loud. The experience was decadent and luxurious and I felt it was something I should do every day from now on, maybe after my studies, just to unwind. The mud was quite dense and I felt buoyantly suspended. It tickled as it squeezed itself between my toes and I revelled in the sheer delight of getting so dirty. It clung to my hair and my face, even under my fingernails - every part of me was deliciously covered in mud. And it was exactly at that moment that I turned and saw Isayel sitting at the side of the pool, watching me with eyes full of amusement and... desire.

I was shocked, seeing him there like that, as if it was the most natural thing in the world, as if he could just turn up, whenever he felt like it.

"Get... out..." I whispered, my voice suddenly lost to me.

"No." His answer echoed through my mind. He sat quite still, watching me with those incredible eyes, and I became still too, hardly daring to move or to breathe as I watched him watching me. Then I felt it. A tremor rose inside me as his presence formed in the mud beside me. How could it be? He was still sitting at the side, some distance away and yet I could feel him right next to me too. The sweetest of tortures ripped through me as I felt the pressure of his body entwined with mine, mud slipping between us, bonding us closer as we slipped and slid against each other.

"No, this isn't happening... this isn't real." I shook my head, trying to clear my thoughts, but I could feel his hands upon me, holding me to him, coiling around me, claiming me as his. I closed my eyes and traced the sinew of his muscles with my fingertips, exploring him, drinking in his grace and strength, needing him as much as I knew he needed me. I felt his lips graze my neck, and his fingers deftly working along the muscles each side of my spine, relaxing me, stroking and coaxing me, fanning the flames of my desire that I'd tried so hard to extinguish.

"No, it's not real... it's not happening," I whispered again, forcing myself to remain calm, and when I slowly opened my eyes, the moment was over. There was no sign of Isayel, and I wondered if he had ever been there at all, or whether my imagination had simply got the better of me. The bench was empty and I was completely alone.

◆ ◆ ◆

The party invitations had asked all guests to arrive for 8.00pm Earth Standard Time in holographic world number 4. It had been programmed with absolute precision, overseen not just by Cassiel but by the technical director and his team, who ran the HWs. I hadn't actually seen the finished world but Cassiel had assured me that I would absolutely love it.

At 4.00pm I was whisked to hair and make-up, where I was preened over and given an absolutely out-of-this world makeover. Cassiel had sat with me, chattering idly about the cake and the catering, who said what and how it was all going, whilst enjoying a manicure of his own. I wanted to talk to him about what had happened earlier in the day but the more I thought about it, the more embarrassed I felt. It seemed like it was something my mind had just imagined, all by itself.

"Where's my fairy godmother?" I asked, trying to take my mind off the strange encounter. "Shouldn't she be able to fix my hair and make-up in a jiffy with her magic wand without all this?"

"Really? You think so?" Cassiel laughed, "maybe if you wasn't so ugly" he teased, ducking as I threw my magazine at him.

By the time the stylists had finished, even Cassiel had stopped talking and gaped at me with his mouth open. I could hardly recognise myself. The hairdresser had highlighted my hair with various shades of blonde, lifting my natural colour, and painstakingly creating a head full of ringlets that were held in place by a delicate circlet of flowers. Then the beauty therapist had smudged dark blue kohl around my eyes and accentuated my cheekbones with subtle use of blusher. My lips were a pearly shimmering pink and my eyelashes had been thickened and darkened to produce a grand sweeping feathery arc of lashes. All the mud from earlier in the day had been washed away and my skin was soft and glowing.

Christie came by my room at just after 6.00pm so that I could try on my dress. Together, we carefully lifted it over my head and she tightened the corset at the back. As the folds of silk floated around me I felt like I was someone else, someone beautiful. The lower layers of the dress were scalloped and tiered, and they sashayed in the most wonderful way as I walked, reminding me of ladies of the Victorian age.

"I love it so much," I breathed as I twirled in the full-length mirror. Christie had done an amazing job.

"It looks stunning on you. It's definitely your colour. Just think, when you start your training with me, you will be able to make these sorts of things for yourself, and so much more besides." I smiled, but said nothing. There was no way I would ever be able to make something that looked as amazing as this dress.

"And don't forget, if you want to feel more comfortable later, the whole of the crinoline section can be removed and you will be able to dance to your heart's content without the restriction."

At 8.20pm, I made my fashionably late entrance, walking into Holographic World 4 on the arm of Cassiel, who was dressed in a superb white and blue pinstriped morning suit, complete with tails and a top hat. The skies were a deep dark indigo, lit up by a sparkle of fireworks that showered the heavens with an array of falling stars. It was truly magical and the castle stood out as majestically as if Walt Disney had placed it there himself. Trees stood regally each side of a central pathway, lit up with an array of colourful paper lanterns and fairy lights, casting a magical rainbow over the lawns.

"Am I dreaming?" I'd asked Cassiel, to which he had replied that I most definitely was not. I knew that it was probably the very worst time to well up with nostalgia, but a lump rose in my throat all the same, and I blinked back tears as my mind turned to my family. As usual, I wondered what they were doing and whether they missed me. I imagined that today they did, probably more than at any other time in the past, because you only get one chance at being eighteen, and they would never again have the opportunity to share it with me. I imagined Amy a little more grown up and if dad had been alive he would have taken us all out bowling or to the cinema. Mum would have baked a cake, there would have been ice cream and party food, and we would all sing Happy Birthday and make up silly alternative verses.

Before I could wallow further in my feelings, I became aware of all eyes on me as I ascended the staircase, heading towards the main hall. A band was playing and guests everywhere were chattering, laughing and generally having a very good time.

"Do you know..." Cassiel ventured thoughtfully, "I do believe this is the first party we've had on board this ship for years."

"Really?" I was amazed. "I'd have thought you would have parties and celebrations all the time, with the holographic worlds here to create whatever you want."

"You would think so, wouldn't you? But, actually, when it comes down to it, apart from my good self here, angels aren't that great at parties."

Cassiel was the perfect escort, making sure my glass was always brimming over and keeping me giggling with more of his wicked stories. He swept me onto the dance floor and chaperoned me as we danced through the ages of Swing, Motown, Disco, Rap and just about every other style of music I'd ever heard of. It was surreal, but I enjoyed every second of it, panting for breath as I twirled and whirled in my big balloon of a dress, not yet wanting to remove the bulkier layers.

I'd been inside the castle for over an hour before I saw Isayel and I'd begun to think he wouldn't be coming. My heart fluttered as I watched him. He was standing leaning against the wall next to a table of drinks and looked so sad, so far away and out of reach, that all my previous annoyances with him seemed to dissolve. Dressed in a dark grey suit, instead of his feathery robes, he looked every inch a man of quiet confidence and power. I took a step towards him, fuelled by my birthday drinks.

"Hey" I said, as I approached him.

He turned to look at me, and his eyes went all the way through me as if he could penetrate my mind and read every scrap of my thoughts. Gently he brought his hand up to one of my ringlets, smoothing it between his fingers before he let it go again and it popped right back into place.

"Happy Birthday Luna. You look very beautiful, like a

Princess," his words flowed around me but I couldn't feel any emotion behind them. I remembered our conversation from long ago when he said I looked like a mermaid and how that encounter ended.

"Would you like your present?"

"Is it a guinea pig?" I teased, "because if so, I will have it later."

"No, it's not that," he replied very seriously, as if he hadn't realised I'd been joking. "Turn around."

I did as he told me and then felt his arms gently rest on my shoulders while he fastened a white gold necklace around my neck.

It was a truly stunning gift, a circle of hearts, which spoke to my own heart of love but not of exclusivity.

"What does it symbolise?" I asked.

'That we are all connected, that each heart is precious." My eyes started to brim over again, I was having a very emotional kind of day. At least he had been thinking about me on my birthday and had gone to the trouble of finding a gift for me, even if I would have preferred something a little more... well... I wasn't sure, only that this gift didn't feel very personal to me and I didn't feel a single ounce of gratitude for it.

"I would wish that you didn't cry on your special day."

"I can't help it." I sniffed back the sob that threatened to erupt from me. "I'm so tired Isayel. I'm tired of wanting you and waiting for you. You have no idea how much you hurt me, over and over again, just by not caring and not taking the time to be with me, to get to know me or be interested in anything that I do."

I saw his shoulders drop slightly and he sighed a deep, heavy sigh.

"Let's walk," he said as he guided me down the steps of the castle and into the grounds. The moon hung low and large in the sky, lighting a silver pathway that we followed, down to a tranquil boating lake. Small boats bobbed about on the surface and the reflected moonlight cast shadows all around us.

"Luna, how can I explain to you all that is in my mind? You are never far from my thoughts, you need to know this. I keep my distance for a reason, because this connection that we have affects me just as much as it affects you. But our similarities end there, and although you are a light in the world, it's a mere human light, that will flicker and be extinguished all too soon."

"I don't understand what you're trying to tell me." I felt defensive. Whatever he was saying, I didn't like the sound of it.

"Angels hold a much greater imprint than humans. We have interacted and caused change over millennia and our strength and influence multiplies over time. Everything we do is magnified, every action and every thought. We can no longer just go with the flow of our feelings because we need to consider the very real repercussion of cause and effect."

"I know about cause and effect, it's a universal law."

"Indeed it is, and we all reap what we sow. How would it be if I followed my every whim and folly? If I gave into my feelings for you... what then? I'm not trying to belittle you Luna, far from it – I'm trying to save you, because there is far more to your life than you can ever imagine. You are a woman now, no longer a child. Do you comprehend what kind of future will be yours?"

"How can I know the answer to that? I do everything you tell me to do. I train and study hard, I listen to the broadcasts, I stay away from you, and yes, I wander around chatting and making friends with other people. What else can I do with my leisure time?"

"Leisure is a strange concept. Humans strive to have time to do things that they think they will enjoy, but these things are merely distractions from what they should be doing. No man is ever happier or feels more rewarded than when he is helping others. Remember that."

I groaned inwardly. Isayel was giving me a lecture, today of all days. I looked down to the floor, scuffing the ground with the toe of my new boots, hidden beneath my voluminous dress.

"You should spend some time thinking not about your friends or your leisure time, but in consideration of God Luna."

"Yeah, well, that's not really where I'm at right now, is it?" I didn't want to talk about God. It was a subject I had no interest in whatsoever.

"There is a part of you, and a part of everyone, that belongs to God. You may call it your spirit, that eternal flame that exists within each man, woman and child. When you die, that part of you will be reclaimed by God himself and he will experience in full all the moments of each life."

I watched Isayel's face light up when he spoke about God, the luminous shine of his eyes that seemed vivid, even in the dim twilight of the evening. He was going full flow and I felt powerless to stop him, although I was cringing inside at the religious turn of his talk with me. I was pretty sure that God had never helped me with anything, and I still didn't believe he was a real being, despite anything anybody tried to say to convince me otherwise.

"God searches for his own enlightenment through the accrued knowledge and experience of others. He also has to overcome the torment and suffering of those fractured souls, of which there are many. Each act of love, kindness or selfless generosity restores the balance. This is a continual process that will go on without end, unless God decrees that humanity should cease to be."

"How can God be looking for enlightenment, I thought he was meant to be perfect?"

"No-one is perfect, Luna. Enlightenment continues, even for the greatest of beings. God seeks to purify all parts of himself and eradicate suffering from the hearts of mankind."

"I'm sure the Bible says that God is supremely good and kind, oh, and that he's always right."

"Ah, then perhaps you must not believe everything you read, little princess. We all fight the battle of dark and light, some more than others. A good deed will bring good results. A bad deed will bring bad results, but it is the results of your own deeds that will count the most."

In the distance I could hear the joviality of the other party-goers. Everyone was having a good time it seemed, except me. Isayel had picked the worst possible moment to give me his in-depth commentary on spiritual matters. It was absolutely true what Cassiel had said, angels were rubbish at parties.

"You should loosen up. You're far too tense for an old guy."

I saw Isayel prickle at my words. The corner of his mouth twitched as his eyes studied me.

"This God of yours, he doesn't like parties then?"

"I would not know." He replied stubbornly.

"Well, you already said he's not perfect... maybe he would enjoy a good dance, to let his hair down a little? When I die and he is up in heaven somewhere crunching through the juicy bits of my life, maybe he will come across me here, at my eighteenth birthday party, standing with you, talking... what's he going to think about that?"

"He will think you behaved yourself."

"Would he? But the night's still young... and as you said yourself, I am a woman now Isayel." I traced a finger across the line of my dress, cut low to expose my cleavage. My figure was more curvaceous than a couple of years ago and the swell of my breast threatened to spill out of the tight corset. I knew I looked good.

"You need to behave yourself." His voice was tight, strained, and I wanted to hurt him, just a little bit, to make him feel some of what I'd been feeling.

"But I'm reckless and only eighteen. I've got some wild seeds to sow... and I don't believe in your stupid God so I really don't care what he thinks of me – Demon!"

Isayel grabbed my wrist. "You don't know what you're saying. You're drunk."

"No, I'm not drunk enough." I shouted up at him and twisted my arm away, stomping back towards the castle. "I've had it with you and your self-righteous ways... telling me how grand you are... well, I know the truth... you've lusted after women for centuries haven't you? You've had your pick of all the beautiful women in ages past... and now you stand there, telling me how devout and good you are.... like I'm not good enough or desirable enough or something".

I could feel the storm behind me, but I had opened my own emotional floodgates and couldn't stop the outpouring of my words.

"I've been good, Isayel. I've done everything you've asked of me. Spending most of my time training with The Mothers...oh, and what a sexy little title for them by the way... it takes away their teeth and claws doesn't it? De-sexualises them so that they can appear tame and timid, like old maids. Well, they're not... they are strong, powerful and beautiful women. You and your lot had your way with them, you loved them and left them to shrivel away. You took everything they had, and even then, it wasn't enough, was it? They've devoted their whole lives to you, basking in your shadows... well you're not doing that to me. I'm not from the Dark Ages, you're dealing with a modern twenty first century girl, an atheist at that, and I won't let you do that to me."

I heard him behind me then, and before I could even turn to continue my onslaught, his hands were around my waist, pulling me down, pushing me onto the soft dewy grass.

He groaned as his mouth plundered mine, intense, all consuming... and I met him kiss for kiss, anger and frustration fuelling my passion.

"I love you.... and I hate you too" I said, biting hard on his lip, tasting his blood before he thrust himself against me, pulling my hair back and crushing me to him.

"You..." he said, between his kisses, "... are the most infuriating, annoying, desirable woman..... I've ever.... met."

"And you... are.... a...a.... bastard." I replied as the petticoats and outer layers of my dress fell away from me and the cool breeze wafted against the exposed skin of my thighs. I pulled my legs up tightly around him, my new boots digging into him as I pressed him closer to me. His hands scorched me, roaming over the swell of my breasts, down and down, and then his fingers were edging beneath my lace undergarments. No one had ever touched me there before and I burned with such intense desire that my whole body started to tremble.

"How can you say that I don't want you? Look what you are doing to me" he rasped as his finger circled around the tender centre of me, enflaming me, as he began to rub and tease the nub of me between his fingers.

"I want more... I want you to love me. Just me, no-one else. I want to be your one and only." I panted breathlessly into his ear as he continued his teasing strokes.

"Oh Luna..." he buried his head into the side of my hair. "You don't know what you ask."

It took all my strength and every single ounce of determination to withdraw myself from him then, because just as suddenly as the flame of my passion had been aroused, he had doused it with his reply. I needed more than he could give me.

For all his size and weight, as soon as I pushed him away, he fell back. I could see his arousal straining through the fabric of his trousers and the look on his face, crushed, hurt and bewildered.

"Isayel, I don't want you. Go back to the party and don't bother me again."

He stood up to his full height, looking down at me where I lay on the grass, dishevelled, ringlets tumbling down my back and around my face, bare legs poking out from my crushed skirts.

"I forgive you, because you are young and foolish. But, trust me, I will not let this happen again." They were the last words he spoke to me and I, in my hot-headed frustration shouted out to his retreating back that I would never, ever let him touch me again.

CHAPTER 13

"One should see the world, and see himself as a scale with an equal balance of good and evil. When he does one good deed the scale is tipped to the good - he and the world is saved. When he does one evil deed the scale is tipped to the bad - he and the world is destroyed."

- MAIMONIDES

The day after my encounter with Isayel I lay in bed, clutching the bed sheets, the room swimming and a pulsing headache pounding through my head. Maybe he had been right, and I had been drunk. Just like my mum, I thought, and it seemed as if I could forgive her just a little bit more for all the times I'd seen her throwing up in the toilet. I heaved then, wishing death would take me.

Instead I suffered, alone in my misery until later in the morning when Elisia came to find me.

"Ahh... I thought so." She said as my bathroom material-ised and she went to soak a flannel in tepid water. Gently she wiped around my mouth and my face, rinsing the flannel in cooler water and placing it across my temples.

"You disappeared early," she commented. I knew she was waiting for me to talk, maybe confide my feelings, but it all felt too raw.

"He is handsome, isn't he?" she said at last. "And maybe a bit of a rogue."

"I hate him." I replied, glad that my eyes were closed and obscured by the cloth placed there.

"You're very hard on him."

"How can you say that? I've seen the way he treats you. Teasing you with little snatches of attention but not really there for you at all."

"Is that what you think?

"Yes. I don't know how you stand it."

"Dear child, you have a lot to learn about the nature of love, and hate, for that matter, because one is very close to the other. I know that you are hurting, you feel he neglects you and you want his whole attention, but he isn't human Luna, and he cannot give you that."

"Has he spoken to you about what happened?"

"No, he would not do that. But I have eyes and ears... I've watched you pining for him, the way your eyes follow him during meal times, the things you don't say... It's not good for you."

"I won't be pining for him anymore, I promise you. I'm finished with him."

"That's just your bruised feelings talking. Give it time, everything will sort itself out as it's meant to be."

I'm sure Elisia thought she was making me feel better with her pep talk, but as I lay there remembering the extent of my passion, and how close we got to having that forbidden sexual encounter, I felt flooded with embarrassment and shame. I don't think I could have looked him in the face even if we did meet again.

Slowly I sat up on the bed, there was something I needed to do. I fingered the clasp at the back of the necklace that Isayel had given to me and prised it open. The delicate chain folded into the palm of my hand, the circle of hearts half obscured. It was a beautiful gift and I knew what it meant to him, but I didn't want to be half loved. I felt a stab of pain as I offered the necklace to Elisia.

"When you see Isayel will you give him this, from me."

I kept myself busy and my mind occupied and it wasn't long before The Mothers started to notice. Elisia first commented on how much I'd improved in my training. Over and over again I had practised perceiving the different energies, raising or lowering my vibration, meditating, chanting mantras and tuning into the subtle energy fields that were all around me but previously intangible. I felt myself responding to these energies in an advanced, more complete way until it felt natural to me. I could sense the vibrations of pebbles, rocks, trees, water, flowers, even animals, and a kind of sympathetic or empathetic understanding flowed between us, like a stream of information which passed from them to me, and from me to them. Communication of this kind could be very tiring but it felt incredible to interact with the world in this entirely elemental way. The opportunities to practice my craft were all around me. When I bathed or brushed my teeth I merged with the water, feeling the spirits, connecting in blissful gratitude and peace. It was the same with all the elements and when I watched the flames in the braziers it was almost as if I became one with the fire spirits. The earth supported me, as did the breath in my lungs and I became thankful and indebted to this process of creation of which I was part.

Sofia, too, was delighted with the art work I was producing. I loved sketching portraits the most, capturing those special moments in time, the light in my subject's eyes, or a certain expression around the mouth. I never drew Isayel again though, and his picture lay wrapped and tucked away in one of the many cupboards that adorned the walls, all but forgotten.

"We will work with oils next" Sofia had said, always pushing me to improve and expand my skill. "And, as a special treat, next week we will go visit Rembrandt." I smiled, I loved our excursions and often they concluded with ice cream or some other wonderful surprise.

Even Corrine said my focus and concentration had improved. I was pleased because I felt my success all around me, my reward for effort and perseverance. In my mind it showed that I had turned a corner, putting behind me some of my more selfish desires and maybe growing up just a little bit more.

I had seen Isayel too, from a distance now and again. He was particularly hard to avoid at mealtimes as these occasions were meant to be social and many people who didn't have the opportunity to see each other in the course of their working day very often mingled and took advantage of these opportunities. We never spoke but he sometimes acknowledged me with a slight nod of his head, and I found myself doing the same. It was a kind of unspoken acceptance of our differences and a begrudging respect, but at the same time I acknowledged it was another sign of my increasing maturity and a step towards some kind of dignity and stand-off between us.

Cassiel continued to be a great support to me and our friendship blossomed. Often we would sit talking or go off into one of the holographic worlds to enjoy different excursions. It was during one of our regular walks together that an almighty alarm sounded. I jumped in surprise, I'd never heard an alarm like it before.

"What's that?" I'd asked, a feeling of concern unravelling in the pit of my stomach. Cassiel looked almost as shocked as me.

"It can't be..." he said, "come, we have to get back."

"But what is it?" Cassiel didn't answer, only dragged me along beside him as I struggled to keep up with his long stride, half running and half walking, breathless and bedraggled by the time we arrived back on the ship proper.

"Go directly to your room and don't leave unless I or one of the Mothers come to fetch you. Is that understood?"

I nodded miserably. Something terrible was happening. People were running like mice, all through the corridors, and it seemed as if all the holographic worlds opened up at once, with swarms of people pouring from them. I had no idea so many inhabitants were aboard the ship, many of them running this way or that way, creating a chaos all around them.

I pushed through the throngs, elbowing people out of my way, as a renewed sense of urgency overtook me, adrenalin pumping around my body, making me feel edgy and alert. When I finally reached my chambers I ensured the doors were sealed and breathed a deep sigh of relief. No one, except the Mothers or Cassiel, would be able to enter unless it was with my express consent. That was just another privilege that had been passed onto me during my time on-board.

I supposed Isayel might have that privilege too, but I doubted he would ever come to visit me again. I'd been on board for three years and it was hard to believe that it was over a year since our last physical encounter. It seemed every time we met we'd ended up clashing in a truly awful way so although I thought of him often, my feelings had been tempered with time. It left my heart feeling heavy but I felt, at last, that we were both doing the right thing by avoiding each other.

I was totally trusted now too, a true resident of the ship, and it's not like I could just get off and run away so I was much more able to come and go as I pleased.

In the early days I'd longed for home and foolishly thought that if I could find the exit door I would be able to find a way to escape back to the canal where they'd found me, but when I'd found out we were actually travelling in space, rather than still parked up, my last shred of hope had died. I'd wept for my home and family then, more than ever, and entered a kind of lingering depression. Actually, if I'm honest, I'd cried for my dad most of all, because he'd been the strong, supportive influence in my life, the one I'd always gone to with my problems. I doubted if even his ghost could find me now and he felt doubly lost to me. Everyone else seemed so far away that their faces blurred in my mind when I tried to think of them and the memories became more and more indistinct as time went by. Amy would be thirteen now and I couldn't imagine what she would be like as a teenager. I wondered what she would be doing and whether she was coping with life as an only child.

As for mum, we'd had so many arguments before I left that for the longest time I just felt annoyed about her. Slowly that feeling had left me and I'd started to understand that she'd been in a very emotional place herself, struggling to bring up two kids and coping with the death of her husband. All the silly, trivial arguments seemed pointless now and my deepest regret was that I couldn't tell her how sorry I was for the things I'd said and done. I was no longer that foul-mouthed little girl who was so full of her own self-importance that she couldn't see beyond her own selfish little world. My dreams of home became faded snatches of memory and I realised that it was unlikely that I would ever see the people I cared about again.

I waited for long hours and nobody came. Restless, I paced the room, watching the flickering walls and waiting for news. Cassiel had definitely told me not to leave my room and I didn't want to defy him but... where was everyone? My chamber was soundproof and totally isolated from the main part of the ship, what was I meant to do? Eventually I could bear it no longer and opened the doors, half expecting something terrible to be waiting for me, but everywhere was quiet and still. In some ways that felt even more ominous. I made my way to the training rooms, Elisia would perhaps be able to tell me what was happening.

On entering the room I saw that it was empty and the brazier, which always simmered with herbal incenses, had been left to burn down, the remnants of ash and blackened roots cold in the pan. I'd never known her to be too far away from this beloved space of hers and although I called her name I wasn't surprised to be met with the cold echo of silence. Trying to gather my thoughts I decided to connect through the elemental realm. I sat next to a large tree that was growing through the room, branching out and seemingly supporting the outside wall. Leaning back against the trunk, I deliberately slowed my breathing and my thoughts, lowering my vibration so that I could understand and merge with the tree's energy field.

I let my auric field expand so that myself and the tree existed in a pulsing vibrational field that allowed us to merge. Gently I probed, asking permission to communicate. I felt the tree was agreeable and sought the knowledge that I longed for.

"Where is Cassiel?" I formed the question in my mind. After a few moments the answer resonated within me. "Gone". My heartbeat quickened as I tried to keep the connection.

"Where is Elisia?"

The tree gave the same answer, "gone."

"And Isayel?"

"All gone".

These answers became a knowing in my mind, knowledge that had been filtered through from the tree's consciousness, but I couldn't understand how it could be true. The tree must have been mistaken because we were hurtling through space at thousands of kilometres per hour... and they couldn't have just disappeared and left me here, could they?

"Where have they gone?" I asked, but I couldn't think clearly enough to hold my vibration in clarity. My connection diminished and all I could hear was a low buzz in my ears.

I thanked the tree and slowly withdrew my energy fields as I steadied myself and got to my feet. I would need to go back through the outer corridors towards the main portal of the ship and see if anyone else could help me.

As I walked, I was aware of other ship inhabitants milling around, ordinary people doing ordinary jobs. Someone was sweeping the floors with a mechanised sweeper while another person was cleaning the inner screens with a bright blue cloth. It seemed so normal and commonplace that I almost questioned my own sanity. Where were the angels? Not one to be seen anywhere.

"What's happened?" I asked one of the workers but he just shrugged and looked at me as if he didn't know what I was talking about.

As I scanned the unfamiliar faces around me, I felt more alone than I'd ever been before. For some reason the angels had disappeared. What could have made them do that? It didn't make sense but the alarm that had sounded whilst I was out walking with Cassiel had been filled with foreboding. I remembered the look of shocked bewilderment on Cassiel's face. What if we had been declared at war or some other disaster had befallen the ship? Maybe the angels had gone to fight or perhaps we were invading someone else's territory? All these thoughts poured through my mind, but each one made me fear even more for the safety of my friends, not to mention my own safety too.

From a distance I saw a face that I thought I recognised, pretty certain that she was one of the Mothers. We hadn't trained together yet and I didn't know what her disciplines were, but I thought she would probably know more than anyone else about what was going on. She was dressed from head to foot in black and in her left hand she held an ornately carved staff, which I'd seen her use more as a prop than a walking aid. In the middle of her forehead a multi-faceted ruby was suspended over her third eye, held in place by an intricate web of lace that capped her dark curls.

"Hey," I called out, pushing through the throng to get closer. "Hey, wait... I don't know if you know me, I'm Luna and..."

She looked up at me then, and as I got nearer I could see that her eyes were red and swollen. She had been crying.

"Yes, I know who you are" she uttered, throwing me a look of distaste. "And just so you know for future reference, I don't answer to the name 'Hey'. You will refer to me as Keysha."

I was in such a state of distress, I let the acidity of her comment sweep over me. The Mothers could be strict sometimes. "What's happening? Please, tell me what's going on."

She paused, as if considering what to do with me, like I was an insect that had just crawled into her field of vision.

"It's not safe here, follow me," she said at last, and ushered me through a maze of inner corridors to her chambers, which were surprisingly similar to my own but at the opposite end of the ship.

"I don't understand? What's happened, why isn't it safe?"

Keysha eyed me sharply, "we never thought it would happen, or even that it could happen... so, it just shows you, you just never know..."

"Never know what?" She was talking half to herself, or as if she thought I already knew the answers to my own questions.

"Keysha? Keysha? What's happened?" I was talking louder now, feeling my desperation rising.

"Yes, you would like to know wouldn't you? I bet you thought you were special, that you would be consulted or considered in some way?"

"I don't understand. What do you mean?"

"That alarm... it has never sounded before. Not ever. You can't even begin to know the implications of that... after all this time..." It seemed to me that she was dragging out the suspense for as long as possible, playing with me, while my mind went on an internal search for what could possibly have happened, and dredging up every nasty possibility that my imagination would allow.

After what seemed like an age, she turned her attention

back to me, her eyes still red-rimmed but showing flecks of annoyance now too. She looked me up and down slowly, as if she was considering whether to tell me or not. She must have decided that if it wasn't in my interests to impart this secret knowledge, then it was most definitely in her own.

"Well, if you must know... It's finally happened, hasn't it? The thing we never thought would... the alarm... the signal from the Great Almighty One... that's right... you're as well to look shocked... you have no idea of the magnitude of what's happened... God himself has called the angels back, including your beloved Isayel. They've all left the ship. They've abandoned you Luna, left you here to rot by yourself."

"I don't understand. What do you mean?"

"You wouldn't understand. It's not knowledge that's meant for you."

"But I NEED to know."

"Hmm... well, you will know in time, but all you need to know right now is that God has demanded an audience with all of his angels. Not just those on this ship, but a grand meeting with all the beings who defied him in the Great War, the multitudes who have spread throughout the universes, including the angels who currently rot in hell." I gasped, it sounded... seriously bad and too incredulous to even believe. I still didn't believe in God and to hear other people talk about him as if he were a real entity... well it just made me think they were all deluded.

"Why? Why has he done that?"

"Well, it's obvious isn't it? He probably wants to enlist them on his side again, maybe offer an olive branch or a solution that they can accept without losing face. No one wants to admit defeat in battle, do they?"

"But they wouldn't do that, would they?"

"Wouldn't they? It seems to me that whenever God calls,

they run to do his bidding, even now after all this time. You must have seen this?"

I remembered all the things Cassiel had told me about the discord, the emptiness of an angel's life without God to give it purpose and meaning... and then when Isayel had spoken of God at my party, his whole manner had changed. It was like he had come alive and I had to force my attention on him just to get a reaction... he loved his God more than me.... that much was clear now. Maybe they were like the prodigal son in the bible, just waiting for the right time to go home to heaven.

Keysha stared at me. "If God decides to allow the angels residence back in heaven, then I believe no power on earth will stop them from reclaiming their former glory."

"But what about the Zarns? And the gene pool?"

"What about it? It will be a pointless exercise, a trivial bit of entertainment that kept The Watchers occupied for a few hundred years, nothing more. And your precious little vibrations and energy field will all be for nothing. No angel will lay with a mortal ever again if they reconcile with God."

I felt sick inside, like I'd been kicked or trampled. This woman filled the room with poison and I wondered how she could even be a Mother. The Mothers I knew were kind and loyal, endlessly patient and loving, whereas Keysha had gloated over the bad news she gave me and I could sense her pleasure at my pain.

"I need to go," I went to walk past her but she raised her staff to block me. "Not so fast young one. You may not have liked our little chat but you need to stay here for a while. It's not safe for you. I will go and see what news I can find."

I looked at her, searching her eyes. Was she lying to me? I couldn't tell. What reason would she have to be deceitful? It didn't make sense. "Okay." I said at last. "How long will you be?"

"An hour. I will come back in an hour."

As soon as Keysha breezed out of the room a sense of dread overcame me and the pit of my stomach started to churn with anxiety. I walked towards the door but it was sealed and there was no way to prise it open or get out. I hadn't anticipated this and could only pray that Keysha would be as good as her word and come back for me.

Hours ticked by and there was no sign of Keysha. I shouted for help until my throat began to burn with pain - but there was only silence and the steady bleeping of the flickering bank of wall lights that continued to be active in the background. I had no idea where I was on the ship, and if these chambers were anything like my own, I knew they would be soundproof and practically impenetrable.

Luckily, I was able to drink from the tap in the bathroom and relieve myself when needed. But even as I quenched my thirst, hunger had already started to gnaw at my insides. What if she didn't come back and I just died of starvation in this room? How many days could I live for? I stuck my arms out in front of me... I was pretty skinny, I wouldn't last long at all.

CHAPTER 14

"I am nave and I have fucked up but I tell you something else. I believe in change. I don't mind getting my hands dirty because my hands are dirty already. I don't mind giving my life to this because I'm only alive because of the compassion and love of others."

— RUSSELL BRAND

When the alarm sounded those of my kind made great haste to gather together in the Grand Meeting Room, so called because of the splendour of the furnishings there. Drapes of red velvet and ancient tapestries adorned the walls, complementing the intricate fretwork that had been carved into the oak panelling. It possessed the sumptuous style of a great lodge or majestic courtroom, designed solely for the purposes of serious contemplation and reflection. We enjoyed the grandiose setting, revelling in the artistry of the craftsmen who had laboured so diligently in order to create this environment for us. It was a place where we could feel the weight of our propositions and the responsibility of our decisions. This room was situated in a part of the ship that was off-limits to humans and where we also held our spiritual observances when we felt moved to do so.

Glancing around the large oval table that occupied the central position in the room, I studied the faces of my many brothers. I noted the general perception of concern, furrowed brows and facial muscles held in tension, together with an underlying buzz of activity as whispers hung low and heavy in the air, prior to the proceedings being commenced. This was the place we gathered in order to discuss matters of importance or significance. Democracy would always rule here and each member would, in turn, get the chance to air their opinions and put forward their arguments. Once this was done, we would terminate the proceedings by casting a vote, which would be final.

A silence befell the room as Danjal held counsel, raising his right hand to indicate the commencement of the proceedings.

"Brethren, we find ourselves in the greatest of predicaments. The siren has sounded, which means that God has requested our presence. We are not prepared, despite our previous debates on this very subject." His argument was brief and to the point, culminating in his deepest desires.

"There is no choice. We need to return and hear that which is spoken. We are Angels of God, are we not? Have we not been cast into the darkness for too long?"

"And then?" Cassiel had stood to attendance, drawing up to his full height, entreating his brethren to reconsider.

"What about everything we've worked so hard to achieve? The new colonies will be flourishing. Zarnett-9 is on the verge of becoming self-sustaining. We don't even know what God wants, he hasn't been clear, and I think we deserve more information before we act rashly and abandon our duties here."

Sariel was next to his feet, followed quickly by Semjaza. Each had a point of view and held strong contradicting opinions. Some amongst us nodded in agreement, others remained silent, intently listening to what was said.

"We are free – free from the yoke of our responsibilities to God. Tell me, what will we gain by going back, tail between our legs, humbling ourselves at his command? We are warriors – kings in our own rights, we don't need God." Gadreel banged his fist onto the table, vehemently putting forward his dominant beliefs.

Feelings were being stirred and I could feel the thrumming of tension escalating around me. Gadreel was a persuasive speaker and had long held very negative views about God, which had not tempered with time.

Penemué reflected, holding the space around him in silence until he deigned it appropriate to speak quietly to the waiting assemble. "Freedom is nothing. We fought hard for it, revelled in it while it was still new to us. But what of it?

All we discovered was that freedom brings with it the burden of responsibility and the terror of consequence. I would submit that we are bound more tightly now by our own misdeeds than ever we were in the Mansions of our Lord."

It was my turn to speak. I knew that my opinion would hold weight with many of those present. I had been a trusted companion to God, residing in the Seventh Heavens at his side before the chaotic turn of events pulled us away from him and all that we held dear.

I chose my words with caution, picking over them and turning them around in my mind like polished pebbles, before I uttered them out loud.

"Friends, it seems to me that we are a company divided. The great alarm is unprecedented and, as Cassiel has pointed out, we have very little information on which to consider or plan. However, Danjal, I am in agreement with your sentiments. We have suffered through eternity in the knowledge that we lost the Great Battle, that we were cast down to live in the shadows, to walk amongst men. But, let us not forget our faith. We stood up for what we believed in, which meant that God had to accept the division of heaven. That being so, when we return to God it will be on our terms, not as defeated warriors, but as independent, strong individuals with the right to a voice. Return to him we must, for we cannot deny the nature of that which we are - God's Messengers, still carrying the spark of God's flame – now and for all time. We need to go back to the source to replenish and reflect back on our own existence."

Turel spoke next. "If we ignore God's calling, we risk far more than we can ever know. From our meeting with him, negotiations will become possible, which can only strengthen our situation. Perhaps one day there will be greater understanding and consideration on all sides, so that a true reconciliation can take place. And, yes, I know that is not what we seek – we accepted our fate and have been independent since the dawn of time... but is it not also true that many of us feel homesick? We wish for reacquaintance and, yes, even forgiveness?"

It took over three hours of discussion before every one of us had been heard. A quiet calm descended through the room as Uziel, the final angel to put forward his viewpoint, made his stand. "We have been punished and labelled as demons when, in reality, we have just stood our ground in the name of freedom. Hasn't mankind done the same, without judgement? Wasn't our punishment unjust, because we refused to bow in submission to Adam? Ours is not to question the will of God – ours is to question our own will. Sometimes events spiral out of control and set us on a trajectory that is far removed from anything we would have wished for. It is vital that we learn from our past mistakes, and we can only find peace if we allow this communion with God to take place. We need to remove those negative labels that hold people in fear of us and discover who we really are and if we are no longer meant to be God's Messengers then we need to know how to live without that bind."

A murmur descended upon the room as we took a moment to discuss amongst ourselves the intricacies of the debate before Danjal called for attention. "We have heard from all present. All that remains is for the vote to be cast."

Each of us settled back, eyes closed, and connected to the grid of energy that was all around us. Unlike the voting systems on earth, there would be no whimsical or nostalgic casting of opinion, nor votes submitted to gain a political point or advantage. This process was infallible and intractable. In the middle of the table a shaft of light emerged, oscillating with flecks of colour that cast a prism of light across the wooden surface. The light was generated by the vibrational frequencies of our hearts and minds, which gave a true reflection of our desires and intentions. There would be no escaping the ultimate truth of our preferences and the eventual colour of that prism would indicate with perfect exactitude the final result of our votes.

Minutes ticked by as we sat motionless, generating the necessary altered states of awareness that we needed in order to perform this function. In time, a low hum began to build and intensify, alerting us to open our eyes.

As I came back into the material present the prism of light had stabilised to a pulsating shade of deep blue. Each of us fixed our gaze there, accepting without question the inevitable consequence of our vote. We would be leaving.

CHAPTER 15

"All changes, even the most longed for, have their melancholy; for what we leave behind us is a part of ourselves; we must die to one life before we can enter another."

-ANATOLE FRANCE

anjal had instructed that we had one single hour to attend to any unfinished business before we left The Omicron. My priority, of course, was to find Luna. I imagined her concern, perhaps even her anger, and felt duty bound to instruct her as to the nature of our departure. Cassiel had already told me she was safely in her chambers and I had no reason to doubt him, but when I arrived and found her room empty and in darkness, I was more than a little surprised.

Elisia seemed the obvious second choice and I quickly made my way to the training rooms. These, too, were quiet and unoccupied. It felt strange to me, Luna had never been one to wander too far, and I could only assume she was otherwise engaged with the Mothers.

My chest felt heavy, burdened with the responsibility of ensuring Luna would be well cared for in our absence, but with such limited time remaining I had no choice but to abandon my search. I knew it was unlikely that she would miss my company, as our interactions had been forcibly limited, but Cassiel had been a constant visitor, helping her to adjust more easily to life on board the ship, brightening her days and bringing her much needed amusement. I knew she would feel his loss most keenly. As for myself, she had never been far from my thoughts.

With one final attempt I cast my mind around the ship, searching for her energy signature but I could not find it. In hindsight, I should have searched harder, but at the time I was distracted with the extreme prospect of entering the Kingdom of Heaven for the first time in thousands of years.

We were all leaving together, a mass exodus, like a migration of souls into a place that exists outside of time and space. Many people have wondered how one enters the heavenly realms. I can only say that man enters through the goodness in his heart and that the gates of heaven are closed to those who sin and who are unworthy.

Angels would ordinarily be pure of spirit, mind, body and soul and gain unconditional admittance, but our past misdemeanours condemned us as we stood at the threshold waiting for an audience with God himself. The Gatekeeper of Heaven is known to mortals as St Peter and that can allow for images of a gentle soul patiently guiding people through to the realm of God. The truth is far more terrifying, for the seven headed dragon known as The Great Beast roams these outer worlds and guards the gates of Heaven from those deemed too wretched to enter. The Great Beast does not sleep and his vigil is relentless.

Whilst he watched us with great interest, he did not attack, despite our formidable sins, because when the conflict in Heaven commenced, it was the dragon himself who waged war, seeking victory over God and enlisting us, the ones known as the Fallen Angels, to fight by his side. Once we were allies, but now he looked upon us with hostility, snapping and snarling, eyes red like pokers, pacing backwards and forwards as if on an invisible leash. He did not speak with us, nor us with him, for we parted company in the long distant past. His way is not our way. We are not beholden to him or anyone.

It seemed like an age of waiting when finally a horn sounded and we were escorted through the gates into the lower celestial realms. Little had changed since my last visit here and it felt like a strange homecoming. There was a vastness that stretched as far as could be seen in all directions. Shapes swirled around us, unravelling and reforming, misty and opaque. This realm was not material and therefore nothing in it felt or looked solid. Thought directed matter here, but thought itself is a wispy, whimsical vehicle and on this level even dreamers can influence the surroundings. We had to journey further as these lower levels mainly attracted psychopomps, who guided the souls of the recent dead into the afterlife, and casual explorers of the astral realms. Angelic beings did not linger long in these parts and I was already starting to feel uncomfortable with the onslaught of undirected, confused energy that snaked around us.

"Keep moving," Danjal directed, and we followed his lead in silence. As we approached the higher realms, the ascension created a purifying ripple of bliss that washed over us, building into a crescendo of emotion, like a tidal wave of forgiveness and compassion. It was akin to bathing in an ocean of love and serenity, cleansing all the pain, anguish and torment that that been coiled inside us.

I studied the faces of the others, rapturous, contented and, dare I say, angelic of countenance once more. More than this, our great wings began to form, stretching out from the taut skin of our backs, growing in shape and size until they were in perfect proportion to our bodies. I had not realised how much I had missed the glory of my wings until this moment, and my breath caught in my throat as they unfurled, and I felt their great weight and presence. Closing my eyes, I immersed myself in the sensation and euphoria of the moment. The sound of my wings beating, the currents of air being displaced by the powerful impetus of the movement, a cascade of joy and self-righteous power, all cascading around me, the depth of which I could only just fathom.

With the formation of our wings we soared higher and further than any mortal being, straight into the realm where God himself awaited our arrival. It seemed to me that my soul was expanding with love and acceptance as the weight and sorrow of my past misdeeds were released from the darkest, deepest part of me, a transmutation into something gentle and pure.

God's presence was all around us, a tangible illuminating energy that penetrated into the very centre of our beings, lighting us up with an ephemeral sense of wellbeing. God does not sit on a cloud as popular opinion would suggest. He has no form or solid structure, and yet he is everywhere and encompasses everything. Within us and without us, God exists. He is the breath that we breathe and also the lungs that are doing the breathing. He is the ground, the sky, the laughter of a child and the teardrop of a saint. In everything he is expressed, and this expression is his way of expanding his knowledge of life. You may think that historical texts and my chauvinism authenticate that God is of male gender and I now confess to misleading you in this matter. For God is not he or she, but something far greater than this, beyond those barriers of language. To call God "it" would imply that God is a somehow lesser being, or even something without life, soul or spirit. God is not that. In contrast, to call God 'she' would stir up a radical minority opinion that would in turn create fanatical or impassioned debate. So, I will settle with the word 'he' to describe God, and God will, for the time being, express himself in this way too.

When God speaks, he does so through the valley of the mind. His presence is such that he can talk with each of us in a singular moment and still be fluid to the direction of each conversation. When God spoke with me, he communicated his longing to be reconciled. "For too long," he said, "has there been hostility" and my heart replied to God in concurrence with his words. He knew my mind and my heart's longing without the encumbrance of speech, and as I bathed in the serenity of his love, I felt renewed in my vows of worship and obedience. The thousands of years cast away from God became like nothing, a blink of the eye, a speck of dust in the infinite universe.

At that moment I was suspended, cradled from harshness

or discord, separate from all of my experiences and even separate from the nature of myself. What of Luna, you might ask? She was lost to me and for a time I could not even comprehend her existence. Within me a cellular regeneration was taking place, where I could rejoice in my oneness with the spirit of God. Nothing else mattered and the memories of Luna had been all but erased from my mind. In this state of suspension time was irrelevant and I dangled in the void, like a hanged man without shackles.

I could have existed in that state for eternity were it not for the Ceremony of Farewells. From the depths of my deepest bliss, God pulled me back, reeling me in slowly, allowing me to wade through the layers of thought and feeling until I was fully present once more. Looking around me I could see my brethren undergoing the very same process. Some were still drowsily absent, stumbling back into their own bodies and minds from that suspended state. It was uncomfortable to return, similar to having been rudely awakened from a sound sleep to the realisation that there was no going back to the dream state once the cold light of day poured in through the windows. There was only forward motion and the prospect of a future that was as yet unwritten.

I flexed my wings and waited for the Ceremony to commence. I had attended a handful of such ceremonies in the past and whilst not always pleasant, they completed the cycle for beings who were considered elevated enough to be worthy of this sacrament. In terms of similarity, the funeral rites on earth were the closest approximation to what we were about to observe.

Music commenced in the distance, a heavenly choir that diligently raised spirits but suppressed joy, droning on in rapturous glorification. I turned my attention towards the ensemble that processed towards me. There were several figures, all veiled, dressed from head to foot in white lace. Their forms seemed to float a few inches above ground level, propelling them ever nearer, much like a sinister conveyer belt of faceless bodies.

At last, and with a final lyrical burst of enthusiasm from the choir, the group came to a halt in front of us, where a cloaked figure commenced his litany. The minister's face was obscured by the hood of his cloak, and his voice was slightly muffled, as if coming from a distance.

"We are gathered here today to allow for the onward journey of these souls....."

A nice touch, I thought. Someone had obviously taken the pains to actually be present at a similar occasion on the earth plane.

"Lives entwined, friends until the end. The passage of time brought these souls wisdom and knowledge, more than most ever receive. These lives were blessed in countless ways..."

The words rambled on and my mind, which had been dredged back from the deepest of slumbers, started to become alert to the sentiments being expressed. The six figures in white, all motionless, still veiled, stood to attention like vertical corpses. They unsettled me in a way that was disquieting. Something wasn't right and my heart trembled with a dreadful fear that seemed to come from nowhere.

"We cast these souls into the holy fire to be purged in the name of God. The sins of these spirits will not contaminate those that go after them. Their seed will falter and perish, and the earth shall reclaim that which is hers as God's Will be done. Let it be so"

As the presiding minister spoke, the violet flame of St Germain flickered into life, growing up around the bodies until it created a wall ten feet high. This flame was searing hot and yet cool at the same time, oscillating within the red and blue colour spectrums to create a spiritual fire that enabled the transmutation of sin and negative energy. Anyone afflicted with despair or disease could walk through the holy flames and gain protection, healing and metamorphosis, but these flames could also burn into the inner chambers of the heart and deeper recesses of the mind to vaporise learnings, wisdom, personality and individuality. If somebody basked within St Germain's fire for too long, they would become a shadow in the world, or what could be thought of as a shade, neither dead nor alive but trapped in the underworld for eternity.

My mind wrestled with the growing unease I was feeling, a tremor cast through me and I could not prevent myself from intervening.

"Stop," I shouted, calling a sudden halt to the minister's words. "I need to see the faces of these souls." At once it seemed that the minister's voice changed, and his cloak dropped away, revealing a presence of light energy that radiated brighter than any flame. I knew this to be Metratron, the Angel of Life, through whom God spoke. His mission was often to deliver God's messages to the physical realm and now, here he was, representing God in this heavenly sanctuary.

"You, Isayel, have no jurisdiction here."

"Who are these souls. I need to see with my own eyes."

There was a moment of silence and all angels looked to me, almost in disbelief that I had been bold enough to utter what I knew they were all thinking.

"It is of no consequence to you."

"Are you sure that is so? I lay down the challenge and it seemed I was right back in a situation where the will of God was once more put to the test.

"You are foolish to even ask that question." Metratron's voice boomed out, ringing with the authority of God's own power. "Do you not know the grace that you have received from God? That he has been willing to forgive all your former transgressions? The disobedience you have displayed throughout time? Your gratitude for such a gift should be ten thousand fold, and yet here you stand before God's Holy Assembly, and you demand... yes... demand the right to knowledge that is not yours to know."

"Metraton, with respect, we have fought Holy Wars side by side together in the past. In unity we have served and supplicated to the Will of God. Let it be known that we have been created equal and I will not bow to you or your superior attitude. God can speak with me directly, if he so wishes. But right here and now, I am asking to see the faces of these souls for I believe this knowledge should be mine."

As we continued to exchange words I could see that Cassiel was edging forward, soundlessly stepping closer to those veiled forms. I kept my eyes on Metraton, considerate not to alert him to what was happening behind him. He was self-righteous in his stance, offering no compromise or true reason as to why the veils could not be lifted. My intuition was screaming at me that I should persist in my requests.

Within a millisecond of time Cassiel had removed the veil of the first figure and there, staring out of white, vacant eyes, her face but an inanimate mask, was the Mother Elisia. No longer living and yet not truly dead.

My beloved Elisia, who had been a treasured companion for decades. She who was the Mother of Tri-ane, and Luna's closest guardian. Luna. It was as if a shroud of forgetfulness had lifted and thoughts of her flooded back into my mind. What terrible fate had befallen Luna and those still on board the Omicron? Did she still live? A crushing weight filled my chest.

Metraton observed the proceedings silently, resigned, as Cassiel lifted the veils, one after the other. Sofia, Corinne, Christie, Maylene and Karin, all Mothers of exceptional talent and ability, all of whom had been chosen to share their diverse knowledge and wisdom with Luna.

I staggered backwards as shock ran through my body and I closed my eyes to the ghoulish site of the Mothers, once so animated, their forms lifeless instruments to be tossed into the flames. And if the Mothers were here, I wondered who was taking care of Luna?

"Is God responsible for this?" I asked at last.

"It is better this way." Metraton replied. "God requested a sacrifice, something sacred to you, that would represent your true repentance in his eyes. My understanding was that this had already been agreed by you."

"My repentance? I don't understand. I did not ask for repentance. We are here because God called us back."

Metraton shook his head. "That is not my understanding."

"What do you mean?"

"God received your signal, a total surprise to him. A clear request from your ship that The Watchers were ready to once more serve their God, that they had denounced their insurrection and wanted to come home."

"That cannot be." I searched the faces of my Brethren, each of whom shook their heads in confusion and disbelief. We had lived with our sins since ancient times and not one of us had considered our previous uprising to be wrong or out of place.

I thought back to only moments ago, the rapturous bliss of being forgiven, the comforting density of my wings wrapped around me, the absolution of my sins... would it be worth this? The annihilation of The Mothers? I looked at their blank eyes, the soulless, lifeless shells they had become, like puppets without a master. I did not have the right, nor the inclination, to cause such suffering to those I held in such great esteem.

"Metraton, there has been a grave misunderstanding. For it was *us* that received the message from God. We came back at his request, not ours."

Metraton looked dubious. "How can this be?"

"It would seem that each side has been put into this position by an outside source. Who would have the power to do that, I know not, but this ceremony has to stop now. The Mothers must not be harmed."

"Isayel, you know the rules. No mortal can return from this place. It is unheard of."

"Who makes those rules? Your God? Our God? Rules are made to be broken, are they not? I challenge God to understand the great wrong that has been done here, to these innocent women."

"Hardly innocent. They cohabited with you, raised your children, unholy seed that should not have been born."

"Life is sacred... all life is sacred... and the Mothers have done no wrong, for is not love a pure thing? Is not love precious beyond all? Did not God himself say that love is the greatest power in the whole of the universe? These women loved and in return, we loved them also."

"Isayel, I understand your sentiments. This matter is very grave indeed and one that will need careful thought. I will give you my oath that until this matter has been settled by God's hand I will personally see to it that the Mothers shall remain in suspension, untouched and unharmed, awaiting God's verdict. I can do no more than this."

It was all I could have hoped for and the Ceremony of Farewells halted right then, the violet flame extinguished and the Mothers taken away into a safe suspension. No heavenly choir resumed, for which I thanked God, and myself and my brethren were left to consider these new developments, alone together once more.

CHAPTER 16

"Sometimes two people have to fall apart to realize how much they need to fall back together."

-    MAYA ANGELOU

T here is no time in the heavenly planes, for time is a manmade construct, and because this is so, I could not say how long we waited in this dormant state, expecting tidings from God. There was, however, nothing, no word, only silence. Metraton had advised he would hold an audience with our Lord in the near future, but who knew when that would be?

Our future, past and present seemed to merge together, fused into a meaningless strand of events that circled around, looping backwards and forwards so that nothing seemed clear or straightforward. Perhaps we were meant to feel like this, to keep us off-centre and unclear about what we should be doing. You cannot put plans in motion if you cannot understand the concept of tomorrow.

We neither ate nor slept and nothing stirred our senses except, that is, for Cassiel. He was more alert than ever, pacing around, trying to engage in conversation and inject some enthusiasm into our sorry selves. On this particular occasion he approached me more forcefully, and yet still I sighed and demanded he leave me alone. He was like an annoying fly who persisted in alighting on the flesh despite being swatted away.

"Isayel," he whispered frantically in my ear, "you must listen. This is urgent business."

"Nothing is urgent" I swatted, and missed.

"Do you know what day it is?"

"Why should I care? We are not bound by time in this realm."

"Well, you may think that, but I am the Angel of Time, and it follows me wherever I am, so I know exactly what time and date it is."

"So?"

"So, if you want to save everything we've worked for, and if you want to honour the memory of the Mothers then there is something you must do."

"I will do nothing, except wait for Metraton to deliver unto us the Will of God."

"Do not even say that." Cassiel's voice was interjected with a desperation. "In two days from now it will be Luna's twenty first birthday."

"What?" I was confused, how could that even be possible. I couldn't comprehend how long we had been away for.

"If you want to do something right and save Zarnett-9 and the future of the Zarns, you must return to the Omicron to seek out Luna. You must lay with her on her twenty first birthday and she must become a Mother."

"It is not possible. I cannot do it. Besides, she would not have me now."

"It is meant to be, it is what we have waited for, for so long. You must do it. Her frequencies are aligned to only you, so no other can go in your place. God knows, if I could help out here I would, but it is not to be that way."

I felt wretched, and buried my head in my hands. All that Cassiel had said was true but how could I find the strength and motivation to leave this place?

"You must do it. You must leave tonight. Penemué can go with you, and act as your advisor and aide should you need it."

At the mention of Luna's name my heart had fluttered in my chest. Could it even be possible that two days from now I could legitimately hold her in my arms and become her lover and her consort? The prospect was of such serious magnitude I knew that I could not dismiss it. The pull to be by Luna's side at this time was at least as strong as the need to stay in heaven. I had to make a choice, and quickly.

Descending from heaven required a lowering of our vibrational energies. It is something that can be cumbersome and unpalatable, like blunting down the senses and engaging with the immediate environment in a deeper, denser way.

Penemué and I had agreed that we would leave that evening, and spent our last moments saying goodbye to everyone. I was still doubtful about whether I was doing the right thing but Cassiel could be very persuasive when he set his mind to it.

Navigating back to the Omicron would take around five hours in human time, this being necessary so that we could acclimatise ourselves to the changes in air pressure and environment. To reach a moving target our trajectory had to be perfect and we had decided not to use the bridges that could have sped up our journey. Wormholes sometimes had a nasty way of taking us somewhere else entirely and we could not afford to take the chance that we would not return in time.

"Tell Metraton I am sorry," I had said to Cassiel, only to hear Metraton reply from behind me.

"Tell me yourself, on your return." I turned to face Metraton. He looked both concerned and resigned. I felt his apprehension and the old bonds of friendship renewing themselves, wrapping around my heart, even after all this time. We embraced then, with the unspoken understanding that, whatever the outcome, we would still regard each other as brothers, despite our divided loyalties and disagreements. With one last look at those we left behind, myself and Penemué set off for our encounter with The Omicron.

There are different ways we can travel through space. There is the scenic way, where we drift slowly towards our destinations, observing the planets and star clusters, and soaking up the total tranquillity of this nebulous landscape, or we can obtain thrust-drive speeds, pushing through barriers of light and sound, so that we can arrive at destinations almost instantaneously. For reasons of my own, my return to The Omicron had to be a slower journey. It felt like I had left Luna far behind, long, long ago, and now my mind needed time to reverse-engineer those feelings. I was quite aware that Luna would probably think I had forsaken her. She would no doubt be angry and bitter. Laying with her might prove more complicated than I anticipated and yet, I knew she would find it hard to resist the pull of our energies when we were together once more.

Penemué was silent for much of the journey and I suspected he was busy chronicling events in his mind for later use. In those early times it was Penemué who gifted the knowledge of writing and storytelling to the ancient humans. He patiently sat with them and taught cuneiform, runes, hieroglyphics and alphabets so that history [his story] could be handed down from generation to generation. More than this, he touched their minds with a creativity so powerful that the urge to bring stories into existence has remained with man throughout all time. It was this gift that I believe transcended all others, as without Penemué none of the Holy Scriptures could ever have been written, nor the great works of masters such as Chaucer, Shakespeare, Dickens, Bronte or Austen. The written word changed the very histories of mankind.

Penemué was aware of each word that had ever been chiselled, scratched, etched, painted or written throughout the ages, whether on cave walls, clay tablets, papyrus, wood, parchment, paper or, in modern times, even on screens. Under his direction the Muses would visit those destined to create, forging inspiration in the head and the heart, so that great works of literature could educate and inspire all those who had a mind to read and learn.

I had witnessed, too, Penemué's own suffering and dramatic interludes in life. It seemed he courted adventure and adversity in equal measure, perhaps so that he could continue to perpetually create with passion and sensitivity throughout the ages.

I remembered back to a time when Penemué was lost to us, rejecting his angelic heritage in order to fully appreciate the hardships and suffering that human life endured. It was during this period that he became involved with Nairie, a mortal woman with whom he had fallen in love. By day he would exchange casual pleasantries with this woman, limited to "good mornings" and "how do you do's". He ensured their circles crossed with regularity and that she would take note of the way he looked at her, with eyes that could see into her heart's desires.

However, not able to show his true form, he would visit Nairie in her dreams, stirring her night time visions so that she would awaken each morning touched by a phantom lover that she could not explain. Nairie became charmed by this nocturnal love to the extent that she withdrew from life. She had a husband who could no longer please her, despite his best intentions, and to whom she no longer felt an affinity. Then, when her passions could no longer be denied, Nairie departed from her husband's side without notice or warning. She abandoned her home to travel far distantly and take up residence on a remote windswept island far, far away from neighbours or friends. Penemué should not have influenced a human in this way, putting his own needs before those of this woman and her family, but he had loved with the heart of a poet and had wanted her singularly for himself.

Angelic love transcends time and although the flesh of man ages, withers and eventually dies, this does not concern our kind. We see the soul inside, which ripens and becomes more precious with age. And so it was that Penemué, in the transient form of man, lived side by side with Nairie as husband and wife. This arrangement, you understand, was not acceptable in the eyes of God for Nairie had already chosen her husband in years past and so Penemué and Nairie committed the sin of fornication and adultery. Such acts, which seem so commonplace now, were considered the greatest of violations in those times and when Nairie passed from the earth only Penemué mourned her loss as all others had been deserted. More than this, Penemué never confessed to Nairie his true nature and only on her deathbed, when the veil from her mortal soul had been lifted, did she understand her life with Penemué had been built on lies and deception. He carries with him the scars of this duplicity and waits, even now, for her reincarnated soul to once more be born into the flesh so that he can make amends. During her next incarnation, which may still be hundreds of years from now, Penemué has pledged to guide her life with selfless love and kindness so that she will experience a lifetime of joy, success, wealth and happiness – a rare life, filled also with a love that will quench the karmic debt he owes her.

I turned my attention back to the moment, and could feel the weightlessness around me as we progressed through the many layers of space. In the far distance I recognised the girdle of Orion, and shuddered in apprehension. In this place, scattered amongst the constellation of Nephilia, we had despatched our despicable offspring, the Nephalim, to rampage and, we imagined, to destroy themselves, thus saving Earth and the human race. As far as I was aware, no angel ever returned to investigate what happened to those ancient Nephalim and for thousands of years we could feel contented that their existence had been eradicated.

My senses started to tune into The Omicron which was now circling the dwarf planet Ceres, where it had no doubt recouped its fresh water supplies. I had every reason to believe that the crew would have continued to follow instructions and that the android contingency would ensure that the continued smooth running of the ship would be a priority.

Anticipating how I would approach Luna loomed large in my thoughts. Had I been away for almost two years? It hardly seemed that a moment had passed but I knew that, for Luna, each day would have dragged out interminably. How would she have survived, without the nucleus of the Mothers to guide her and show warmth and affection? Would she have encouraged further friendships with the human or android crew? I hoped she had, and that she had matured gracefully into a more understanding version of herself than the one I had left behind.

As soon as we landed on board The Omicron, materialising at photon speed within the vacuum chamber, I felt the familiarity of the ship welcoming me. Luna was a priority, but first I needed to look presentable and purge myself of the accumulated space dust. I thought that on seeing me, particularly with my newly re-established wings, she would probably go into deep shock. Penemué and I parted company and I headed straight to my chambers where I had the luxury of immersing myself in the foaming healing waters of my bathing complex. It felt so good to let the fluid wash away the grime and the negative thoughts I had been experiencing. It would be alright. I took a deep sigh, I hoped it would. I still hadn't attuned to her energy signature but thought that perhaps she had learned to cloak it from me. Some of the Mothers had crafty tricks they may have taught her.

It was heart-breaking now to think of the Mothers, waiting in limbo, their fate yet to be decided, and I shook my head to clear my mind. When Luna and I mated, my heart, body and soul had to attune to hers in a very specific way, and negativity could not be part of that melding process.

It was one hour before Luna's birthday as I strode through the familiar corridors towards her chambers, remembering that the last time I was here I couldn't find her and had no way to communicate what was happening. My stomach churned in apprehension, and part of me wanted to turn back and return to my Brethren in heaven, but I knew this was something I had to do.

Cassiel and the others were relying on me to plant my seed

to ensure the continued success of the Zarns. It was more than that though, because I'd longed for this moment too. Despite the words I had spoken to Luna in the past this was far from just a mating ritual for me. Luna held a special place in my heart, I loved her even though our time together had been difficult, the problems caused by overwhelming emotions on both sides. Sometimes it is this way with great love because the intensity and the power of it is so unsettling.

I knew my feelings for Luna would be timeless... it was destined that we should be together. She had not been mature enough to hear how much I loved her before, but maybe now she would be.

What is more, I would do everything I could to put her mind at rest. I would be gentle with her and learn to understand her vulnerabilities and needs. My heart was ready to commit to her fully, just as she'd asked me to in the past, and I imagined how happy this news would make her.

As I approached the door to Luna's chambers I felt a strange nervousness overtake me and, taking a deep breath, I buzzed the identifier panel located outside her door. It was a fraction of time but seemed like a lifetime before the entrance swished open. As the interior of the room revealed itself to me, I blinked to meet the unwavering gaze of Luna, smiling up at me in a way that I had never expected in a million years.

"I knew you would come back for me." She said and wrapped her arms tightly around my neck. It was all I could do not to fall over into her welcoming embrace as she pulled me to her.

"Luna, my love," I whispered, surprised beyond measure at her civil welcome. "You do not know how I have longed for this moment, how it was the thought of being with you again that has kept me going all this time. You have been the moon and sun to me since my departure." There were some untruths in my statement, and I used a little poetic licence, but I did not feel it would help our relationship to tell her that all thoughts of her had been wiped from my mind for most of my stay away. We were at a delicate point in our relationship and I wanted to court her properly before the ultimate seduction.

"You've come back for the mating?" she asked, tilting her head, as I looked deeply into her eyes. Time had not been kind to her, I could see. Beneath the surface beauty there was a glittering, brittleness about her that perturbed me.

"I've come back so that I can make you mine, and be a father to our child. We can be a family."

"That's what I said," Luna replied to me, flashing me a bright smile. "Can we do it now?"

"No, in a few hours. We need to prepare our energies in the modulation chamber first. I must say, your enthusiasm is a little... surprising?"

"Surprising for you, maybe. But I've been waiting for this day since you left." She seemed agitated and impatient, not engaging with me in the way that I had anticipated.

"Are you not curious to know what has happened and where I have been?"

"No, it's okay... I'm cool with it. What you do is your business, isn't it? I'm not bothered really." She stifled a yawn, as if the whole conversation was tiresome. "Can we go to the modulation chamber now?"

I walked at Luna's side as we made our way to the chamber. When I reached to hold her hand, she made a point of quickly moving it away, bringing it up to her hair as if rearranging the strands that fell in an untidy mane down her back.

"Did you miss me, my love?" I asked, hoping to inject a little romance into the proceedings.

"Yeah sure, you've been gone a long time. Not much to do around here is there?"

"How did you manage, without the Mothers, without Cassiel?"

"How do you think?" As she flippantly batted my questions away I perceived her defensiveness, but was still hopeful that the softer, more vulnerable side of her nature still existed. I wanted to be with her more than ever.

"Luna, how would you like for us to be married after the birth? We can continue to spend our time together and grow in love. I would honour and respect you, and even if we could no longer make love physically we could merge on an energy level, which is an amazing experience, perhaps even more so than physical lovemaking."

"Isayel, you know your problem? You talk too much and you're starting to sound like my mother, always going on. I don't want to get married, okay. We'll have the kid and that's it."

I was dumbfounded and we entered the chamber in silence. This should have been an exceptional moment for me... for us, and instead it had been rendered nothing more than some kind of business transaction. Was she just trying to get her own back? After all, that is how I'd described our union back in the past. I closed my eyes as the modulator began tuning our frequencies together, aligning us and co-joining our energies so that we could begin the process of creation. None of the previous pleasure I had felt in her company was there any more and I put it down to my long absence. I would resign myself to laying with Luna, creating our child, and then giving her space to decide what she wanted for her future.

It took over two hours for our energies to be brought into synchronisation, far longer than usual, and there was still a discrepancy in Luna's energy signature. I put it down to an electrical malfunction. Clearly, without the angels on board things had lapsed. I would be speaking to the technical team first thing in the morning but for now... now was the approaching moment of seduction.

CHAPTER 17

The hardest thing about being broken, isn't the love you don't receive, it's the love you long to give that nobody wants.

-       DINESH KUMAR BIRAN

L una watched, standing a foot or two away from me, as I programmed the Holographic World. I'd asked if she had a preference and she'd just shrugged as if it didn't matter to her, one way or another. I dialled in what I considered to be a romantic date night scenario for people from Earth.

As we stepped over the threshold we were transported to an intimate, candlelit restaurant, with the quiet, comforting murmur of other diners enjoying the delights of Italian cuisine.

An olive-skinned young man approached us, impeccably dressed in white shirt and black trousers.

"Sir, Madam?" he bowed slightly and raised an eyebrow, waiting for my request. Before I could even utter a word, Luna had barged ahead.

"Table for two, that one over there." She pointed to an alcoved seating area and the waiter politely led us over to Luna's preferred table. She was being uncharacteristically rude, and I wondered if The Mothers' previous training had worn away whilst she'd been left to her own devices.

We ordered Brunello di Montalcino from the burgeoning wine list and then went on to select grilled crostini for starters. Our conversation was stilted but I persevered with my questioning.

"What have you been doing during my absence?" I asked.

"Oh, you know, nothing much, watching the screens, using the Holographic Worlds to get away from it all."

"Oh? And who organised that for you? They were only accessible to you when accompanied before I left."

"Key… I mean, I spoke to the technical guys and they let me have some passwords."

"They are not allowed to do that." I was bristling with annoyance by now. My romantic evening was far lower than any of my expectations.

"I'm not asking for your approval. You weren't around to give the all clear, was you?" Luna continued to swig back her wine and the more she drank, the more her eyes shone with an unnatural brightness.

Conspiratorially she leaned towards me and covered her mouth with her hand, "do you know what I think we should do?" she asked, not pausing to await my reply, "I think we should just fuck all this and get on with it, don't you? You don't need to seduce me Isayel, I'm a sure thing."

I took a huge draught of my own wine then, and grabbed her tightly by the arm. "Come on then, let's get this over and done with." My mouth was clamped into a tight line. This woman was like a stranger to me now and it would be all I could do to rouse myself to please her and implant the necessary seed.

We stepped out of the Holographic World and I briefly entertained the idea of programming a new one, perhaps a chateau with a grand four poster bed and twinkling fairy lights scattered amongst the trees outside, similar to her eighteenth birthday scenario. The Luna I remembered would have been enchanted with such a landscape. I looked down at this challenging, unpleasant woman at my side, who seemed like a stranger to me, and decided we would just go to her chambers and get the deed over with.

As we lay together, my mind was not in a good place. To awaken my interest and stir life into my body I had to recreate in my imagination those other times with Luna, when my mouth had searched her out and it was all I could do to hold myself back. And so it was that my mind created a fantasy Luna, the version I had loved so well, who had been demanding and yet insecure, hiding behind the façade of confidence when I knew that inside she was like a tiny bud, waiting to unfurl into womanhood. The woman I kissed, therefore, was not the woman lying next to me in the bed. Instead, I kissed the woman of my dreams, gently holding her to me as we merged and became united in our lovemaking.

The reality was far different from my dreamscape. Luna clawed at my skin and pushed me into her, thrusting her hips into me in an aggressive, overbearing way. In turn, I pushed back, not even mindful of her virginity, as she seemed to be unconcerned at any pain or discomfort this would bring. The rhythm of our sex was hurried and savage as we propelled headlong into climax. As quickly as it had begun, it was over. An unsatisfying closure on a moment that I had anticipated with tender contemplation during the waiting years. As soon as the act had been concluded Luna immediately rolled away from me, sat up and stroked her belly. "This is the one" she said, with a smile on her face – the first time I had seen her looking genuinely happy since my return.

"I'm pleased you are looking forward to your impending motherhood."

"Oh I am," she had replied, "you have no idea how much."

As she sat there, turned away from me, I studied her back, in particular the freckles that tracked along her body like a road map. A memory stirred within me but I could not grasp it. Her nakedness was different to what I had expected.

"You can go now," Luna waved her hand, as if to dismiss me and I felt no motivation to stay. I began the process of dressing.

"I will come and see you tomorrow," I had every intention of being there for the full pregnancy and maybe it was better that she didn't want a relationship with me. In time we would learn to respect each other and honour the act of bringing up our child peaceably and with nurturing love.

"Don't put yourself out," Luna casually dismissed the idea. "I'm going to be busy tomorrow."

Those words followed me as I marched back to my own chambers and as I lay in bed I couldn't help but toss and turn. Something felt so wrong. Why hadn't I connected with Luna like I should have? This had never happened before. We should have been swept up in a rapture so great that the culmination of our love making would have been joyous and special beyond all reckoning.

Deep in the back of my mind, a nagging thought intruded into my conscious awareness, but I couldn't recall what it was. Do angels forget? Yes, sometimes, because we have so much time, and experience any number of ordeals and adventures. Eventually I fell into a fitful sleep, haunted by sadness and a gulf that was opening like a chasm in my belly. Dreams of Luna in her party dress, Luna swimming towards the waterfall, Luna enjoying the spa, or bent lovingly over a piece of artwork. She had always wanted me and I had always felt her love. Until now.

Hours ticked by and I felt ragged when I finally dragged myself out of bed, unable to endure the mockery of sleep any longer. Pacing the corridors, I went in search of the head technician. We needed to sort out the fault in the modulator chambers, perhaps that's why everything had been so off-key.

Raab was already busy when I approached him, his head disappearing inside the cavity of one of the control panels on the lower deck. Much of the ship's mainframe existed here and only authorised personnel were allowed in these quarters.

On seeing me, Raab's face broke into a wide smile.

"Sir, so good to have you back on board. We'd heard rumours last night but no one had seen you and we wondered…"

We chatted amicably for a while, nice, open talk that I had missed with Luna. Finally, I turned to the subject of the Modulator Chamber.

"I can vouch myself that the Chamber is in tip-top working order sir. I keep a regular check on it myself and, see here," Raab quickly punched some codes into the panel at the side of where he was working and brought up a log of dates and service information. "This is the service log. It's a pristine environment up there, everything working like clockwork."

"Thank you Raab, good to know." That left me with an even bigger problem because I realised that I had been hoping for a malfunction which would explain everything away in a nice simple way. This was not to be.

I took my time, pottered around and made myself busy. I checked in with those I had left behind, reacquainting myself with old friends and smiled at their stories as they filled in the gaps since I had left. My mind was not strictly with them though and I kept thinking back to Luna.

It was an hour before lunchtime when I finally decided to end my misery and go to see her. Maybe things would be better in the cold light of day. Perhaps her attitude would have softened and I could accompany her to the dining hall where we could catch up properly.

My mood lifted as I created a future scenario which was so much better than yesterday's reality. Things would be better, I knew it. We had just gotten off to a wrong start, which could happen to anyone in the circumstances. She had been under duress, after all. I stopped off along the way to visit the shopping arenas where I picked up a huge bouquet of yellow and white roses and a box of delicately flavoured chocolates. I would win her heart and get back the Luna that I had fallen in love with.

Armed with my gifts I waited patiently outside her chambers but the door never opened. I tried again, only to be met with continued silence and an obstinately shut door. There was nothing to be done except to use my internalised key code, which in theory could open any door on the ship by using my mind to project phototonic frequencies at the identifier panel. It was a last resort, as I didn't want Luna to feel threatened or vulnerable in the knowledge that I could walk in whenever I wanted. I could have left, walked away and decided to try again later, but something about the whole situation still didn't sit right with me.

As I projected the frequencies into the panel it lit up with the message "access revoked" in bright red lettering. Revoked? How could that be possible? Nobody had the authority to revoke my rights here.

A feeling of dread washed over me, what if Luna had collapsed inside her chambers? What if the pregnancy had gone wrong? Maybe her out-of-character behaviour was a symptom of an infection of some kind? Maybe a brain trauma? There was nothing left except for me to slipstream into the room, materialising directly inside the space. I aligned my energies to the axis bearings, something far more difficult to do at close quarters than from a distance, but I was met with a force of resistance that blocked even this mode of entry. I could not get in.

I threw the flowers and chocolates to the floor, uncaring that they scattered in wild disarray across the corridor, and went straight to find Raab for the second time that morning. He looked alarmed as I told him the problem, and echoed my thoughts, "sir, it's impossible. Nobody has the authority to revoke you here." "Well, it's happened and I need you to fix it."

"I will get my best team on it now and oversee it myself."

"Good man."

Minutes ticked by, turning into hours. Raab was beginning to look more and more unsettled, and a film of sweat beaded his brow.

"What is it?" I could see that he felt under pressure, probably more so than usual as I had decided to sit and wait for the repairs to take place, carefully monitoring progress.

"Sir, we've tried everything. The problem is that it's not a malfunction, at least not an electronic or technical one. Everything is working fine. What you have here is a magical force being exerted, which is preventing the identifier from picking up the frequencies."

I was perplexed. Luna had not been taught in the ways of witchcraft, only simple elemental communication. Who could be responsible for this?

"We need to break down the doors. I don't care what it takes, I need to get into that room."

"Impossible sir. This craft is designed to withstand brute force. There is no way to force open any of the entrances or exits. It was specifically made this way in case of attack."

Abruptly I left the technicians, still scratching their heads about what could be done, and no doubt putting in place some kind of contingency plans should an occurrence like this happen again in the future.

I needed to find Penemué, who was exactly where I had expected him to be, in the ship's library, gorging himself on the volumes of literature that lined the walls. Explaining all that had happened, I could see Penemué's mind working overtime, no doubt, logging everything as a legendary story to be recited at some time in the future. Whilst I had a memory that could easily overlook something, Penemué was blessed with the most amazing brain I had ever encountered.

He was thoughtful for a moment, looking considered,

drawing out a long breath and staring with a vacant look into the air in front of him, while I impatiently waited for him to say something. I could tell he was up to mischief because his eyes suddenly sparkled with merriment.

"I don't think now is the time for your amusement Penemué," I reminded him scornfully.

Penemué laughed then, a hearty chuckle, and never had I felt more like hitting him for displaying such mirth.

"I see the problem," he said, and laughed again, so hard that I thought he might choke on his own self-indulgence.

"What's so funny?" I glared at him, as he laughed some more, holding his sides and creasing over in a guffaw of mirth. Rarely had I seen him looking so gleeful, Penemué was usually quite dignified in his manner. After what seemed like an age, he pulled himself together and simply said, "why didn't you use the secret panel?"

"What?"

"Don't tell me you've forgotten. The secret panel!" He looked at me as if I should know exactly what he was referring to, but I hadn't the faintest idea what he was talking about.

"Come on, I will show you." Penemué drew himself up to his full height, replaced the book he had been reading back on the shelf, and strolled out before me in the direction of Luna's room. Once there, he created a small glowing green flame in the palm of his hand, and recited an old Arabic verse in supplication to the fire elementals, requesting the aid of the Djinn. At once a glowing green doorway appeared in the side of Luna's chamber where before there had just been the blank surface.

"Hmph" I glowered at him. "I don't do good with fire, as well you know".

Penemué smiled, "after you," he replied as I entered the chamber without restriction.

It took less than a few seconds to glance around the room and realise that it was totally empty. Luna had gone.

CHAPTER 18

"People trust their eyes above all else - but most people see what they wish to see, or what they believe they should see; not what is really there"

— ZO MARRIOTT

At that moment, I felt as if I'd been side-lined. I had been concentrating on the wrong thing, expecting that Luna had been passed out in her room or some other tragedy had befallen her, when all that time she wasn't even there.

Just at that moment Raab came racing down to meet us.

"Sir, there has been a violation of Code 9. Someone has taken one of the capsules and left the ship." My heart sank.

"Luna?" I asked.

Raab shook his head, confused. "No sir, I haven't seen Luna on board since the day you departed. I thought she had left with you."

My blood froze in my veins as my mind worked feverishly to try to put the pieces together. What was I missing? I went over events with Penemué, down to the finest detail of my meeting with Luna last night. When I described our lovemaking and her turning away from me, he sighed deeply.

"The freckles on her back, I know of only one who is marked as you describe. Keysha the Sorceress. Her back is a map of some of the star systems, including the constellation of Cassiopeia and Orion if my memory serves me."

Oh, how stupid I was. It made glaring sense to me now. She must have used some powerful dark magic, a glamour charm, to trick me into believing she was Luna. That would explain the energy signature being off frequency.

Keysha... oh we had history, Keysha and I... how long had it been? I counted perhaps four hundred years, when she had first approached us to become one of The Mothers. As it was, she was sullied and had violated her own body, prostituting herself to gain power and knowledge, not to mention an accumulation of wealth, which she had used to further ingratiate herself into households of influence. There was nothing of goodness in her and we had turned her away, but she had been persistent in her petitions.

It had been a cold wintery evening when Keysha had appeared in my bed chambers, naked as the day and just as brazen. I remembered how she had tried to stimulate my senses... using every trick she could conceivably think of to seduce me. How little she knew me, to think that her brand of lovemaking could entice me. I had not been interested in Keysha's advances and rejected her forthwith.

Yes, I had seen her back before, as she retreated from my rooms into the night, cursing me under her breath. It made me sick to the core that she had tricked me into sleeping with her, and now, a child growing inside her womb. Not just any child but an abomination, one of the Nephilim race. That was another problem all of its own. My thoughts turned to God, knowing he would be ill-pleased and my recent redemption was, in all likelihood, going to be very short lived.

How Keysha got on board the ship in the first place I could only guess, but with her sorcery I could easily see how she could remain undetected, shapeshifting when it suited her, causing illusion and planting ideas in people's minds. My guess was that she had been the one responsible for triggering the great alarm, all as part of her scheming and cunning ways.

As much as that sickened me, my thoughts turned overwhelmingly to Luna. Where could she be? Was she lying dead somewhere? I could not even begin to imagine the horrors she may have endured while I had been away. I doubted even Keysha would have killed her because to do so would have sent a signal to the whole of the angelic hosts and we would have descended upon her in our thousands. She had to be alive, although I could not find her energetically.

"I want the whole ship searched, let no chamber be missed, and I want each of the holographic worlds closed down. Everyone and anyone who is on board this ship needs to be accounted for and go through the process of identification. Is that clear?"

"Yes sir. We will get to it immediately."

I knew it would take some considerable time, there were hundreds of people who worked on The Omicron and many of those had families who also stayed on board. It was late in the afternoon when I received the alert. A locked room on the far side of the ship had been discovered, which nobody had been able to enter.

"Come on," I called to Penemué. "I need your Djinn to do a bit more work."

With Penemué's help, getting into the chamber was straightforward as he set about revealing the hidden panel. As soon as the seal was broken, a terrible smell flooded from the chamber, causing a few of those present to step back, gagging. Something very unpleasant awaited us. The room was almost totally in darkness and it took a moment for my eyes to adjust before outlines started to emerge from the shadows.

There was a form lying still on the bed and I felt a numbness creep over me as I imagined the worst. Part of me wanted to leave right then, without having to witness what might come next, but I needed to see with my own eyes what terrible fate had befallen Luna.

"Lights" I commanded, and the room slowly illuminated.

"In the name of God" Penemué cried, for there on the bed was Luna, bound at the ankles and wrists by coarse rope, lying in a pool of blood and excrement. She was skeletal and etched onto her skin were two mystical sigils which I could not immediately interpret but which seemed likely to be of sinister purpose.

I took a pace forward to release her from her shackles, but Penemué put a hand on my arm to stop me.

"Don't touch her."

I looked aghast at him.

"She is still breathing, let the medics take over from here. We need to understand what those symbols mean before you go anywhere near her."

I nodded mutely as the capable medics took over, deftly untying her and lifting her up onto a mechanised stretcher. It seemed as if her eyes had sunk deep into the recesses of her skull and her cheek bones, always beautifully chiselled, looked even more prominent. Her hair was a mass of knots, fouled with any manner of disgusting detritus and my heart was filled with pain as I witnessed the proceedings.

I moved aside for the paramedics as they wheeled her out into the corridor to transport her to the ship's hospital and all I could do was wait, hope and pray.

It was another few hours before I was allowed to visit Luna. She was still unconscious but they had managed to bathe and dress her in one of the standard hospital gowns. As I looked at her, my heart felt heavy with the suffering she had endured. The doctors had set up a feeding tube, which was being administered through her nose and her hair had been shaved off too. She looked tiny and vulnerable, pale and still against the hospital sheets. I wanted to reach out and hold her hand but wires protruded everywhere, hooking her up to monitors that bleeped with a comforting regularity to show that she was still breathing.

I adjusted my position at the side of the bed, feeling awkward and too large for the space we were in. Resting on top of the blankets, Luna's arms lay limply at her sides. They were thin like reeds and she looked like she could have snapped into pieces with wrong handling. Visible on her left forearm were the symbols, which looked as if they had been tattooed deep into her skin.

"My love," I whispered, "what did she do to you?" I hadn't expected a response and nor did I receive one. She was trapped in some inner world that I could not reach unless... unless I decided to meet her in the dreamscape. It was easy enough for an angel to do, and was one of the more common ways that we interacted with humans when we wanted to pass on messages in a subtler way.

With Luna it was different. I didn't want to chase her through those twilight dreams, appearing as an illusion without form or substance. I wanted her to open her physical eyes and see me standing before her, real and solid, as someone who would never leave her side again.

I looked once more at the symbols, but could not place them. Not for the first time since my return, I felt fortunate that it was Penemué that had been chosen to accompany me. I had no doubt that his knowledge of the written word would prove invaluable in helping to decipher these sigils.

It was a short time later that Penemué sat quietly at Luna's side, studying the symbols that were etched into her flesh.

"This one," he said, "is a symbol representing sustenance. It's likely that this is how Luna survived without physical food for so long. Keysha was not stupid enough to leave her to die but kept her too weak and emaciated to do anything for herself. In some ways it's a fortunate symbol to have and it will do no harm to keep it there."

"What about the other one?"

"Ah... that's a little trickier." I watched as Penemué held his hand a few inches above the sigil, working with the vibration of it, trying to unpick its purpose. As he did so, it radiated with colour, casting jade coloured threads along Luna's skin, poisonous veins creeping slowly up her arm. Luna, still unconscious, started to breath laboriously and her body stiffened and shuddered on the bed, her face grimacing with pain as the threads trailed further along her arm towards her shoulder, neck and upper chest.

Penemué withdrew his hand and the jade threads retreated back towards the sigil. "I see what's happening. I've come across this only once before. This is dark shamanic magic and serves as entrapment. It's like a mental prison. It can't be unpicked from the outside and it will bind Luna to the inner planes for all eternity unless we can remove it."

"What's its nature? I asked.

"It's fluid. Although on the surface of the skin it presents as permanent it's actually not so. Think on it Isayel. I am sure you will find a way to break it."

"Indeed I will." The thought had already occurred to me, and I knew exactly what I must do. But first, we needed for Luna to get stronger which, thanks to the hospital staff, she would do quickly enough.

CHAPTER 19

"Evil may be strong, but love - love breaks any curse, any spell - any sort of magic."

— CHANTAL GADOURY

It was November, eight weeks since Luna had been discovered in that bed of filth and contamination, where Keysha had left her to exist in a state that was not death and yet not living.

Each day I had visited and sat by Luna's side. I talked to her of ancient tales and wonderous escapades, both real and imagined. Penemué, too, had proven his worth as a storyteller beyond compare.

She showed no outward sign of being able to hear us, although occasionally I had witnessed movements underneath her eyelids when I described fantastical landscapes and adventures. Her hair had started to grow back, and her face and features had softened as she gained weight from the nutrition she was now receiving.

I had felt impatient with the slow passage of time, wanting to proceed with releasing Luna from this oblivion, but knowing that to rush ahead before she had regained her strength and health would have been a miscalculation in judgement. Now, however, I knew she was ready to come back to us and had arranged for the nurses to remove her feeding tubes so that she could be released to me.

Carefully I lifted her from the bed, nothing more than a feather in my arms, and carried her over to Holographic World 3, where I had already instigated a spa programme. Once inside, curls of steam coiled up from a bubbling natural spa set amongst ancient rocks and tropical greenery. At the nearside there was a shallow pooling of water where the rock fell away into a gently sloping recline. I positioned Luna carefully so that her whole body was submerged but her head remained above the water. Once she was in position, supported by the rock and the natural buoyancy of the water, I undressed and submerged myself. I cast myself into the middle of the pool and raised my hands skyward in supplication to the Lord, through whom I knew all things were possible and to whom I still gave my thanks.

Plunging deep within the waters, I revelled in the texture of the liquid against my skin. This was my domain for I, Isayel, was Keeper of the Waters. This was my strength and my foundation. Water, that lifegiving source that nurtured all living things from the smallest of raindrops to the infinite boundless oceans, where water existed, I existed also. I dropped into the folds of the water, allowing it to flow over me and through me and I felt myself merging into the infinite space between the atoms of the fluid. The simplest of chemical compounds, H_2O, hydrogen and oxygen molecules as described by humans, was the place I felt most at home, and where I ultimately became a more powerful version of myself. I disappeared then, into the depths, becoming one with the water itself and luxuriating in the fluidity of movement that allowed me to tumble into nothingness.

I turned my attention towards my purpose. I needed to gain access to Luna's interior so that I could dilute and draw out the enchantment that kept her ensnared. I guessed that the fluid moved between the layers of her skin and that the most difficult part would be to gain entry without hurting her. Humans are reasonably waterproof so I would either have to enter through the mouth or through the mucus membranes and search out a channel from there. I decided to go through the mouth, creating a small vortex which allowed me the necessary propulsion down into her throat. Briefly she spluttered and I found myself jostled around, but down I went, sliding rapidly down the esophagus towards the stomach. I needed to divert into the lymphatic system from which I could circulate through the body and leach out as interstitial fluid.

It was not difficult and I had travelled around many other life forms in the past, particularly when I was much younger and cared for such explorations. As I approached the entrapment symbol, I could feel it beginning to activate and the jade liquid oozed towards me. It was an onslaught that I was well prepared for. I pushed forwards in a way that could have been described as "head down" in manner, had I possessed such a body part at this time. I surged at the liquid, attacking from the sides and from above and below. My one mission was to dilute and disintegrate its form and therefore render it useless. As I pushed forward it was swept along by the intensity of my thrust, like a tidal wave dissolving everything in its path. I had it in my grip now, a foul enchantment but no match for me. I plotted our exit, out the way I had entered, and within moments Luna started coughing and spluttering, ejecting both me and the green fluid that had caused her such misery and torment. Once it had been flushed out, there was nothing it could do except disintegrate into the void, lost in form and substance with no cellular structure around it to keep its formation.

Luna blinked and rubbed her eyes, a look on her face that perhaps indicated she could not quite believe what she was doing in the middle of a pool of water. She looked around, seeing nothing only the scenery and the depth of water that she was lying in. I was still in my watery form and had not quite decided whether I should show myself or not. Had I been in any doubt, the moment that Luna let out a cry of deep despair and started to sob settled it for me. Shifting back into my original form, I rose up out of the water like a god in the myths of old, my wings expanding in opulent showmanship as I rose to waist height within the foaming swirls.

Luna startled and cried even louder, staring at me in disbelief as I waded through the waters to be by her side.

"Welcome back, my love." I kissed her forehead and she

wrapped her arms around me, clinging to me as if she would never let me go.

"I love you," she whispered in my ear as I wrapped my arms around her, gently rocking her and holding her to me, letting her feel safe and protected as her salty tears streamed from her eyes, dripped from her chin and cascaded down into the waters below. "And I hate you too," she added, in a smaller, softer voice not meant for my ears.

CHAPTER 20

"Temper us in fire, and we grow stronger. When we suffer, we survive."

— CASSANDRA CLARE

When Keysha had left me in that room, I thought I would never see her again. I remembered the way I'd stuck my arms out in front of myself and wondered how long I would survive. As it happens, she did come back, hours and hours later than she said she would. By then I was frantic, and as soon as she opened the door I tried in vain to push past her to get out, but she was strong and it was the first time anyone had used magic against me. Stretching out her hand in a violent forward motion, I was flung back through the air and onto the bed, cracking my head on the wall behind as I landed with force. A trickle of blood ran down the back of my neck but I was too terrified to even investigate.

"You're going nowhere," she'd said. "In fact, I think it will be quite amusing to keep you here, as my little pet."

Nothing had prepared me for her cruelty. It was as if she hated me without even knowing anything about me and she took great pleasure in making my life a tormented hell.

Sometimes she would eat in front of me, knowing that I was starving hungry, and then throw small parcels of food onto the floor near her feet, laughing recklessly as I scurried over to pick up the scraps, devouring them as quickly as I could before she changed her mind.

"You're pathetic," she said. "Like an animal. Why would Isayel want you?"

I couldn't answer her. I felt like an animal. She had reduced me to a level of inhumanity and degradation that I didn't know I could stoop to.

When that amusement got tiresome she brought me maggoty grubs to eat. The old Luna would not even have been able to look at such nasty little creatures, but as my belly rumbled and kept me awake through the nights with bloated emptiness I gobbled them up and was thankful. Often, I just lay there, too weak to move, and thought back to my life on earth. I missed my home and the people who cared about me. Simple things, like homework and chats about boys with Tara. Eating all the red Smarties first... oh I hadn't tasted chocolate in so long... stupid, trivial, inconsequential thoughts... I was too numb to cry.

Then, as if torturing me with food was no longer enough, Keysha began engraving symbols onto my skin. She didn't do this with a visible implement of any kind, but the pain I experienced felt like a thousand razor blades were slicing through me, one layer at a time. Beads of blood would bubble to the surface and I would wince with pain. After a few days the incisions would scab over and settle, but these symbols would be actively working inside me, causing all sorts of terror. Oh, she laughed at this new game and it was like she was testing me, or herself, experimenting to see what would happen if she did this, and this... and this... she created hallucinations in my head and night terrors that stalked me even when I opened my eyes, so that I felt sure I was going crazy.

One symbol created an illusion of Isayel being there with me, and it was such sweet torment, and such a relief from the horrors. I began talking with him, telling him all about the wicked Keysha. Too late, I realised that the vision of Isayel was just another one of her amusements, caused by her rotten symbols. She had slapped me then, over and over again, so hard that I was covered in bruises and welts. I was not to say anything bad about her ever, ever again, because if I did, she would know and she would make me suffer tenfold for what I'd done.

Then sometimes she used her staff to hit me, just because she felt like it, or because I had looked at her the wrong way. I learned to avert my eyes and keep my mind blank but each day it became harder and harder just to survive.

I lay there broken and crushed, my spirit ebbing away as I retreated into silence. I think that is when she decided that I was too boring to bother about anymore. She had prodded and poked me for long enough, and my responses had increasingly diminished. Not yet dead, but wishing I was.

"Ah well," she had whispered in my ear. "All good things come to an end, don't they? It's been fun Luna, while it lasted... But to be honest, it's started to become a bit of a drag. I can't kill you... that would be too good for you... and we don't want to alert the wrong sorts, do we? No, I'm going to put you into a different kind of box."

Whenever a symbol had served its purpose she removed it, and in this way kept thinking up ever more twisted scenarios. This time, I was so far removed in my mind that even the pain she created within me seemed distant and dim.

"I can't be bothered to feed you anymore," she muttered as the first symbol was placed. "You'll live, you'll get just enough nourishment to keep your vital organs functioning... no more than that... hmmm, let's see.... you might lose your fertility... no problem there for someone as useless as you... your teeth might loosen from their gums, rot and drop out, don't choke on them now if they do... and what else? Oh yes, that hair of yours, those silky strands, might just drop out too as your hair follicles shut down. Poor sweet little Luna... oh you will look a fright, won't you?"

As she etched the second symbol into my arm I felt myself withdrawing entirely, into a space where nothing existed and nothing mattered, what's more, it seemed more real than anything else up to that point in my life. Far from being the prison that she had threatened, it felt like she had given me an escape because although my body was captive, my mind could drift in endless suspension, safely away from Keysha's cruelty. Had she known the relief I felt I am sure she would have pulled me out of that twilight world immediately, but she could not follow me into the abyss. I was safe.

It was while I was in this void, with the darkness all around me, that something strange happened. Drifting from nowhere the Mothers came into my inner field of vision. I wept to see their beautiful kindly faces again as they poured their love over me. Elisia held me and comforted me, while Sofia sang lullabies and Corrine stroked my hair. "We have not deserted you," they said. "we will support you here for as long as we can."

"But how are you here?" I asked, thinking this might be another of Keysha's foul tricks.

"That's not important but we're going to help you. We will keep you strong and safe."

True to their word, the Mothers visited me in this realm for long tranches of time, telling me stories and continuing my education in a different kind of way. I think I learned more at this time than at any other. We talked about Isayel too, and what he had meant to all of them and I saw how pure and wonderful their hearts were and why Isayel was right to love these women, just as I now loved them too.

"This has been an initiation for you," Elisia said one day. I had questioned what she meant. "True shamans walk between the worlds and have to go through a death within life. Their old selves fall away as a new self emerges, like a phoenix from the ashes. Your experiences have given you the wisdom and courage of the shaman." She was right, of course, because the suffering had become a spiritual experience for me. I carried the invisible scars of a life that could not ever be the same as it was, but within each scar was a story with a depth of pain and suffering which now defined me in an entirely different way.

As for Keysha's evil prophesies, the Mothers would not let

more harm befall me. Each day they administered a spirit medicine which I felt circulating through me, healing me enough so that I wouldn't succumb to the physical decay that Keysha had gloated about.

One day Elisia came to me on her own. Our souls rested in quiet companionship together and I felt her graceful love flowing all around me. "Something wonderful is about to happen," she said at last. "Your freedom is coming, I sense it."

"Freedom?" I actually already felt pretty free where I was, away from the pain and all the horrors of the past.

"This isn't a place you want to stay forever, not yet anyway. You have a whole life to live, children to raise and, maybe one day, grandchildren."

"I don't think of my life in that way."

"I know, child. How can you possibly think such a normal life can be yours, after everything you've been through? But, trust me, you will carve your own future in time."

I smiled and blessed her on the inner planes with a thousand rainbows, imagining them sparkling and shining all around her, bathing Elisia in a wonderful magical light. She deserved everything good in her life.

Over the course of the next few weeks the Mothers began to fade away. On one level I knew they were still there but it was as if I could no longer see them as clearly or feel their presence close by, like a veil had been gently drawn, rendering them ephemeral and ghostly until, one day, they just weren't there anymore.

They left a great, searing emptiness inside me but part of me recognised that it had to be this way. In their place I began having dreams. In them, Isayel was talking to me, telling me vibrant stories about shipwrecked sailors and lustrous mermaids, fire-breathing dragons and kingdoms lost beneath the sea. I looked forward to hearing these legends come alive with his words and my mind fizzed with activity and mental imagery. Just hearing his voice had been a soothing healing balm and I longed to be able to open my eyes and see him there in front of me.

I was regaining my strength now, a little bit more every day, and I counted minutes by the steady rhythm of my heartbeat circulating blood, oxygen and nutrients around my body. For the first time in what seemed like forever, I decided that I wanted to live. It became the song in my veins and my every thought in the twilight hours.

When I finally opened my eyes and found myself swaying gently to and fro with the lapping waters supporting me, I was disorientated. It took me a while to take in where I was, and the fact that I was away from that dirty stinking bed and the foulness that Keysha had forced me to endure. I could do nothing except burst into tears, and then there *HE* was. Isayel had come back to me.

CHAPTER 21

"I thought I was stronger than a word, but I just discovered that having to say goodbye to you is by far the hardest thing I've ever had to do."

— COLLEEN HOOVER

T he next few months it seemed as if Isayel and I never left each other's sides. It became comfortable and kind, moving away from the intensity of our previous encounters, but evolving into a more fulfilling, loving relationship.

Isayel was keen to explain some of what had happened whilst we'd been apart and when he spoke of the Mothers, a lump rose in my throat – so that was how they had found me, for they too were trapped in that twilight world. I hoped that one day I would be able to help them, just as much as they had helped me.

On the whole, it was a blissful, simple time and Isayel and I enjoyed each other's company in a way that we'd never quite managed to do before. On a few occasions Isayel had broached the subject of Keysha, wanting to know what happened, but each time he did so I froze, remembering the beatings and the threats, still convinced she could hunt me down and take out her revenge. I could not speak ill of her and Isayel learned not to probe too deeply.

As much as my feelings for Isayel grew stronger day by day, I also started to feel restless and Isayel noticed too.

"Tell me, what's troubling you?" He had entwined his hands with mine as we sat cross legged, facing each other in a park setting in HW7.

"I don't know... I just feel... well, like something is missing."

"You've been through such an ordeal... I know why you won't talk about it and it's alright, but sometimes after we've endured so much, it's almost an anti-climax when normal life is returned to us."

213

"Yes, I guess so." I said absently, wondering if I could tell him what was really on my mind. I had no choice, the words slipped out of me even before I could properly consider what I was saying. "Is it true that I can't be a Mother anymore?"

Isayel bent and tenderly kissed each of the knuckles of my hands before he looked me squarely in the eyes and told me about Keysha pretending to be me, how he had been fooled into sleeping with her and that growing in her womb was a monstrous Nephilim being.

"You've fathered a beast?" I looked at him, eyes wide and the familiar fearful feelings pricking around my edges, together with a huge jolt of jealousy.

"It would seem so… unintentionally."

And it was at that point that I hated Keysha more than anyone else in the world. Strange as it sounded, I could have forgiven her for locking me in that room and even for the way she had abused me, but to lay with Isayel whilst using enchantments to pretend she was me – that was unforgivable. She had taken my one chance of physical love with Isayel and used it for her own gain. I felt cheated beyond all measure and the thought of him lying next to her, sharing himself with her made me feel sick.

"It's too late for us now," Isayel had looked so forlorn when he spoke. "The timings are very specific. I had to join with you on your 21st birthday. It's the only astronomically correct time for a Zarn to be conceived. It's why I came back when I did."

"No other birthday? No other time, not ever?"

"No my love. One window of opportunity and that has gone."

Our conversation left me unsettled and a sadness lingered within me as I mourned for our unborn child and a future that could now never be.

It was a couple of weeks later when Isayel came to see me with a big smile on his face.

"Follow me, I have a surprise for you."

I wasn't sure I liked surprises anymore, but Isayel was positively beaming and I trusted him one hundred percent. We walked down the corridors towards HW2.

"I'm going to leave you here for a little while. Have a look around and enjoy yourself."

"You're not coming with me?" I was intrigued and a little scared. I didn't like being left on my own for long anymore.

"Not this time. But it will be alright. Trust me."

And so, I stepped hesitantly forward into the HW2 scenario of an enchanting forest. Mighty oaks burst upwards towards an azure blue sky and, nestled amongst them, holly, ivy, ash... a thriving world of lush undergrowth and foliage. I was immersed in an amazing energy bath that was so strong and vital it pulled me into a whirlpool of healing and restorative energy. I quietened my mind to connect, just as Elisia had trained me to do so long ago. It was such an amazing, touching experience and I bubbled with emotion, swept along by the infinite love and healing that the plants poured over me.

I sat with my eyes closed, listening to the sounds all around me, the gentle rustle of the trees as a breeze tinkered through their leaves, and birds singing high in the tree tops... for what is a tree without its companions? I gently stroked the bark of a wizened old oak tree, the texture warm and gnarled underneath my fingertips. All my senses became absorbed in this dreamy paradise when a voice cut into my thoughts.

"Hello old friend," I startled, jumping a foot out of my skin, and quickly opened my eyes.

"Cassiel!" I jumped to my feet and ran to give him the biggest of hugs. He stood there, large as life in front of me, smiling just as much as Isayel had done earlier.

"Thought you'd got rid of me, did you?" He said as he swallowed me into a big bear hug.

"Oh it's so good to see you. I can't believe that you're here, I've missed you so much."

"Just for a while. I have a few things I need to do before I have to leave again."

"You haven't changed a bit." I said to him, smiling at the lavender cloak he was wearing in a very self-assured kind of way.

"You've changed though," he commented, his voice suddenly serious.

"I guess I have. Lots of things have happened."

"So I've been told. But what I want to know is, how are you really doing?"

I knew that I could talk to Cassiel about anything and that in some ways he was far easier to speak with than Isayel. It wasn't long before I was pouring my heart out to him, even telling him about my time with Keysha. His face was grave as he listened, careful not to interrupt me as I revealed my deepest, darkest thoughts and feelings.

"You've been through so much, and I feel the responsibility falls to me somewhat, because I was the one who left you here and told you to stay in your room, although at the time there was no other choice."

I nodded miserably. It was a relief to speak about things, but it brought everything right back to the surface of my mind again.

"Can I offer you an opinion? And please don't feel you have to take my advice, but I do have some experience in these matters."

I looked up at Cassiel. My true friend, the greatest of allies, perhaps even my guardian angel. "Yes," I said. "You can tell me anything."

"My very strong advice to you is that you need to go home. Settle back into your old life. Reacquaint yourself with your old friends, make new ones... live in the real world once more and do ordinary things with ordinary people."

"Go back?" I was stunned, that thought had not entered my mind in so long. "But how?"

"If you want to go back, I can arrange it. I'm here for three more days before I have to leave again. It's a big decision, and not one that anyone can make for you. The alternative is to stay on this ship, maybe settle on Zarnett-9, enjoy your time with Isayel and others you might befriend along the way. It could be a good life, but it won't be home, and it will never be what you wanted it to be."

The sigh that escaped me came from deep inside, and my mind quite suddenly felt overloaded with problems. If I left, it would mean leaving Isayel behind, who was the love of my life... but with whom I could never share true intimacy... And the mothers had gone... Cassiel might not be around much. I wondered how long I would be happy for, especially if we settled on Zarnett-9, where the Zarns would outstrip me in intelligence, beauty, charm... everything in fact. I would grow old and Isayel would not.

Isayel was extra attentive to me that evening and I knew that he sensed something was wrong.

"Didn't you enjoy the surprise I arranged for you?" he asked as we sat for our evening meal in the Main Hall.

"Yes, it was lovely to be there, and to meet Cassiel again."

"So, why so sad, my love? You look troubled."

"It's nothing," I lied. I could not tell him my thoughts. I didn't want to hurt him, but with each moment that passed it felt more and more important that I should go home. The more I thought about it, the more the memory of my family burned in my mind and I became homesick all over again. I'd been gone far too long.

Cassiel spent plenty of time with me over the next couple of days and he didn't mention our chat again, giving me lots of space to think about things. He was his old self, funny and outrageous, saying things that other people would not dare to, but making me laugh with his particular brand of humour. I made sure I spent lots of time with Isayel too. In some ways, I knew I was saying goodbye to him. I held him close to me and breathed in the scent of him.

"I do love you very much," I said to him, taking him by surprise, because I'd always been cagey about using those words.

There was a moment of silence, as if he was waiting for my usual add-on... it never came and he cocked his eyebrow in surprise. "But you hate me too, right?"

I smiled a sad, slow smile. "No Isayel. I never hated you. I just didn't understand you, but more than that, I didn't understand myself."

He held me with such gentleness and caring that I silently wept for our love, the wetness of my tears seeping from my closed eyelids and sliding into my hairline. I slept cradled within the feathery fold of his wings that night, tucked against him, feeling his breath on the back of my neck. We hadn't been able to fulfil a physical relationship and as much I felt broken by what Keysha did to me, I knew that Isayel was plagued with feelings of remorse and guilt too. She had cheated and hurt us both. As I slept I could feel Isayel's love all around me and I tried to draw it into the very heart of me so that I would always remember what it felt like to be that close to him. This would be my goodbye.

The next morning I awoke early and, leaving Isayel sleeping, went to search out Cassiel in his chambers.

"I've made my mind up," I said to him. "I need to go home."

"I know it feels difficult, but it's the right choice Luna."

I nodded, I knew it was, it felt right.

"I can transport you back using the slipstream. It will be very quick. You will need to be shielded by my aura, which will protect you from the space environment."

"Will I be able to breathe?" I'd asked, wondering how this whole thing would work.

"Yes, and in fact you will have arrived back on Earth before you even take your second breath."

"That fast?"

"Oh yes... faster than you can even imagine."

"Can we go now, before Isayel wakes up?" I felt the lump forming in my throat and tears threatening to spill once more from my faulty, leaking eyes.

"Yes, if you're sure."

I gave Cassiel a big hug, and my small body shuddered with the pain I was feeling inside, to leave this place. "I will miss you all so much."

"I know, but we will always be with you, one way or another. You've been kissed by an angel, remember that."

"Will you talk to Isayel for me... tell him..." Words failed me but Cassiel nodded, he knew my heart so well.

"Don't you worry little Luna, I will make sure he knows."

I held onto Cassiel as he unfurled his giant wings, impressive and glorious, and folded me inside them. I was overcome with a feeling of pure love and compassion, which intensified as a golden shimmering auric shell materialised around us, cocooning us within a vibrant energy field.

"Ready?" he asked. I nodded. Never more so. It seemed

only seconds later that I found myself standing all alone at the edge of the canal, where I'd first witnessed The Omicron. The canal looked dirty and grey, as did the sky above me, with no sign of the ship or anything else out of the ordinary. I had expected that Cassiel would have been with me, at least for a little while, but he was gone too.

I felt cold and shivered as I pulled my coat around me. Looking down I could see I was dressed in black jeans and black jacket, just like when I had left this place… but I was bigger now, so they couldn't have been the same ones, could they? I reached into the pocket of my jacket and fingered my phone. It seemed like ancient technology now. I turned it on and it started beeping crazily at me, as hundreds of messages poured into it.

"Where are you? Your dinner's ruined… Mum x"

"Luna, answer me, where are you? It's nearly midnight."

"If you don't call me this minute I'm going to call the police."

"Luna, please answer me, I'm really worried about you. Where are you?"

The messages went on and on, lots from my mum, some from Tara and a few other friends from school, even Amy… and then… and then silence… not one message after I'd been gone for around a month. It was shocking to read all those messages and part way through them I had to stop and turn my phone off again.

As if for the first time, it suddenly dawned on me that I couldn't just walk back into my old life. I couldn't begin to imagine what I could say to them all about where I'd been all this time. I definitely couldn't tell them I'd been abducted by angels, they would think I was crazy. I would need to either lie, make up some kind of believable story or just give them the least information that I could.

CHAPTER 22

"The Bible tells us to love our neighbours, and also to love our enemies; probably because generally they are the same people."

- GILBERT K. CHESTERTON

L ooking down at my feet I noticed a large white feather on the ground beside me. At around two feet long there was no doubt in my mind that it had belonged to Cassiel. It was probably the best reassurance I could ever have hoped for that I hadn't just had a knock on the head and imagined it all. I picked it up gently and, as I smoothed the fronds of it beneath my fingers, I knew that I would treasure it always as a departing gift.

Walking slowly back along the canal, everything looked familiar but so different. The reeds poking out from the water, the stumps of grass along the path, the twisted hedgerow... none of it held the same kind of beauty as the natural worlds I'd experienced on the ship and even the greens weren't as green as I remembered.

"But this is the natural world" I said to myself, heading towards the bridge and to my old life beyond.

Passing the row of houses on Sanville Lane, they all appeared a little shabbier now too. My eyes fell to the net curtains of the house beyond the magnolia tree, and I was surprised to see the net twitch once more. I turned away sharply, quickening my pace. I felt more spooked then than I did in the past, almost certain the house was haunted or that a very twisted person lived there.

I put the thought aside as I commenced walking down those strangely familiar streets, my mind thrummed in anticipation of what awaited me... almost home... home... my heart was racing as I thought about the reaction of mum and Amy. Mum would probably have a heart attack and collapse at the door and I could imagine Amy bursting into tears.

I had no key, I hadn't taken one out with me all those years ago, and so I stood on the doorstep and gave the doorbell a nice long ring. There was a new car in the drive... I guessed the old one must have broken down or something... and new curtains. Mum had sure been busy sprucing up the place, I guessed life really did move on. She'd even put hanging baskets out each side of the front door. Mum never did that. All the little differences started to jingle inside me... maybe it was a mistake to come back. Their lives would be very different now. Perhaps they wouldn't want to see me again. They'd be angry, for sure and what if there was a big argument between us?

It seemed like an age before the door opened and when it did a middle-aged man stood in the doorway. He pushed his glasses a little further up the bridge of his nose and gave me a smile. "Hello? Are you collecting the charity envelopes?"

"Erm... no..." I cleared my throat, which had suddenly turned dry on me, rendering my voice a frail croak. "I'm looking for my er... looking for Helen Mason... she lived here a few years ago."

"Well, let's see now, we've been here..." he turned and shouted over his shoulder, "how long have we been here Sally?"

A female voice came from a distance away, "oh, quite a few months, now." The lady, presumably his wife, came scurrying to stand next to her husband, wiping her hands on an old-fashioned apron that she had tied around her waist, "but the house was empty when we moved in."

"Empty?" I must have sounded shocked. Mum would never leave this place; she loved her friends and neighbours too much.

"Yes, a terrible business... repossession it was. We got it for a good price, didn't we Bill?"

"Best investment we ever made." He beamed at his wife.

"Sorry, we don't really know more than that."

"But… you said it was a terrible business??" I prompted. "Why did you say that?"

"What? Oh, that.. no, you mustn't mind me. I'm not one to gossip. Goodness me, what would they say at the church if I spread rumours around about those less fortunate. No, love, sorry we can't help you there."

The nice Christian couple firmly closed the door in my face, politely and irrevocably telling me that our conversation was over. Should I knock again, insist that they tell me everything they knew? I loitered there for a minute or more, wondering what to do next. Harassing these people probably wouldn't be my most sensible choice and I dejectedly made my way back down the drive.

As I wandered up the road, clutching my angel feather close to my chest, it dawned on me that I had no home anymore, and that I didn't actually know what I needed to do in order to find my family. As it was, I was probably on the police missing persons list myself, or even registered as dead for that matter. If that was the case, I truly was a nobody, somebody who didn't even exist in the eyes of the law. When I took in the full implication of my situation, I realised I hadn't actually thought this through properly at all.   "Cassiel," I whispered, looking up at the sullen sky, "you've got a lot of explaining to do when I see you again."

I had hoped that the heavens would just open up right there and then and that I could be whisked back on board The Omicron and resume my life with the angels, but nothing is ever so straightforward. It was all I could do to put one step in front of the other as the dirty grey pavement stretched ahead of me.

It seemed hardly possible that beyond what my eyes could see there were different universes pulsing with life, and decisions being made by beings who belonged to greater civilisations than ours. I hoped Cassiel was somewhere up there, maybe looking down on me to check I was safe and, if I was lucky, helping me a little along the way. My heart was heavy, too, with thoughts of Isayel and just how he would react when he found out I was gone.

Just then, a familiar figure came running from her front door to the gate, legs wobbling in their haste to reach me.

"Luna? Luna Mason… is that really you?"

"Mrs Clarke!" I gasped in surprise. If anybody knew what had happened to my mum, she would… they'd been thick as thieves back then.

"Oh my God, it is you, it's really you. Oh… oh…" she stood there with her mouth opening and closing like a fish struggling to breathe out of water, looking truly stunned. I almost felt sorry for her.

"Your poor mum… what's she's been through… we thought you were dead!"

For a moment I just stared back at her, wondering what I could possibly say that would improve the situation.

"I'd love a cup of tea" I finally remarked, which I knew was pretty much the answer for everything.

"A cup of tea?" She looked flummoxed for a moment and then seemed to rally round. "Oh yes, of course… come on in… I'll put the kettle on. Oh, my goodness, I can't believe it. Luna Mason turns up after disappearing for six years and asks for a cup of tea!" I followed her through into her kitchen. It was pristine, with a combination of black glittery worktops and units with grey surrounds. It all looked very affluent, right down to the twinkling lights that cast their glow from beneath the cupboards.

"Oh heavens," she said again, for about the fifth time, before sitting down heavily on one of the kitchen chairs.

"Well, I'm sure I just don't know what to do with you now. Have you been to see your mum?"

"I don't know where my mum is." I answered flatly.

"Oh dear, oh what a carry on. Of course, you wouldn't know, would you, you disappeared without trace."

Mrs Clarke looked so much older than how I remembered her. Somewhat curvy back then, she was now positively heaving and it looked like she'd tried her hardest to squeeze chubby rolls of fat into clothing that was just a little too tight for her. As she got up to mash the tea, she continued to talk about the day that I never came home.

"I'll never forget it," she said. "There you were, being rude and unpleasant to your mum as usual, poor woman, who never deserved how you treated her, and then just getting up and walking out like that. What was everyone to think? It's no wonder she had a breakdown."

I ignored all the unpleasant things she was saying about me, actually feeling guilty because I realised she was probably right. I hadn't been a very nice teenager.

"A breakdown?" I asked. "What kind of breakdown?"

Mrs Clarke looked at me over the rim of her glasses, which I remembered was a particular habit of hers. Her blue eyes were still fizzy and kind of accusing. "A mental breakdown of course." She poured the tea and carried the dainty cups and saucers over to the kitchen table, where I was already sitting.

"Your disappearance was in all the local papers, and on the radio... Your mum was beside herself and then there's Amy... hardly surprising how she turned out, is it, with all that carry on."

My head was reeling from this patchwork of conversation that I was trying to put together out of the scraps of information she was throwing me.

"Please, can we start at the beginning? I don't know any of this."

"How could you not know, for heaven's sake. Anyone

would think you'd been abducted by aliens or something." I nearly choked on the mouthful of tea I was drinking, if she only knew the truth!

"I've not been watching any news" I said, which was partly true. Mrs Clarke sighed, and started a longer explanation of events.

"That day you left, your mum had been planning on buying you that puppy, do you remember?"

"Yes, I do." I smiled at the thought, I'd been excited about the prospect of having my own dog, but was too pig-headed to admit it back then.

"What happened to the puppy?"

"Your mum couldn't collect it and she ended up losing the deposit too. The last thing she wanted was a dog in the house, with all the commotion going on. She couldn't really afford it anyway, she was just trying to make you happy."

"Well she always seemed to have enough money for drink." I'd said, bitterly remembering the cheap bottles of wine that had started to spring up with increasing frequency around the house.

"Well, that's as may be, but have you ever stopped to wonder why she started drinking? After your dad died you were always causing trouble and upsetting her. She'd never been a strong lady."

"I know what you're saying and you're absolutely right. I was too wrapped up in my own feelings to notice before."

"Yes, you need to keep in mind what she's been through and why she turned to drink… it got a lot worse after you left too." I nodded and sighed, this was not how I'd planned my homecoming, sitting in Mrs Clarke's kitchen going on a guilt trip about my absent family. My angel feather trembled in my hand as I listened.

"I guess I was a little shit back then."

"That's not a word I would use Luna Mason, but you always did have a crude tongue in your head."

It was like watching myself slipping back into bad old ways and it took a moment for me to remember that I'd changed. I wasn't the same girl anymore.

"I'm sorry, that was uncalled for. I don't actually swear much these days, can you believe it?" We shared a smile and Mrs Clarke patted my hand affectionately.

"That's good to know."

"Where's my mum? I need to go see her."

"It's a little tricky, you see, she's been in rehab and not very stable. I think they'll sort her out now though, she's in the right place. I can give you the visiting hours, I'm sure she'd love to see you." I took the offered leaflet and turned it over in my hands,

"The Charlesworth Unit at Fieldhead Hospital?"

"Yes dear... as I said, she's not been coping very well."

"Wow, mum's in a mental home. A lot really has happened since I've been away."

"Just the tip of the iceberg dear."

"Just the tip? I dread to think what else I've yet to uncover. Thank you for the tea and the info, you've been really helpful, and I'm sure mum's really appreciated your friendship over the years."

Mrs Clarke's chin wobbled and she looked away quickly, "oh, it's nothing... that's what friends are for aren't they? Your mum helped me no end when my David... Mr Clarke... left me for another woman."

The emotion I felt right at that moment in Mrs Clarke's kitchen hit me like a train. This poor woman who I had misjudged and criticised for so long, had stood by my mum through all the difficult years. Stuck in my silly, teenage world

I hadn't noticed any of the problems and difficulties of the people around me. Maybe throughout all these years I'd got it all wrong.

" I'm so sorry. That must have been really tough."

"Yes, well... it wasn't easy... but anyway, we need to see that you're alright too, don't we? There's so much you have to catch up with. Where are you staying?"

"Nowhere at the moment, I guess I'm homeless."

"Well, we can't have that. Tell you what, I'll make up the spare room and get some dinner ready for us, you will be hungry after you come back from seeing your mum."

"Are you sure that will be okay? I don't want to put you to any trouble."

"Absolutely, I insist. The truth is, I have so much time on my own, I'd be glad for a bit of company."

And so it was that I made an unlikely friend in Mrs Clarke and learned a very important lesson about judging people at the same time.

CHAPTER 23

"Children are the anchors that hold a mother to life."

- SOPHOCLES

I'd phoned the hospital in advance, my hand trembling as I punched in the number. It seemed right that I gave them prior warning that I was coming just in case my mum reacted badly. I waited on hold while I was connected to the ward and then, with some difficulty, tried to explain who I was. The nurse seemed to know a little about me but was very wary about giving out any information.

"I can't tell you anything about the patient, due to data protection regulations. We would need your mum's consent before we could discuss her treatment with you."

"But I haven't seen her in years, how can I get her consent?"

"You can still visit your mum, but we won't be able to disclose personal information unless she agrees."

Well, that was a right good start, I thought, as I headed off towards the bus stop. Mrs Clarke had kindly given me twenty quid and it felt so good to be able to hold real money in my hands. I hadn't needed currency at all on The Omicron and now the prospect of actually spending it seemed like such a weird thing to do.

I'd left Cassiel's feather on the kitchen table and Mrs Clarke had agreed to keep it safe for me, after all it was the only thing I possessed in the world apart from the clothes I stood up in.

I walked into the hospital with trepidation. There were locked doors on both sides of the reception desk and I had to give my mum's details and the name of the ward she was on, together with my own name and relationship to the patient. After staring at her computer screen for a minute or two the receptionist pointed to a door on the left. "Follow the signs, straight down and round. There will be a buzzer and the ward staff will let you in." The walls of the corridor were adorned with brightly coloured abstract art, and for a moment I was transported back to Sofia's wonderful classroom and the amazing adventures we used to share. I wasn't much of a Picasso fan and never visited his studio with Sofia but I smiled as I remembered some of the other artists we had ventured to see. They were good times and I suddenly realised how much I'd missed Sofia's exuberance and the artistic part of my life.

I stood for a moment outside the double doors with the small panel of glass separating me from that world beyond – an extraordinarily different world, even for me. I buzzed for admittance and after a moment a nurse approached, took my details and ushered me into a large communal room with sofas, a television and some tables and chairs. There was an open door at the far end that led out into a courtyard area and I watched as patients regularly wandered in and out, some of them pacing in a very unsettling way.

Sitting quietly at one of the tables, I tried not to stare at the people around me. Nurses sat around, some of them engaging with patients and others just observing the area. This was a mixed ward with men and women shuffling around me, some staring or pointing, others engrossed in what they were doing. I felt nervous and out of place but it was nothing compared to how I felt when my mum walked through the doors. Her once shiny blond hair was a dishevelled uncombed mass of grey and she was wearing an old blue cardigan which was misshapen due to the buttons not being correctly lined up. Her once attractive face looked downtrodden and wrinkled, much older than her years, and far different from when I last saw her. Her eyes were bagged with dark rings underneath them and her skin had a mottled red look about it too.

For a moment she just stared at me, a weird, looking-right-through-me kind of stare, and an uncomfortable shudder ran through me. She put her hand out towards my face, and I tried not to flinch as her fingers touched my cheek, dragging at my skin.

"Luna?" she queried and I just nodded, tears beginning to trickle down my face as my mum sagged into the chair in front of me.

"But you're dead," she said, and my heart snapped and shattered into a million tiny little pieces.

The visit was nothing like I'd expected it to be. My mum didn't seem to comprehend that I was really there at all and the nurse, seeing I was distressed, told me that it would be better if I came back another day.

"It will be alright," she said, "it's just the medication... it confuses people. Come back in a few days and I'm sure it will be different again."

Walking away from my mum and leaving her in that place was probably one of the hardest things I ever had to do. She didn't seem to grasp the reality of me being there and after such a long time apart it was almost like sitting with a stranger. As I said goodbye, her cardigan sleeve rode up her arm a little and I caught a glimpse of thick bandage bound around her wrist. I couldn't even bring myself to ask her what she'd done but in my mind it was glaringly obvious. I sank a little deeper into the darkness that was forming inside me as I thought about what these last years must have been like for her.

After seeing mum, I didn't feel like going straight back to Mrs Clarke's house. Instead I caught the bus and got off a stop early, near to the park where I used to hang around. A couple of young lads were playing football but I didn't recognise them. As they shouted to each other and passed the ball back and forth I couldn't help but wonder what the point of everything was. We come into the world and get conditioned by the people around us, our family values, the choices that we make every day, and we go about our lives in what we think is a normal way. But, really, I wondered if anything was actually ever normal at all. People change, we grow up, grow old and eventually die, sometimes way too soon, like my dad.

I wasn't old, but I'd matured enough to understand how little I knew, not just about myself but about all the other people in my life.

The wind blew across my face, whipping my hair in front of me, and I closed my eyes as I listened to the sounds all around. So, this was life. Life was just feelings and thoughts, nothing more. Feelings generated by events, bubbling up from somewhere inside me like a simmering pot of water, threatening to overspill. I didn't want to feel this way. I didn't want to feel the responsibility for other people's pain and be the witness to the broken pieces of the lives I'd left behind. The question was, whether I would be capable of putting all those pieces back together again.

Looking back at my life before the abduction, I revisited that younger version of myself, remembering how I'd always brushed off mum's attempts at having a proper conversation with me. I would tell her to leave me alone and stomp away from her like the brattish child that I was. Then, to add insult to injury, I would lock myself in my bedroom and talk to dad's memory, as if he was more important than my still-living mum. I'd chat with his ghost, not that I could ever feel his presence around me, but it felt somehow easier to do that, telling him what I'd been up to, how school was, what was doing my head in, and I always ended this one-sided conversation by telling dad how much I loved and missed him. Throughout all of this, mum had been there in the background, my backbone, trying her best to be the mother that I so callously rejected. I could now understand all too keenly how she must have felt back then.

It was little wonder she started drinking, drowning out her own pain when I'd been rude or dismissive, leaving her on her own for long periods of time whilst I sought refuge with my friends. More than anything, I saw that the brush I'd used to give colour and texture to my life story had not been the right one at all.

"Luna!" A voice suddenly startled me and I opened my eyes to see my old friend Tara standing there right in front of me, a pushchair out in front of her with a little bobble hatted child inside.

"Tara…"

"Bloody fucking hell… I can't believe it.. We thought you were dead."

"Yes… so I've been told. Who's this little chap? Don't tell me you've had a baby?"

"Oh yeah… this is Charlie, soon be three. Say hello to Auntie Luna, Charlie."

The little child looked up at me, an unimpressed expression on his face, which was half hidden by the bright blue dummy he was sucking on.

"Oh my God, when you disappeared like that… I was the last person you contacted – that text message you sent me, I replied but you never answered. Then that weird as hell phone call that wasn't even registered on the network… you remember? The silent one, that really creeped me out because when the Police took my phone to investigate, they had no way of tracing where that call came from. Everyone was questioned, missing posters went up, I was even interviewed for the tele. It was like I was fucking famous or something."

"You must have enjoyed that!" I tried to joke but even as I spoke the awkwardness of our meeting was all too apparent.

"So what happened, where did you go?"

"I can't tell you. I… I don't know what happened. The last thing I remember is going for a walk along the canal, sitting on the bench… and then… nothing, until earlier today.. and I was right back there in the exact same place and all these years gone by." It seemed so much easier to pretend that I couldn't remember anything.

"Fuck off Luna... you must remember something?"

"No, really, it's all a blank."

"I don't believe you. Are you fucking for real? No one forgets everything."

"Honestly, I don't remember any of it."

"I bet you shacked up with someone." Tara narrowed her eyes, looking at me as if she was weighing me up. "And you sound different."

"You don't..." I replied, all too aware of how much she was swearing. I'd never noticed it before but back then I was probably swearing right along with her.

"I guess you've heard all the news have you?"

"No, not really."

"Oh my god, it was a total fuck-up. I mean... your mum going off the rails like that, and then Amy having to go into care. Your whole family turned into one big freakshow."

I'd been so preoccupied with dealing with my mum, I hadn't even got around to getting all the details about Amy's whereabouts yet.

"Why did Amy go into care?"

"She was way out of control... made you look like Little Bo Peep... she was doing serious drugs, stealing... hanging around with a whole bunch of fucking losers and as for your mum, she couldn't even look after herself, never mind Amy."

I shook my head and closed my eyes, as if by doing so I could blot it all out. I wondered why no-one on The Omicron had thought to tell me all this was happening to my family. Cassiel had urged me to go home – perhaps he had known and that's why he'd encouraged me to return, but Isayel had never mentioned my family at all. I felt angry with them then, they should have made sure my family were safe. It was all their fault because they'd stolen me from my home and started this whole mess.

Like an echo from the past, my mind filled with images of Amy's tiny frame, and our last special time together when we'd had that picnic. I remembered how she would cling to me in that annoying way, her big eyes following me wherever I went. I'd told her I'd never leave her and then disappeared. How could she ever trust anyone again after that?

"Do you know where she is?"

"Sure, the big old house up near the fire station... you can't miss it."

I wanted to visit her as soon as I could, but right now I needed to eat and sleep. It had been one of the most traumatic days of my life.

Tara continued to look at me in a funny kind of way.

"What?" I said at last.

"Nowt... it's just dead weird to see you here."

"Weird to be here too." I added. There was an awkward silence as she continued to study me, her eyes sharp, but not as sharp as her tongue had been.

"Well, I gotta go. Charlie needs his nap. We'll have to have a real catch up soon and a gossip. Can't wait to tell the others that you're back. They won't fucking believe it."

With that Tara trailed away and as I watched her retreating back I shuddered in apprehension. Maybe I'd turned into a snob during my absence but I didn't think a catch up with Tara would be a life enhancing experience at all.

CHAPTER 24

"You only lie to two people in your life, your girlfriend and the police."

- JACK NICHOLSON

T he following day dawned bright, with soft rays of sunlight spilling into the cosy bedroom that Mrs Clarke had made up for me. The walls were painted a sunny golden yellow too and this added an extra layer of optimistic warmth to the room. It all seemed so normal, and so very different to the chamber I'd become accustomed to, where I'd woken up each day to the gently flickering bank of coloured lights that had bathed the room in a rainbow hue of loveliness. I snuggled down a little bit deeper into the comfy duvet, just a few minutes more... but instead of sinking back into the peaceful abyss of sleep I was brought wide awake by a loud, incessant banging at the front door.

I jumped out of bed, stubbing my toe on the side of the dresser as I rushed out onto the landing, almost colliding with Mrs Clarke. I hung back a little, letting her pass so that she could clamber down the stairs first. "I'm coming," she called out a moment before she opened the door to two police officers, a male and female, and I couldn't help but smirk at her unfortunate turn of phrase.

"Good morning, we're just following up a line of enquiry and need to ask a few questions. May we come in?"

Mrs Clarke showed them through into the lounge and then busied herself making tea while I was left to answer some "relevant and important questions". As I sat there in the oversized flannel pyjamas that I'd been loaned I couldn't help but feel a little ridiculous.

"Can you confirm your full name and date of birth for us please?" I knew they probably already had all of that information about me, and guessed that Tara must have blabbed that I was back from the dead.

"Luna May Mason"

"Date of Birth?"

"18th September 1995"

"Luna, on Saturday, 7th August 2010 the police received a report of a missing person, namely yourself. At that time you were still a minor and as such would have been in a vulnerable position. Can you tell us anything about what happened on that date, and in particular the events leading up to your disappearance?"

Mrs Clarke made a timely reappearance at that moment, tea cups rattling on their saucers as she unsuccessfully tried to stop her hands from trembling. I had a vision of her tripping on the rug and then the house would be filled with flying saucers of an entirely different kind. I stifled a smile and tried to look serious as the police officers continued to take notes.

"Really officers, it's too much for Luna to take in right now. She's only been back a day and there's a lot of family problems to deal with. I'm sure all this questioning can wait, can't it?"

"Unfortunately not ma'am" replied the male Officer in a very official tone of voice. "We need to take a statement while everything is still fresh in Luna's mind. This has been an unsolved case for many years and we need to get the paperwork done."

They went through the process of reading me my rights, reassuring me that I hadn't done anything wrong and that they just needed to get some understanding about what had happened that day.

I closed my eyes, hoping that meant they couldn't read my expression, while I tried to compose my story. When I opened them again everyone was looking at me expectantly, even Mrs Clarke, who was probably just as eager to know what had happened as the police were.

"To be honest," I said, drawing in a big deep breath, "I don't remember any of it. I'd gone out, called for my friend Tara who wasn't in. Then I decided not to go home straight away but just go for a little walk. I walked over the canal bridge to the canal and was sitting just up from the Lock House. I think I must have fainted. Next thing I'm back there, and all these years have gone by."

"We know this is hard for you, but there must be something you can tell us. Are you protecting somebody? Has somebody threatened you?"

I shook my head, earnestly wishing that they would leave. I'd never been any good at lying, that's why I'd had so much detention at school.

"We frequently get reports of vulnerable people going missing across the whole country and quite a lot of activity in this area is related to sex trafficking offences and modern human slavery. Whatever anyone has done to you Luna, it's alright. We know it's not your fault and we can help you get the support you need."

Big fat stupid tears welled up in my eyes for no reason, except that I missed Isayel, Cassiel and the Mothers so much, that even my earlier anger with them had subsided. I wished they could be with me to help me through this.

"We want you to come to the station with us Luna. A doctor can give you a full medical examination and we can talk a bit more about things. Is that alright?"

I looked across at Mrs Clarke who just nodded at me, a worried look of concern on her face.

"Can I say no?"

"Yes, we can't force you, you're not under arrest or anything, but we want to clear up a few details and your co-operation would be greatly appreciated."

I decided to go with them, out of courtesy more than anything, but as I rode in the back of the police car I felt like a criminal, minus the handcuffs. A few heads turned as we drove down the smaller streets before reaching the main road. Curious people, all wondering who I was and what I'd been up to, no doubt. Thinking of what was going to happen next, my stomach started to churn in apprehension. I knew I hadn't done anything wrong, but I still felt like I was guilty of something really terrible.

As soon as we arrived, I was booked in at the front desk and then taken to one of the interrogation rooms, or whatever they called them. I was pretty relieved to see it was just an ordinary looking room with a desk and a couple of chairs, no 3000-watt lamp or torture equipment to be seen anywhere.

"Okay, let's start at the beginning, nice and slowly and just tell me everything you can remember about that day." The lady officer who'd arrived to take my statement smiled at me and looked very friendly, making sure I'd got a nice cup of tea in front of me and a bag of chocolates, which she'd placed on the desk at the side, indicating to help myself.

With each question that she asked me I just shrugged, told her I didn't know and had no idea what had happened during the last five and a half years. It got ultra-boring very quickly and I could see the officer's brain trying to work out what else she could do with me. She seemed to ask me the same question lots of times in many different ways, expecting more details maybe.

"Are you sure there's nothing else you want to tell me?" She asked finally, and I told her no, that was all and no, I wasn't protecting anybody.

"With your consent we would like you to undergo a thorough medical examination. We can't force you, but it will be in your own best interests if you truly have lost your memory about all events. This can sometimes happen when someone has been involved in a traumatic experience and we would like to rule out any physical harm that might have been done to you. Will this be okay?"

I nodded my agreement.

"The examination will be with a female doctor and another female officer will also remain in the room, alright?"

"Yes, that's fine," I said and followed her through into a room with a screen, a couch and various other medical looking implements.

"Wait here please."

Ten minutes later a doctor arrived, followed by yet another female officer who stood at the door, giving us a little bit of space and privacy, if that were possible. The doctor asked me questions about my medical history, which again seemed very sketchy. I couldn't remember when I'd had my vaccinations or anything major that had happened to me, no broken bones, no major diseases.

"Okay, undress behind that screen, put the gown on, opening at the back and then hop up on the couch for me."

I did as I was told as she gave me a variety of instructions, checking my pulse, blood pressure, weight and height – all the regular things. Finally, she asked me to put my legs into stirrups so that she could check my more delicate parts. I felt totally exposed and embarrassed as she prodded around and took a vaginal swab. I hadn't been expecting this and my stomach muscles clenched as I tensed up.

"Your hymen is intact, you're still a virgin Luna?"

"Yes".

"Okay, that's quite unusual for a girl of your age." She sounded surprised and I realised she probably thought I'd disappeared into the seedy underbelly of prostitution or worse.

"Thank you, you can lower your legs now," she said, organising the urine, blood and vaginal specimens that she'd now taken.

"And what's this here?" The doctor pointed at the symbol that had remained active on my forearm.

"Erm... it's a tattoo." I looked at the silvery, almost metallic looking outline that had a mercurial appearance to it.

"Did you have it before you disappeared?"

"Yes, I think so."

"You think so? But you're not sure?"

"No, I'm not sure, I can't remember... it's a long time ago."

"I'm sure everyone remembers their first tattoo Luna. It's quite a strange colour too, I've never seen one quite like it before. Interesting, it almost looks like it's moving."

She said no more on the subject and I was relieved when she told me I could dress. I desperately needed a change of clothing and that was on my list of things I had to do today. I would have to appeal to Mrs Clarke for a bit more cash. It took another hour of hanging around before they finally told me I could go.

"Well Luna, seems that you're in good health. The doctor says you don't even have any fillings – remarkable. Wherever you've been over the last few years it looks like no one has abused or hurt you. We are going to close the case, but if you do remember anything, anything at all, that might shed some more light on this, we can re-open our investigations and make further enquiries."

"Thank you," relief flooded through me that I was free to leave and I was particularly relieved that the beatings I'd received from Keysha hadn't left any lasting scars. That would have been so much harder to explain.

"And please take these."

The officer handed me some information leaflets.

"Should you feel that you need any counselling services or psychiatric evaluations you can call one of these numbers. As someone who has been involved in a missing person's case you will be entitled to get help should you feel you need it."

"Thank you, I appreciate it."

"And you will probably need to speak to the HMRC, get issued with a National Insurance Number and also visit the Job Centre. I'm sure you will want to start getting on with things. The local Borough Council can also help you with housing if you have nowhere to stay."

My eyes glazed over as he talked, there were hundreds of things I needed to sort out, all the boring mundane things that I'd never had to deal with in my life before.

Finally, the whole ordeal was over. I scraped the chair back on the floor as I stood up, head down, browsing the literature I'd been given. I didn't even own a handbag to stuff all this into.

"Can I be dropped off near the Fire Station?" I'd asked the desk sergeant on my way back through to the main entrance.

"It's not a taxi service love," was the curt reply and I found myself back out on the streets, having to find my own way across town.

CHAPTER 25

"There is a language every sister knows, a language tender beyond words and rarely spoken. It runs like a string between two hearts, and we only pluck that string in times of trouble. This night […] we speak as sisters."

- KATHLEEN BALDWIN

I traipsed along the streets feeling a little violated and all alone, wondering why everything was so damned difficult. And on top of everything that I'd already been through I now had to go and see what was going on with Amy. I couldn't help but feel crushingly sad for her. If I hadn't gone away maybe she would be okay now and we would always have had each other to rely on for support.

The children's home was situated in one of those old Victorian buildings with big grey windows, set back in its own grounds. I could have done with a taxi just to go from the gates to the main entrance. Walking up to the central pathway I imagined I was about to enter a workhouse or some other sinister place. I counted the stone steps as I approached the front reception area, twelve, then a plateauing out and another seven. By the time I reached the reception I just wanted to sit down.

The inside of the building was very different from what I'd been expecting though, much lighter and brighter and not a barefoot, sackcloth-wearing child in sight. I wandered into a brightly lit reception area and gave a quick summary of who I was and who I'd come to see.

"You will need to fill out some forms. I'm sure you understand, we have to safeguard our children here."

"But I'm her sister"

"I'm sure you are dear, but anyone could walk in and say that, couldn't they? Amy hasn't spoken about you and you've never visited before so we need to be certain."

"I'm sure you must know our family history. I've been away."

The lady threw me a sorrowful look. "We need some ID.

Do you have a passport or a driving licence?"

"No."

"A utility bill in your name or some other form of ID with your address on it? Maybe a bank statement or a post office account?"

"No. I have nothing. Literally just the clothes I'm standing up in. I'm homeless, jobless, have no money, no friends, no history, no life, no house, no bank account, no prospects and now, for God's sake, if I can't even visit my sister, then I might as well have no family either." My voice, which had started off calm, began to rise in pitch as my frustrations took over.

The woman looked sympathetically at me. "Oh dear, this is a sorry state of affairs, isn't it? We obviously try to do everything we can to encourage visiting and for families to stay in touch. Wait here and I will see what I can do."

Around fifteen minutes later she came back. "I've had a chat with Amy and she's confirmed she has a sister named Luna May... interesting that her name is Amy Nula... your mum and dad must have had a very funny sense of humour."

I didn't think there was anything funny about it at all, and just smiled weakly as I followed her through into a common room which looked a little worn but cosy. A bookshelf in the corner was home to all sorts of books, and there was a ping pong table set up at the far end of the room. There were board games, and an assortment of other toys in the corner on the opposite side. Anyone living here would probably find it quite comfortable, I thought, reassured in a good way that it wasn't at all what I expected.

Amy was sitting on an overstuffed sofa and I took an intake of breath as I looked at her, hardly recognising the transformation. At fifteen she was the same age as I'd been when I got abducted. She had dark black eyeliner around her eyes, very similar to how I used to apply mine, and blond streaked hair that was cut spikey and sharp. It was like looking at a more dejected version of my younger self because her face showed an immense amount of suffering and there was a kind of hopeless resignation behind her eyes.

"Amy," I breathed and her face crumpled into a million folds as she ran over and clung to me as if clinging onto a piece of shipwrecked driftwood in a tempestuous, swollen, sea. She'd always been a cling-on and I smiled at the memory of her.

"Luna… you've come back."

"Sshh… yes I have, and everything is going to be alright now." I held tightly onto her, breathing the scent of her hair as I folded my arms around her. My little sister, who had been through so much. "I'm going to make everything better, I'll do whatever it takes to make things right again… get a job and find somewhere to live and you can come and live with me. We can be together as a family again."

She looked at me then, with oily black mascara running down her face. "Will you? Can you do that? I want to have a real home again. It's not like a home here."

"I promise I will do everything I can, but it's going to take a bit of time."

"You said you'd never leave me. Did you run away?" Amy asked as she settled down a little and we sat huddled together on the cosy sofa.

"No, I didn't… it was nothing like that."

"What happened? Why did you go?" If there was anyone at all I wanted to tell the truth to, it was her, but I didn't know what she'd think of me or whether she could even keep a secret to herself…. It had been so long, I needed to get to know her again.

"I can't tell you.. not right now… I want to hear about you instead. You're so big now… a grown up nearly… and you were still such a little thing when I left. What's been happening?"

Amy started to cry big sloppy tears as she told me her version of the last few years. She looked tough on the outside but was so vulnerable and afraid on the inside, it made my stomach do somersaults.

"When you didn't come home that night, mum went crazy. I'd already gone to bed but she woke me up in the middle of the night to see what'd happened during the day and whether you'd mentioned running away."

"That must have been awful. What did you do?" I asked.

"I told her I didn't know anything but I don't think she believed me. None of your stuff had gone though and she started to get really worried. The police came round, searched everything, questioned all of us and did a door-to-door investigation of all the neighbours as well. Every day she was ringing them up, but they couldn't find anything. Mum said she thought you were dead, that someone had murdered you, and after a while that's what we all thought."

"That must have been a nightmare. I promise, if I could have come back or sent a message I would have."

"Were you locked up then?"

I didn't know how to bat off her questions without making things worse. "Something like that, but I can't talk about it right now."

"Why can't you talk about it?"

"I just can't alright? You need to trust me on this. One day I will be able to tell you about it, but not right now, okay?"

Amy looked at me suspiciously but just nodded and I asked her to carry on telling me what happened.

"Mum was drinking and started picking on me all the time. I hated it, I couldn't do anything right and felt like running away but I didn't because I felt guilty about leaving her alone like that too and sometimes she wouldn't even get out of bed."

"You were too little to deal with that."

"I didn't know what to do, so I started pretending I was the mum, and started doing more stuff around the house, like cleaning up after her. I learned how to use the washing machine and took her bank card so I could go to the shops. I made it a game and it seemed to be okay for a while."

"Wow, you were a smarty-pants, doing all that."

"Yeah, well I had to. Then she seemed to rally around for a bit and sometimes she was okay. She told me how sorry she was and that she wasn't going to drink anymore. It went on and off like that for a couple of years."

"Then what?"

"I dunno. Something must have happened because she got really sad and depressed again. She stopped getting up to go to work and I worried like mad that she'd get the sack."

"Did Mrs Clarke help you?"

"Mrs Clarke? That old bat? No, she didn't. As soon as mum got ill she stopped coming round."

"Really? That's surprising... I thought they'd stayed close. How ill was mum then?"

"You know... mental like... drinking, sleeping, drinking some more, acting stupid, saying bad things. Eventually she got the sack from work. Too unreliable."

"How did you manage if she stopped working?"

Amy crossed her arms around herself. "We got some benefits but they wouldn't pay the mortgage." I saw Amy's face close down and she drew herself into a tighter huddle.

"I don't want to talk about it, okay? Just like you don't want to talk about what happened to you."

"Okay, it's alright... I guess we have a lot of catching up to do. You were just a kid when I left and now look at you, all grown up."

"Yeah, grown up and stuck here."

"Don't say that, we'll have you out of here. Do you ever get to see mum?"

"No, I don't want to visit mum."

"Really? But I think she really needs you."

"She doesn't need me, she needs you Luna, not me. She didn't give a toss about me, not ever."

It was hard to hear Amy talk like that and my first instinct was to deny it, but maybe there was some truth in it. Maybe we always want the person that is no longer there, just like I used to ignore mum and pine for dad.

Amy's tears dried on her cheeks, and despite the emotional outpouring she looked dead on the inside when I looked into her eyes.

"Do you have any friends?"

"Some" she said.

"That's good. Listen, I'm back now and I'm going to come and visit you every day if you want me to, but I need to try and get a job too and save some money so that I can rent a house so we can live together. Would you like that?

"Yes."

"Remember I love you, I'm not going to leave you again. We're sisters, nothing and no-one can change that, okay?" I squeezed her hand tightly, observing the chewed down finger nails, and the ragged skin around the nail beds where she'd obviously been biting them.

When it was time to leave I said as cheerful a goodbye as I could manage but there was a lump in my throat and a dagger in my heart as I did so.

CHAPTER 26

"He who fights with monsters might take care lest he thereby become a monster. And if you gaze for long into an abyss, the abyss gazes also into you."

- FRIEDRICH NIETZSCHE

T he moment I awoke I knew she had gone. There was a new emptiness inside me where I had held her memory in my heart. Her vibration, that had echoed like a heartbeat, a twin flame, in my chest was silent. I got up slowly, with a determined calmness, showered, dressed, and then... only then... followed my instincts and went in search of Cassiel. I found him in HW3 and as I moved through the entrance I was immediately engulfed in a searing heat.

The landscape was mountainous, with wild red rock, cacti, and a surface of red dust beneath my feet. The simmering air was rent with the piercing shrieks of carrion crows and other feathered beasts. It did nothing to calm the feelings that were bubbling up inside me. I drew in a breath and the heat burned my throat. This was truly a hellish environment.

I observed Cassiel from a distance, although he showed no indication that he had noticed me yet. He was crouching down, studying a desert rose, looking deep in contemplation. As I strode towards him my feet kicked up a flurry of dust and my fury swelled inside me. I broke into a run, my wings beating furiously as I rose into the air, propelled forward until I was hovering above him. My wrath was so great I could no longer contain myself.

"Cassiel! You have betrayed me. Tell me, what have you done? Where is she?" My voice boomed from me, slicing through the sweltering air that swirled around me.

His eyes flashed at me as he turned to face me, sparks flying from him. "I did what was right, and gave Luna the choice. She has gone home."

"Home? This is her home now, she has no other."

"You are wrong. She has people who need her back on

Earth, and yet you would keep her here for your own selfish reasons. She asked me to tell you goodbye."

"She couldn't tell me herself? After all that we've been through?" I roared with anger as it coursed through my veins, like a red-hot lava flowing through me. "You had no right."

Cassiel drew himself up, staring coldly at me. "I had every right." His voice was snake-like, detached and immovable. "You were getting too close, something we vowed we would never do again."

"It was different this time. She was different. There was a future for us. I loved her."

"You forget quickly that I loved her too. I was her friend and, as any true friend would, I put her needs above my own. It was the right time for Luna to go back to where she belongs."

"You need to fetch her back, she belongs here with me."

"No! She does not belong with you, or any of us. She can no longer fulfil her role as a Mother... the very reason we brought her on board to start with. I've given Luna her freedom and the chance of a normal life."

"A normal life... I think not. How could Luna have anything like a normal life after this? You knew we were in love! She was mine!"

"Yours? You really think so? I did not force her hand in this matter. You can say whatever you want to me, but the fact is that it was her choice to leave, not mine. She chose to leave you Isayel."

There was a moment of silence between us, a split second where we eyed each other up and the next moment Cassiel was in the air at my side, his own wings beating wildly as we took our anger to the next level. Rushing forwards, we crashed bodily, attacking and defending with unprecedented speed and precision. Cassiel rained blows upon my chest and head, pounding into me, and I, in turn, sliced through him, attacking and letting out all my pent-up emotion. Physical pain mingled with my emotional pain as we fought on, equally matched for strength and agility. My muscles screamed with exhaustion and I could feel the sinews being stretched relentlessly as I pummelled into him. Both too furious to admit defeat or truce, we continued in this barbaric quest to prove a point. A matter of honour.

Then, without warning, the HW3 scene shut down. We were plunged into darkness and tumbled to the ground as if weighted down by gravity itself. I hit the floor hard, the breath knocked out of me for a moment and the shock of the fall distracting me from my anger. It took a moment or two for my eyes to adjust to the darkness but as they did so, I could see an outline beginning to form near to the entrance.

"Metraton?"

"Yes, it is I."

There was another protracted silence before he spoke again.

"Just like old times, is it? Fighting over the daughters of man? This is not Sodom and Gomorrah. You have discredited yourselves with your pettiness."

"This is the price we pay for having feelings Metraton. You should try it some time."

"I have all the feelings I need. You, on the other hand, forget who you are. You forget your lineage, bickering like children over a toy. How did you become so lowly, so removed from your own supremacy over man?"

Metraton's words were true. I'd behaved foolishly and attacked without provocation. The taste of blood was in my mouth and I swallowed it down, a bitter draught. I'd acted like a human, jealous and emotional, attacking Cassiel not just because he had encouraged Luna to leave, but also because she had chosen to confide in him over me.

Now that my anger had been exhausted, I decided that my emotional pain had not been improved by my actions. Slowly I reached out a hand of friendship towards Cassiel but he refused to acknowledge my gesture, looking right through me before turning away and walking towards the exit. I would not offer again.

"You will both accompany me back to the First Heaven. Your actions will be held in judgement against you."

I got shakily to my feet, following Cassiel's retreating back. I had no fight left in me and there was nothing onboard The Omicron worth staying for. Without Luna and the shining souls of the Mothers, it seemed as if all the joy had been drained from my life.

We used the slipstream to arrive back at the threshold of the First Heaven, and the Great Beast was there waiting for us as we touched down. His eyes flashed and snapped as he surveyed us, his multiple jaws foaming with pleasure.

"Come to me," he snarled. "You're worthy of so much more... God cannot judge you... you don't need God..."

I closed my ears to the suggestions of the Beast but as we waited there, his voice became louder in my mind.

"Come to me Isayel. God doesn't want you. You're not good enough for him or for heaven.... You're weak for the flesh of woman... follow me and we can do whatever we please... renounce God and I will show you all the delights you could ever want... you can satisfy all your pleasures... power will be yours, people will adore you, your life will flow with wealth and abundance... you don't need God, you're not fit to serve him... come, follow me."

I waivered, an instant of uncertainty, which allowed the Great Beast deeper access to my mind, like a doorway that had been prised open, allowing him to probe my insecurities and vulnerabilities. I had failed, lapsed into wicked ways and now the temptation of the Beast dominated my thoughts and my feelings. Maybe the Beast was right and I wasn't good enough for God. I had proven myself unworthy, so what more could I lose? I had already lost Luna... it would be so easy to fall into a life of sin... a life of pleasure, unadulterated passion and hedonistic gratification. The Great Beast was right... God could not judge me. He burrowed further into my mind, swirling all around me. I saw the red glint in his eyes, felt his strong desire to ensnare my soul to his own. His words became my words...

"Isayel?" Metraton pulled me out of my stupor, looking deep inside me, his eyes kind and full of wisdom. "The choice will always be yours."

He knew... he knew my torment. I stood for a moment, the Great Beast to the left of me, showing me the left-hand path that led into darkness and power. And to the right of me, the gateway to the First Heaven, where retribution, punishment and judgement awaited me and, perhaps if I showed redemption, the love of God. The choice was mine alone.

CHAPTER 27

"Each morning
I wake invisible.
I make a needle
from a porcupine quill,
sew feet to legs,
lift spine onto my thighs.
I put on my rib and collarbone.
I pin an ear to my head,
hear the waxwing's yellow cry.
I open my mouth for purple berries,
stick on periwinkle eyes.
I almost know what it is to be seen."

— DIANE GLANCY

Mrs Clarke continued to show me nothing but kindness. She insisted on giving me some more spending money and drove me to the local retail park so that I could pick out some new clothes and personal items. When I'd objected, she'd told me to think of it as a loan, I could always pay her back later.

Observing my reflection in the floor length mirrors it was hard to believe I'd ever been a Goth. My choice in clothing had matured since I'd been gone and Mrs Clarke encouraged me to try on all sorts of different outfits. There were bold printed dresses, fitted blouses and skirts, some colourful, some classically inspired, and casual lounging around clothes too.

I was amazed at how different I looked and, if I'm honest, how much better. My hair had grown back strong and thick since it'd been shaved off on The Omicron and it now hung down my back in soft blonde waves.

"You're very beautiful, you know" Mrs Clarke commented as I gave a twirl in a flowing turquoise summer dress. "You remind me of myself when I was your age."

I smiled at the compliment – even if it was really directed at herself. For the first time since my eighteenth birthday, I actually did feel quite pretty.

The shopping trip had been totally amazing and Mrs Clarke seemed to have a list in her head of everything I might need. By the time we returned to the car we were weighed down with dozens of shopping bags, stuffed with all sorts of wonders. In return for Mrs Clarke's kindness I volunteered to help her around the house and garden. My knowledge and love of plants meant that I was truly transforming the dull flowerbeds into a really colourful, sensory experience and I spent many hours pottering away, digging through the rich brown earth and planting up seedlings.

"My, you do have a way with you," Mrs Clarke said as she witnessed the slow but steady transformation taking place. "I don't think you had much aptitude for gardening before you left, was it something you learned while you were away?"

"I think so," I had replied, not wanting to get into a conversation about it. I was aware that the more lies I dished out, the more tangled I would become in my own web of deceit.

When I was in nature my mind always turned to Elisia and I imagined her supporting me in my efforts to coax life into the tiny seeds and buds. Nature was also the big sky that pressed down upon me every time I was outdoors and as I stared up into the infinite blue beyond, I couldn't help but wonder where The Omicron was and whether Isayel or Cassiel ever thought about me. There was many a sigh that mingled with my breath on the breeze as I bent my back to the work.

There were other matters to deal with too and the Job Centre had now registered me as looking for employment, which meant I was able to get some benefits to help with my cost of living. I also managed to get some money towards rent so that I could start to give Mrs Clarke a little for my upkeep. She'd done so much for me, my gratitude was overflowing.

"I really don't know what I'd have done without your help." I said to her one evening as we were having dinner.

"It's the least I can do. Your family has been through such a terrible ordeal. I'm pleased I've been useful." She was such a good soul.

"Has Amy told you anything else about what happened while you were away?" she asked, slicing through a piece of carrot and spearing it with her fork.

I remembered Amy calling Mrs Clarke an old bat, but thought it best not to mention that particular insult. It was probably just Amy being defensive – I'd been the same at her age.

"No, I don't think she's ready to talk to me about everything yet. She told me she had to go into care because of how mum was, but not much more than that."

"She didn't go into care until after your mum lost the house Luna. She ran away too, but the police brought her back."

"She never told me that." I was surprised Amy hadn't mentioned this; I was pretty certain she'd told me the opposite.

"She'll tell you when she's ready." Mrs Clarke paused while she concentrated on chewing a slice of roast beef, dabbing at her mouth with a napkin to capture a trickle of beefy gravy that had started to run down her chin. It all looked so ordinary, like a normal family scene. In an alternate reality Mrs Clarke could have been my mum and we were just enjoying a meal together.

The days rushed by and I'd made a point of visiting mum regularly. It wasn't until my fourth visit that she appeared almost her old self and understood that I wasn't actually dead but was really there, her flesh and blood long-lost daughter.

"I haven't had a drink for seven weeks," she confided in me.

"It's been really difficult and the cravings can go through the roof.. I've been so stupid, ruined my life really. You don't drink do you?"

It was the first time she'd asked about me and I could almost get a glimmer of my old mum buried underneath all that medication.

"No mum, I don't drink, hardly ever." I hadn't had a drink since I'd left The Omicron and felt justified in saying so.

"Don't ever do it. It will kill you. Promise me…"

"It's okay mum, I won't let drink take over my life. I promise."

She sat forward in her chair then, and I could almost see her mind racing behind her eyes as her gaze darted around the room in an unsettled kind of way. Her hands were in her lap and she twisted her fingers round as if agitated and fidgety.

"I'm worried about leaving this place. Did you know they're looking to put me somewhere? I'm not sure I can cope on my own now."

"It's alright mum. I'm here now and I'll help you however I can." She smiled and reached out to squeeze my hand with her fidgety fingers. "You're such a good girl now. I hardly recognise you."

It was a double-edged compliment but she was right. The old me would never have been so thoughtful or considerate. I was actually starting to like the new Luna because somewhere along the way I'd realised that helping people was a joy in itself and brought far more satisfaction than when I did things solely for my own pleasure. I remembered Isayel had given me that lecture at my eighteenth birthday party. I'm sure he'd look totally smug with this knowledge if I ever got the chance to tell him he'd been right.

We walked out into the courtyard together and did a few laps. It wasn't a very big space and dotted around were some chunky fat red plastic seats that had been bolted into the ground. As we did our second lap I spotted one of the other female inmates relieving herself in the corner. I gagged and turned away. It was hard to think of my mum living here with all these sadly dysfunctional people, each one lost in the mind in some way and not coping with life at all. I couldn't wait to be able to get her out of there and back into the normal world, me, Amy and mum, all together again. We could all help each other.

As well as visiting mum I also spent some time with Amy

every day and we slowly rebuilt our relationship. Seeing her was much easier than seeing mum and I really started to appreciate having a sister, probably the only person I felt like I could properly relax with.

"I hope you get a job soon," Amy said, one afternoon in the summer. I'd been back a few months and was still adjusting to life back on planet earth. Amy had been given permission to leave the grounds and we'd opted to go grab a burger and fries from the café just up the road.

"I'm trying really hard to get a job, but it's more difficult than I ever dreamed it would be, with no qualifications."

"You need to go back to school then," she said and I thought she was actually right. It wasn't that I was stupid, far from it, the Mothers had educated me wonderfully, but I had no paperwork to show for it. Every job I'd looked at had asked for experience and qualifications plus a full working history, and I had nothing to let prospective employers know that I could be trusted with responsibility.

I still thought about Isayel most days too and wondered if he forgave me for leaving him. I even talked to him when I was on my own, much like I used to talk to dad.

Often I would find myself looking up into the sky but there was never any visible sign to show that he'd ever existed. Sometimes I tried to connect with him by pushing my energy fields out like an aura around me, trying to stretch it all the way into space, hoping that I could get some perception of Isayel out there, but I couldn't feel anything. As each day passed I became more and more absorbed with the routine of real life, slowly letting go of that part of me. I was becoming ordinary again.

At 3.00pm on Monday afternoon I made my way down to the

Job Centre to see my Work Coach. For someone who didn't currently have a job, I was constantly busy. A security guard in a navy suit stood in the foyer, eyeing people up as they walked in. I approached him, giving him my name and appointment time. He scanned his clipboard for my details and then nodded and pointed to a bank of chairs lining the wall.

The word "dickhead" sprung to mind as I watched him smugly sticking his chest out, no doubt thinking he was superior to those that were seeking help, just because he already had a job.

I sat down next to a harassed looking woman with greasy hair and a sharp face. She was rocking a baby in a buggy and had another child clinging to her leg. My stomach lurched with an unfulfilled emptiness.

I would never experience the wonder of Isayel's baby growing inside my womb or watch it develop into a little tumbling tot with chubby legs and round rosy cheeks.

The woman beside me snapped at the child round her leg, pushing him away so that she could move. Clumsily she pulled a tobacco pouch out of her pocket and started to roll a cigarette, tucking it back into the folds of the packet for later. She couldn't have been more different from The Mothers, who'd dedicated so much time to helping and supporting me. It was Elisia who'd also settled the ghost of my dad during my first few months aboard.

"Remember the thing you loved most about your dad," she'd said, as she guided me into a deep meditation. "That will be your anchor and will draw him to you." Holding an image in my mind, Elisia had journeyed with me into a spiritual sanctuary where it felt to me as if my dad was actually physically there. I spent a long time with him in that place – a place out of time, between the worlds, where I could tell him everything that had been in my heart since he'd been so cruelly taken from us. I could also finally tell him goodbye and allow his spirit to be released from the pain of my memory. After this, I could think of my dad without getting upset and that made the world of difference to me.

The woman next to me gave me a sharp nudge. "Are you Luna Mason? They've called your name out twice, do you want your appointment or not?"

"Oh, I'm sorry", I stuttered. I'd been so lost in my thoughts I hadn't heard anything.

My work coach was named James and he actually looked as if he genuinely wanted to help me.

"Your case is very unusual," he said. "we've got a letter here from the NHS that gives you special dispensation for not having any previous work history. That's really interesting. So, it says here that you went missing for five and a half years and that you're suffering from amnesia?"

I wondered what any of that had to do with my appointment today, but just smiled and told him yes, he was correct.

"That must have been pretty awful for you. My nan has dementia, poor soul, can't even remember whether she's had her tea or where she put her teeth. What's your short-term memory like now?"

"I can remember everything now, and I definitely don't have dementia," I said. "It's only the time that I was away that I can't remember."

"That's so weird isn't it? Do you ever wonder why?"

"No, I don't. I just want to forget about it actually."

James looked flustered. "Oh, I'm sorry, I didn't mean to get personal... it's just that this job gets very routine and you are... you are so different. I love interesting people." He smiled a lopsided, kind smile and I relaxed a little. I'd spent so long being defensive I often didn't realise how suspicious of other people I'd become.

"There's actually a job here that I'd like to put you forward for. Can you type?"

"Yes, very well," I lied. It wouldn't take me long to practice though and polish up the rough bits.

"What about your spelling and grammar?" I knew my spelling was really good. Corrine had ensured that had been part of my training with her. "Excellent," I replied.

"This job will also involve handing calls, doing a little bit of marketing and talking to people who come into the offices."

"I'm sure I would be able to manage all of that." I was desperate to be given a chance. I couldn't help Amy or mum unless I started earning some proper money.

"Okay, well, let me phone them now and see if I can arrange an interview for you. It's with Blake and Steel, the estate agents on Main Street." That sounded really good to me and I waited with my fingers and toes crossed as James made the call.

"Yes, okay... right, that's great... yes... erm... yes she does... okay... fab... when? Oh okay, lovely, that's great stuff, thanks.... we will set that up then. Thanks for your time. Bye." Listening to a one-sided conversation didn't really give me much idea about what they had been talking about, but it generally sounded positive.

"I've arranged an interview for you on Thursday at 2.00pm. You will need to go to their offices and ask for Mr Blake. He will be conducting the interview, and I'm told there will also be an aptitude test which will take approximately twenty minutes."

"That's wonderful. Thank you, James. You made that look easy. I can't tell you how difficult it's been just trying to get my foot in the door," I smiled at him and he smiled back.

"Let me know how you get on and if you need anything, here's my card." He pushed the small white rectangular business card over to me and our fingers touched as he did so. It was my turn to look flustered. I thanked him again and smiled, things were beginning to look up.

CHAPTER 28

"Producing a great interview requires you to acknowledge the fact that, or to pretend as if, the person you are interviewing is more knowledgeable or interesting than you."

— MOKOKOMA MOKHONOANA

T hursday morning arrived and I awoke in good spirits. Mrs Clarke had helped me to choose a pair of black trousers and white blouse to wear for my interview, together with a matching black jacket. I worked my fingers through my hair, deftly entwining the strands to form a cornrow plait that hung down my back. It was smart and pretty at the same time.

"Now, remember what I said," Mrs Clarke fussed around me. "Just stay confident, make sure you make eye contact and smile. If you need extra time to think about anything, just take some nice deep breaths. You can always ask them to repeat a question."

"Yes, yes... I know... you've already told me a hundred times."

"Oh, but it's so exciting... your first ever interview."

I'm sure Mrs Clarke was more excited than I was and her general attitude had started to give me the jitters.

"Okay, how do I look?"

"Wonderful, just wonderful dear. How can they not choose you? You're beautiful, kind hearted, smart... oh, I can't wait to hear all about it."

I gave Mrs Clarke a quick hug and left promptly, giving myself enough time to take the scenic route. The walk would do me good and maybe calm me down a little.

I'd been walking for around ten minutes and had just crossed over the street when I noticed the figure coming towards me, pushing a pushchair. It was Tara again. I hadn't seen her since my first day back at the park, and now I really wasn't sure about facing her, especially like this. I still felt pretty sure she'd told the police I was back, no doubt trying to feel important. As we got closer she shouted out to me, "Hey Luna, where've you been?"

"Oh hi, just busy sorting things out, there's been so much to do, you know?"

"No, I don't actually. You've been back all this time and not once called round to see us."

"How could I call round? I don't even know where you live anymore."

"Well, it wouldn't have been hard to find out would it?"

I'd decided I hated everything about her and had no intention of renewing our friendship. In the silence that followed she eyed me up and down.

"Look at you, dressed up like a fucking dog's dinner. I guess you think you're too good for us now."

"No, don't be silly," I replied, cringing at her words.

"Yeah you do. Swanking about trying to look posh. Where's the Goth now Luna? Where's your stupid black hair?"

"I've grown up, that's all. You should try it."

"Yeah right..." she sniffed and looked me up and down once more, "where you going dressed up like that?"

"I have an interview."

"Looking for a job now too... well, just in case you missed it while you were off busy doing other things, there's people that've lived here all their lives who can't even get a fucking job, so what makes you think you're going to get one above them? And let's face it, you didn't even finish school did you?"

"Thanks for that," I replied, meeting her gaze for an instant before pushing past her. I wasn't going to get into an argument with Tara in the middle of the street and after my experiences with Keysha I particularly tried to avoid conflict.

It seemed Tara needed to get the last word in, calling out

after me, "and when you see your slut of a sister again, ask her about the fucking sprog."

I almost stopped, almost turned around to defend Amy, but I wasn't going to give her the satisfaction of seeing me worked up. Instead I concentrated on putting one foot in front of the other, walking away and putting a safe distance between us. The sprog? What the hell was she talking about? My mind started to pool with questions. Here we go again, I thought, some more drama to add to my increasingly screwed-up life story.

By the time I arrived for my interview I was a jangly mess inside. All I wanted to do was turn in the opposite direction so that I could visit Amy and ask her what Tara had meant by her comments. Instead I introduced myself and was asked to take a seat. I chose the chair in the corner, next to a large potted Yucca plant, and as I concentrated on steadying my breathing and calming my mind so that I could focus on the interview I could feel the plant starting to connect with me. It wasn't intentional on my part and, to be honest, I was a little surprised when the channels began to open because I'd thought all of that was left in the past. It didn't seem to belong to the ordinary world that I now found myself a part of. Nevertheless, I sent a wave of loving kindness to it and, in return, the plant sent wonderfully calm and harmonious waves back to me.

I started to relax and flow with ease and tranquillity as this sense of wellbeing engulfed me. Then we transcended to the second level of communication. It was a process that I could only describe as being like osmosis, where the plant shared information with me in a non-vocal energetic way. Very quickly I picked up impressions about the place and the people who worked there. The boss loved golf... that could be interesting... the girl at the desk to the immediate front of me enjoyed baking.... another girl suffered migraines and was worried about something. In the few minutes that I'd been sitting there my mind had vacuumed up all the knowledge I could about this workplace, information stored by the plant during the course of its life there, like an imprinted record of everything.

Perhaps the angels were looking after me, after all, I thought, as I was called forward for my interview.

"Good morning Luna, please have a seat."

"Thank you," I replied, remembering to smile and give some eye contact.

"So, let me tell you a little about the company..."

Fifteen minutes later Mr Blake was still talking and I wondered if this was an interview or a monologue. I stifled a yawn and forced my eyes to open a little wider because it felt like I could really use a nap.

"...and so, I think that covers that, for the time being anyway. I'm sure we can go into more detail later. Any questions?"

I was brought back from my totally blank inner mind, where I'd parked my brain while he waffled on. Did I have any questions? I couldn't remember a single thing he'd just spoken about, and I'd practised this part with Mrs Clarke too... questions... what were they? Just beyond Mr Blake's head, as if perched on his right shoulder, I noticed a shiny golf trophy sitting on the cabinet behind him.

"You must be very good at golf?" I said, and then kicked myself. That wasn't a real question at all, it was just stuff I'd soaked up from the plant.

"Oh yes," he beamed and then went on to tell me about his love of the game and how he'd recently been having hypnotherapy sessions to improve his golf swing.

"That stuff really works you know," he enthused and I smiled pleasantly back at him. What a weird interview.

Eventually he got back round to talking about the job, by which time I'd composed myself enough to remember everything I'd practiced in the mirror.

"Well, you just need to do an aptitude test now. Polly has set up the computer and will time you. It's pretty straightforward, she'll give you the instructions and once that's done you'll be free to go. We have two more people to interview today and then we should be able to let the successful candidate know by tomorrow afternoon."

"Thank you so much for your time, I really appreciate it," I pumped Mr Blake's hand with my best firm handshake, gave him my brightest smile complete with eye contact which silently said "pick me" and then left the room.

I sailed through the rest of the interview, Polly seemed attentive to my needs, making sure I had a glass of water too in case I was thirsty.

"You'll easily do it in twenty minutes," she said, and she was right. After twelve minutes I'd completed all the questions and had time left over to re-read them too.

I smiled my goodbyes and, as a final thought, asked if I could give my remaining water to the plant. Polly looked a little surprised but then smiled back, "what a thoughtful gesture, of course you can."

It was much later in the day when I finally had chance to change back into my casual clothes and take the trip across town to visit Amy. She was waiting for me in the grounds and her face lit up when she saw me.

"How did it go?"

"Alright, I think. I did good on the test and Mr Blake

seemed nice."

"That's awesome. Just think, if you get this job you can start saving some money so we can find somewhere to live together. I'm sure they will let you be my guardian. It will be dead good." She was in such high spirits I didn't want to spoil the moment by bringing up what Tara had said. Instead I talked about our mum.

"I'm going to visit mum tomorrow. Do you want to come with me?" For a fleeting moment I saw Amy's face cloud over.

"No, I don't want to go."

"But why not? I don't think you've visited once since I got back. It will really lift her spirits to see you too." I tried cajoling, but Amy was adamant that she didn't want to visit her. I couldn't help but feel that there was more going on than anyone was admitting.

"She's not like a mum to me anymore... and you should know how I feel, because you used to hate her too."

"Oh Amy, that's an awful thing to say. I had problems... but they were my problems, and mum always did her best. I see that now that I'm older. I don't hate her anymore."

Amy was unimpressed. "Maybe she tried to be a proper mum to you, but she wasn't one to me."

"Do you want to tell me some more about it?" I asked, but Amy just folded her arms and looked away, pushing the toe of her shoe into the floor. "I couldn't care less if I never saw her again for as long as I live."

Knowing that Amy felt that way was really difficult for me. I'd imagined a future where we'd all be happy together as a family again but it would never happen if Amy felt this strongly about it.

By the time Friday arrived I was a bag of nerves, checking my phone every few minutes to make sure it was still working, that the ring tone was on and that there was a signal. It wasn't until around 4.30pm that I received the call, and by that time I'd convinced myself that they'd chosen another candidate.

"Hi, is that Luna?" It was my work coach James.

"Hello James, yes... I hope you're bringing me some good news?" I held my breath with anticipation as I awaited his reply.

"Actually I am. Mr Blake said you performed really well during the interview and he has asked if you can start working on a trial basis on Monday?"

"This Monday? Yes of course I can. That will be amazing. Thank you so much for arranging this for me."

"No trouble at all, it's my job, after all." There was a little silence and then James continued, "I know it's a bit against our policy and perhaps a bit out of the blue, but I was wondering, once you're signed off with us, whether I would be able to take you... take you out for a drink some time?"

James had totally caught me by surprise and I answered without giving it too much thought. "Erm... yes, I think that would be fine."

"That's great, I'll give you a call next week and maybe we can arrange a date."

I hung up the phone in shock. Not only did I now have a job but I'd also been asked out on a date. I knew he could never compete with Isayel, but still felt pleased that someone had actually noticed me in that way.

CHAPTER 29

"Nobody trips over mountains. It is the small pebble that causes you to stumble. Pass all the pebbles in your path, and you will find you have crossed the mountain."

—AUTHOR UNKNOWN

T he first few days at my new job seemed much more demanding than I'd anticipated. Polly was a patient teacher though and I hoped she didn't get tired of having to remind me how to do things. Part of the job was pretty boring too, making lots of photocopies, scanning documents and doing the tea rounds. The other girl, Ruth, was quieter and more withdrawn. She was the one who suffered from headaches and I'm sure that affected her mood a lot of the time. Ruth often left the offices so that she could show people around properties, and it was something I was hoping they'd let me do once I'd been trained up a bit more.

As soon as Ruth left the offices it seemed as if Polly brightened up and became more talkative, almost as if Ruth's influence suppressed her somehow. By the same token, Ruth seemed happier when Polly wasn't around, although that was quite rare. There was an underlying tension between the two women that became unsettling when everyone was together. Today, though, Polly seemed in a really good mood and had brought a container full of cakes into work, the result of a baking weekend. "Eat them... help yourself, they've got to go" she said and I didn't need asking twice. Those little gestures made me feel like part of the team but it was still weird to actually be doing a job I liked and getting paid for it. I felt a proper sense of purpose that had been missing when on board The Omicron and, more than that, I was now in control of my own destiny, something which had been taken away from me when I was expected to become the mother of Isayel's child.

Mr Blake also spent a lot of time out of the offices. As the chief surveyor he visited properties that needed valuations, talking to potential customers and providing all the information about our company. Mr Steel was the other partner in the company but I'd never met him and I wasn't sure if he was alive, dead, or merely indifferent.

The policy at work was that lunchtimes were staggered so that someone was always manning the reception and the phone lines. This meant that I didn't get to spend a lot of informal social time with Polly or Ruth. I felt quite grateful for this because making small talk was one of the things I found really difficult to do, and I was particularly vigilant when it came to speaking about my past. Instead, I had taken to eating my sandwiches at lunchtime over in the corner where there was a low table with magazines and a small vending machine area for clients. The beautiful Yucca plant that I'd connected with on my interview lived in this corner too and it felt nice to bathe in the energies around it. I'd christened him Barry, an innocuous sounding name that I thought suited him, and whilst I was sitting close by, I felt a little stirring of emotion about my old life.

Connecting with plants was one of the few things that reminded me of my past, together with the symbol that worked in the background to ensure that I was never too hungry or thirsty. Whatever I was doing or however long I'd been without food or water, that symbol would sustain me. I'm sure that Keysha would never have placed the symbol there if she'd thought it would have been useful to me in any way other than for keeping me alive during my prolonged starvation.

Those days at work kept me functioning but coming back to reality and adjusting to the mundane had been a terrible awakening for me, and Isayel was never far from my mind. Each day when I woke up I wondered if I'd made the right choice, but if I dwelled on that thought for too long it created an overwhelming feeling of sadness within me. It was hard to think that some choices we are just stuck with, for better or for worse, and no amount of wishful thinking could change the new course my life now followed.

I had planned to visit mum after work, and was quite excited about the fact that she would be moving into a flat of her own in a few days. That would be her first step to independence again and it felt really good to think of her becoming settled. I knew it would be a long road but now that I was back to help I wondered what could possibly go wrong. Maybe I was naive because that question tempted fate more than I could ever have realised.

As soon as I arrived at the ward, I knew there was something wrong. The receptionist had advised all visitors to remain in the reception area because the wards were on lockdown. I paced back and forth, worried without knowing why – after all, there were lots of inpatients and there was nothing to indicate my mum would be in any particular difficulty.

Parked outside the main doors was an emergency ambulance and my mind went into overdrive as I imagined paramedics rushing to the aid of an unknown catastrophe. I was fuelled by negative imaginings and ruminations, sitting there chewing the inside of my cheek while I waited for news. Thirty minutes went by and I was aware that visiting time would only last another thirty minutes. Everyone around me was grumbling and speculating, no doubt each of them in their own private little hell of anticipated disaster.

When I could stand it no longer, I approached the desk, "can you tell me anything at all, my mum is Helen Mason on the Briar Ward and I want to know if she is alright?"

"I'm sorry, we can't tell anybody anything at the moment. All I can say is that there has been an incident on that ward." Dread filled me up from the insides, pushing through me like a wrecking ball, never stopping, just sweeping along until I felt sick with worry.

Quickly I fired off a text to Amy. "Hi, I'm visiting mum, I think something bad has happened. They won't let me in to see her." A minute later I received her reply. "So what?" I couldn't understand Amy's continuing hostile attitude towards mum, it wasn't like her at all.

"I think you should be a little kinder to mum. What if something really terrible has happened to her?"

"Luna, it's too late for this. I'm not interested in what's going down with mum, okay? If she dropped dead tomorrow, I couldn't give a damn."

Amy's heartless replies crushed me a little bit more. I felt alone and adrift in a sea of pointless, stupid emotion. What was wrong with everybody?

My fingers flew across the keypad of my phone, texting a reply. It had been on my mind for far too long and wasn't anything I had felt able to ask Amy about face-to-face. "Is it because of the baby?" I asked, and the very second I sent it I knew I shouldn't have. Amy never replied and I was left with a black hole in my chest where my heart should have been.

Most of the other visitors had already dwindled away when, finally, a senior looking nurse came through the locked doors from the ward. Behind her were the paramedics, pushing a stretcher.

"Move back please everybody," she called. "There's nothing to see." Her words had the opposite effect, however, and it seemed that those of us left edged forward a bit more to try to get a view of who was being wheeled out of the ward. The figure lying on the stretcher was covered with a grey hospital blanket and had an oxygen mask around the face, obscuring the features, but from the wild tufts of grey hair that were visible, I was certain it was my mum.

The receptionist advised us that we could now commence our visits and that the visiting times would be extended. On hearing the announcement those visitors left pushed through the doors, away into the corridor leading to the wards. I alone loitered behind, waiting to speak to the nurse who was overseeing the transfer of the patient into the ambulance. As soon as she came back through the door I stood up quickly and approached her.

"Excuse me, I'm the daughter of Helen Mason. I think that's her on the stretcher, isn't it?"

The nurse looked at me for a moment as if trying to place my face and then acknowledged that she would speak with me.

"Come with me," she said. Like a lamb, I followed her into a side room where patients were able to have one-to-one visits with their family members, sometimes for their own safety and at other times for the safety of the visitors.

"What's your name, dear?" The nurse asked me, and I duly answered. "Ah yes, we have got your mum's consent to talk to you now, you'll be pleased to know."

I breathed a sigh of relief. That, at least, was something. Data protection had tied me up in knots for so long, it seemed to make everything twice as complicated.

"There was an incident earlier today which involved your mum."

I was expecting the worst but even so, hearing the news from the nurse pumped me up into an even more agitated state. My mouth went dry and I felt my hands begin to tingle.

"What's happened?"

"Somebody attacked her with a piece of flint. That caused some bleeding, superficial wounds to the arms and a gash to the face. It was dealt with by our staff very quickly but your mum must have been very shocked. She was shouting a lot and appeared very stressed before collapsing. Staff on duty administered some basic first aid and called an ambulance. She's on her way to the Royal Infirmary now."

"A piece of flint? I thought patients weren't allowed sharp objects?"

"That's very true. The offender has indicated that they dug it up from the flower beds in the garden."

"From the flower beds?" I felt a sense of amazement at the ingenuity behind the attack, as if the perpetrator had planned it rather than it being a spur of the moment thing.

"Do you know what caused it?"

"It's quite a difficult situation and there'd been a lot of taunting and name calling going on for some time between your mum and this other patient. It might be as well to ask someone in the family because we don't always get the full story here."

I found the nurse's answer to be a little dismissive and I couldn't imagine how anyone in the family would know anything about mum's relationships with the other patients. As far as I knew Amy hadn't even been to see her and there was no-one else I could think of who would have visited.

"Is my mum going to be alright?"

"I'm sorry, I can't say. I will give you the number for the infirmary so that you can speak to them directly and they will be able to let you know when you can visit."

"Thanks," I felt dismal and deflated as I clutched the piece of paper holding the telephone number and stood up to make my way back to Mrs Clarke's – the place I now thought of as home. Walking towards the bus stop, I decided to visit Amy before going back. We needed to talk and I felt certain that if I spoke to Amy face-to-face I could persuade her to come visit mum with me. Whatever had happened between them, now seemed like a good time to put it in the past.

While I waited for the bus I managed to get through to the Royal and although there was a lot of holding the line and I was transferred twice to different wards, I finally managed to be connected to the right place. After all that, all they could tell me was that the consultant would be doing his rounds later and they would have more idea then about what was wrong with her.

Frustrated and tired, I flagged down the bus and settled back into the seat, vowing that one of the first things I was going to do when I got my first wage packet was to invest in some driving lessons. Public transport was far too slow and cumbersome and as I looked around at the other passengers I couldn't help but wonder at the seeming normality of it. All the other people, totally absorbed in their own little worlds, not just oblivious to the torrent of emotion that was going on inside me but also oblivious to the idea of the countless universes out there, teeming with life, magic and wonder.

When I made my choice to return to earth I couldn't have imagined how difficult life would become for me. In my mind I had pictured walking back into the folds of my family and resuming where we left off. There would have been rejoicing and dancing, a big celebration because I was home, and because I was a nicer, more understanding person now we would all get along so much better. The sad truth was that I'd stepped back into the family from hell.

I dragged myself off the bus and started the walk up the long drive towards the children's home, my feet feeling heavy and leaden. The sky looked turbulent as gusts of wind blew the clouds along, churning the sky up and threatening rain. My mood on the inside felt just as turbulent.

I was a familiar face at the home now and it was almost like I'd been adopted by the staff there. Ann, the lady I had met on my first day, often brought me and Amy drinks and tried to make my visits as nice as possible. As I pushed through the doors into the foyer I gave Ann a quick wave but instead of her usual greeting she rushed over to me, her face very serious.

"Is everything alright?" I asked, as the roller coaster ride inside me did a loop-de-loop and I plummeted once more into that dreadful, fearful place inside my own head. I hadn't heard from Amy since my text message and now all the horrible thoughts I could think of were cramming into my brain.

"Oh, Luna love, I don't know how to tell you, let's go sit down, shall we and I'll ask Pat to make us a cup of tea." And so it was, for the second time in as many hours I was trailing behind somebody, waiting for bad news.

CHAPTER 30

"Let the power of your love change the world, but never let the problems of this world change the beauty of your love."

— DEBASISH MRIDHA

I could feel the heat of The Great Beast's fiery breath, could almost taste the flames that flickered around him. I knew too well how the Beast would try to lure me into temptation with promises of power, privilege and pleasure. But I also knew how that road coiled around the heart like a snake, squeezing and constricting, until all pleasure became tainted with sin. The Beast worked through insecurity and greed but even as I stood there, listening to the dark whisperings in my mind, I could feel the love of God flowing through me like a pure, undiluted river. It was a river that swelled inside me and made me greater than I would otherwise have been. The Beast consumed and used all that he came into contact with, leaving a trail of destruction and despair in his wake. God did not.

It had seemed the longest time had passed during which the dark one had tried to manipulate my senses but, in reality, it was mere moments. I was not immune, but I was stronger than before and had learned how to defend my mind from his disruption.

"Beast, leave me be." I bellowed, turning my back on his monstrous form and indicating to Metraton that I was ready to enter the Gates. Metraton nodded and led the way into the First Heaven as the Beast's eyes rolled to the back of his head and he slashed his tail into the air, frenzied with the agitation of defeat. It would, indeed, have been a great victory for him to have secured the loyalty of one of the Watchers.

These seeds of darkness which the Beast plants deep inside the souls of man only usually touch the outer surface of angels, falling away quickly. It is not always so with the Watchers, who have more choice over their actions and whether to demonise themselves in the quest for power. I knew too well the corruption of that folly.

A person might wonder why God would allow such a being to roam so freely in these territories, but all is never what it seems and the truth is vastly different from the myths that are portrayed in biblical texts. It is known in the higher realms that God allows, and even encourages, the Beast to guard these portals. This is a mutual agreement that suits them both, for those who sway on the cusp of temptation are required to undergo these battles as a true test of their nature before admittance to either heaven or hell. What is more, these two abodes are much closer in approximation than most may realise and the folly of human nature can dismember souls quicker than any blade.

Following Metraton through the Gates of Heaven, a calm serenity washed over me and I felt the influence of the Beast being eradicated from my mind. The Mansions of God were truly the most magnificent of places and I bathed my soul in the true, original fountainhead of hope and love.

Although God's presence is omnipotent, he has the capacity to turn his eye more precisely in the direction of his choosing. As I waited, I felt his presence amassing around me, a brilliant light that dispersed the darkness from my soul. Basking in those golden rays that illuminated my spirit, God's voice resonated through me, not in words, but in fully formed knowing, through the language of the heart.

"Isayel, it is not my punishment that you must fear the most, but your own. You stand before me as one who has let his passions dictate his actions, an unworthy action, unfit for one of the angelic hosts." My shame was a burden, but not unbearable. I had been angered beyond reasoning and even though the fire in my belly had been extinguished, I knew that I would have fought Cassiel all over again if the need arose. Our friendship had withstood much more in the past and in time I felt sure we would be able to reconcile our differences.

"What of Luna?" I had asked, consumed by her memory.

"Luna is of the Earth, mere dust, no longer part of your world. She is of no consequence to you now." I hesitated before speaking my mind to God, knowing that he already saw into the corners of my heart.

"It is my wish that we are reunited."

"She is involved with her family. The karmic wheel of life is turning and events are unfolding as they should."

"But she belongs with me."

"Luna did not choose you."

I glanced over at Cassiel, who had the grace to lower his head. I knew he had influenced her mind away from me. As angels and watchers, we guide and invite changes of direction, for the purposes of strengthening the soul or adapting the soul's journey in some way. I hadn't expected Cassiel to take it upon himself to manipulate Luna's mind in favour of departure.

"The choice, Isayel, has been taken away from you. The environment she finds herself in is one of growth and change, a necessary part of her soul's evolution. These circumstances will enable her to become stronger, emotionally, physically, mentally and spiritually. If she truly belongs to you, then that responsibility lies with her."

"But she has no power of her own to find her way back to me."

"Love is the power."

CHAPTER 31

"The wound is the place where the Light enters you."

— RUMI

A nn made sure I was sitting comfortably and waited until Pat had brought our drinks before she brought the conversation around to my sister.

"I'm not sure how much Amy has told you of her past," she began, getting a feel for how much I might already know.

"Not a lot." I said. "We mainly talk about what we're going to do together in the future. I know she gets upset if I mention what it was like after I left, so I try not to say too much."

"I see... well some of what I am about to tell you may shock you then."

My mind, I thought, was beyond shock at that moment, but as Ann divulged the background to Amy's sad story, I felt the cold weight of circumstance pressing down on me.

"Let me start at the beginning." Ann took a hesitant sip of her hot tea and then continued. "It's a little bit sketchy, but you will get the general idea."

"Okay," I replied, waiting for the big reveal.

"Social services first got involved when we received a report from Amy's school. Her attendance had dropped, she was turning up looking unkempt and generally acting very morose and sullen. Her form teacher had tried to speak to her about her home life but she was very defensive and said everything was okay."

I wasn't sure how to comment, so remained silent as Ann continued with the details.

"Of course, we'd already become aware of your father's death and knew that would have had a great impact on the family. That on its own though would not have triggered an intervention by the social services. Do you remember what it was like at home before you went away?"

"We were all very upset." I recalled. "Amy had become more withdrawn and started being clingy around me, in fact she hardly ever gave me any peace. And if I think about how mum was, well she wasn't handling things well at all, and I felt very angry towards her. I guess I'd always been a daddy's girl and never thought my mum understood me. I feel bad saying it now, but back then I'd wished it was her who had died, not my dad." There, I'd said it out loud. The awful, most shameful thing I could have ever thought. Having given it a voice and brought it out into the open, I waited for the condemnation from Ann, but it never came.

"That's perfectly understandable Luna. You were just a child yourself – confused, angry, and probably rebelling. It's perfectly natural to feel angry about someone we love dying. We feel abandoned and it's easy to start thinking up different outcomes and blaming the ones that we love, who are left behind."

"But she's very ill now and in hospital, and I feel like it's all my fault. It feels like I wished her dead."

Ann gave me a sympathetic look. "We can never be responsible for the actions of other people Luna. When we are young, we don't always make the right choices and we can be spiteful and say the wrong things, but we grow into our responsibilities and life usually makes us more understanding and caring towards other people. You've done nothing wrong."

I sighed, wishing that what she said was true, but not quite believing it. I had been a hateful child.

"Then, of course, your disappearance made national headlines. Your family were plunged into the limelight for a brief time for all the wrong reasons. There was a lot of speculation about what had happened to you, whether you'd been murdered and whether a family member might have been responsible. The Police visited your home, interviewing everyone locally and generally launching extensive investigations."

"It must have been awful. I hadn't really given that much thought."

"It would certainly have created a lot of tension in the home. But, even so, initially it seemed as if your mum was coping. She had some counselling and then was pretty much left to get on with things. The problem was that she had started to self-medicate with drinking and whilst it started as an infrequent binge here and there, it became more and more regular."

As Ann talked, I felt more comfortable with her, opening up to her in a way that I hadn't opened up to anyone in the past.

"She'd already started to drink before I got taken… I mean, before I went away."

Ann gave me a sympathetic look, which, to my mind, indicated she would be ready to listen should I want to confide in her some more. I was still the enigma, my story shrouded in mystery. It would only be human nature to be a little curious about me, I thought.

"Alcoholism is a disease Luna, it doesn't happen all at once, but slowly. So, although there were a few tell-tale signs to start with, it wasn't until much later that serious notice was taken. Amy was fending for herself more and more. Sometimes your mum missed work due to having hangovers, which meant there wasn't always enough money, especially as your mum was spending a lot on alcohol and cigarettes too."

"I was always nagging her to quit. I hated her smoking."

"Well that was a good and sensible attitude you had then."

"I don't know why really… a lot of my friends were smoking but I just never fancied doing it." As I thought back, I realised that maybe it was because of my later involvement with the Watchers. Perhaps even then they were protecting me and preventing me from abusing my body with drugs.

Ann continued, "Amy started shoplifting and got caught. It was bound to happen. The first time the Police let her off with a caution, but she started to become more and more careless and was soon getting into trouble on a regular basis. Then she got involved with wrong crowds of people, and was dabbling with drugs too."

"All kids dabble in drugs." I said, feeling defensive.

"Yes, we know drugs and teenagers can be a big problem, but Amy was totally vulnerable without a stable home life and things began to get out of hand for her. She was more at risk than most other people who just have an occasional dabble."

Ann took another sip of her tea, blowing the top to cool it quicker, before continuing. "There was a bigger problem going on, and we hadn't recognised it."

I felt myself go cold, sitting there, hanging onto every word, as Ann painted a picture of emotional pain, disruption and dysfunctional family life.

"Your mum lost her job due to her drinking. She'd also started dating other men too and there was one man in particular who was a regular visitor to the house. From what we can gather, your mum and her boyfriend used to regularly go out and get drunk together, although he was more of a social drinker and not addicted in the same way as your mum. By this time Amy was pretty much fending for herself but also trying to pull your mum back together. Your mum would break down and beg Amy to give her another chance after she'd been on a particularly bad binge but over time Amy realised that she wasn't going to change - in fact, they rarely do, without proper support. The bills started to pile up and threatening demands were coming from the utility services and also from the mortgage company."

"What a nightmare. I can't believe they weren't getting

any help."

"There's more. Amy was stealing and also getting involved on the peripheries of selling drugs, just so that she could help support the family home. Then, something truly dreadful happened."

Everything Ann had told me so far had been awful, and yet there was more to come.

"Did anything nice ever happen to them?" I asked, feeling somewhat sarcastic. I didn't know how one family's circumstances could be so terribly bad, seemingly without anything good happening to them at all.

"Not really love, at least, nothing notable. I'm sure they had ordinary, regular days in the midst of all of this, but the trend was just a downward spiral, and once your mum had started drinking so much there really was no hope for Amy to lead anything like a normal life."

I sighed, if I had been there, maybe I could have made a difference, or at least protected Amy from our mum's erratic behaviour.

"Sometimes your mum drank until she passed out and this left Amy in a very vulnerable position with your mum's boyfriend in the house. Initially, he started making flirty suggestions to her but she just ignored him, then he began telling her that he would make sure they would be able to pay all their bills, she just needed to have sex with him. Amy knew they were in a mountain of debt and so she agreed to sleep with him for money."

"Sleep with him? Oh my God, no!" I felt my whole body shudder as I thought about what Amy must have endured at the hands of a miserable, evil pervert who had abused her while our mum was in the house, out of her head on booze. It all made sense now, why Amy didn't want to visit mum. And that message... the baby... I had a terrible sense of foreboding that I knew exactly what Ann was going to say next.

"This sexual arrangement continued for several months. Amy was fourteen years old at the time."

"Just last year?"

"Yes. She got pregnant and was beside herself with worry. She couldn't tell anyone, because it would mean her mum's boyfriend would be prosecuted for having sex with a minor and he'd been threatening her to keep quiet about the whole arrangement. Amy had also become used to having the regular money. The pregnancy wasn't showing yet and she was hardly eating anyway, struggling with the stress and the worry of the whole situation. At that time and for the first few months of the pregnancy she was still having sex with your mum's boyfriend."

"That's terrible, poor Amy. I can't even imagine what hell that must have been like."

"She never visited the GP... if she had have done that then she could have had a termination. Instead she kept it a secret for the first four or five months. It's probably just as the pregnancy was beginning to show that she decided to run away from home. This seemed a better option for her, in her mind, than accusing the boyfriend. It also meant that she hadn't received any antenatal care either."

I felt like I couldn't listen to any more of this awful story but my whole body was heavy in the chair, almost as if I had no strength to move. And if I didn't hear it from Ann, there was no telling if I would ever know what had truly happened.

"Let me get you another drink Luna, you've not touched your tea and it's gone cold." I allowed Ann to fuss around me, as I hung my head in my hands, not realising my eyes were leaking until I drew my wet palms away from my eyes.

"I know it's such a lot to take in Luna, and I'm really sorry that I'm having to tell you all this now, but it's important that you know the facts."

I nodded, not trusting myself to say anything, sucking in the air through my clamped mouth. My chin was wobbling as I tried to hold it all inside, only just keeping control and stopping myself from fully bursting into tears.

"Amy ran away to Bristol and was sleeping rough, sometimes on the streets and at other times just on floors or sofas at random people's houses. She begged for money and was also taking drugs again. At six months pregnant she collapsed and paramedics were called. She was taken to the emergency unit and whilst there gave birth to a still born boy child."

So, that's what Tara had been referring to, about "the sprog". What a nasty, vicious thing to say. I wondered how she even knew, but guessed the jungle drums didn't keep anything secret for long.

"After her hospital stay Amy was taken straight into care, and has been doing very well here, even more so since you came back into her life." Ann gave me a quick, nervous smile and I intuited that more bad news was imminent.

"What's happened?" I asked.

"Well, we found Amy unconscious in her room earlier today. She'd taken an overdose."

I stood up sharply, already grabbing my bag so that I could leave quickly. "Is she okay? I need to go and see her. Where is she?" I couldn't think straight.

"We called an ambulance immediately and they came very quickly. They've taken her to the Leicester Royal," Ann replied.

My heart almost stopped beating. "That's where my mum's been taken too." I really didn't know if that was a good thing or a bad thing, but I couldn't help but wonder whether someone up there was playing one enormous fucking joke.

CHAPTER 32

"When you compare the sorrows of real life to the pleasures of the imaginary one, you will never want to live again, only to dream forever."

— ALEXANDRE DUMAS

As it happens, after visiting the children's home I couldn't face going back to the hospital. It was starting to get late and I expected Mrs Clarke would have begun to worry about me, so I made the trek back to her house, ready to tell her everything I knew so far.

Mrs Clarke sat there, grave faced, as I brought her up to date with events. "I'm so sorry Luna, how terrible for all of you," she said as she listened to the drama unfolding.

I nodded, it felt like a terrible curse had befallen our whole family. If ever I doubted it, I felt doubly sure now that if there was a god, he would never have let such awful things happen to my family.

"I tried to be a good friend to your mum over the years Luna and at one time we were very close but, well, once she started going off the rails like she did, we drifted apart a bit. I'm not one for drinking myself and I really didn't like seeing her so out of control like that."

"I don't think you could have done anything more." I sighed, "I guess she wasn't a very good friend to you."

"Don't say that Luna, we never know another's struggles or another's pain. She was obviously very, very depressed. When the house got repossessed, I think things were at rock bottom for her."

As I listened, Mrs Clarke's voice became increasingly emotional. "Amy had run away, you were gone, your dad was dead, even the ratty boyfriend had slinked off... she had no-one...."

I waited as Mrs Clarke paused, took a deep breath, and then continued, "and she didn't even have me Luna, because when she came knocking at my door, drunk as a lord, asking for a place to stay for a few days, I'm ashamed to say that I turned her away and actually gave her a piece of my mind."

It was Mrs Clarke who started to cry then – not just a small cry either, but a real anguished outburst. Out of nowhere it seemed that her whole body just crumbled. The table juddered with the violence of her sobbing as she collapsed into her folded arms which were resting on the table top. She doubled over, her body racked with this emotional outpouring as I did my best to console her. Maybe she'd been feeling guilty all this time too.

"Please don't cry Mrs Clarke. It wasn't your fault. No one could have helped my mum then."

She tried to talk between the sobs, gasping for breath, her voice a strangulation of sound in her throat. "You don't understand Luna, because… after I turned her away, that's when she tried to kill herself." Another series of convulsions commenced before she could continue and I strained to hear what she was saying between her breaths. "She slashed her wrists… over on the park… with the jagged edges of an old wine bottle."

I closed my eyes briefly, flashing back to the tell-tale bandages that had been wrapped around my mum's wrists in the hospital. That made sense now.

"She could have died Luna… truly it broke my heart when I heard…"

"Sshh… it's alright," I soothed, not quite knowing what to say. Mrs Clarke had been a diamond to me, maybe it was partly because she was trying to make amends for how she'd treated my mum. She didn't give my mum a room when she asked, so she gave me one instead.

"It.. It… it was just luck that someone found her when they did. She'd hidden herself away in some bushes."

I rubbed Mrs Clarke's thick back, feeling the vibration of her sobs under my hand, which were gradually subsiding as she started to regain a little composure.

"She'd passed out right there, lost quite a bit of blood. A man walking his Collie dog spotted her."

"I really don't know what to do now." I said. "It's all one big hopeless mess." So, my mum had tried to kill herself at the park, where I'd been drawn to when I first arrived back, but I'd had no idea at the time. My preternatural senses obviously weren't so focused in my real life as they used to be.

Mrs Clarke finally regained enough composure to straighten up and wiped her eyes and nose with a soggy bit of tissue. She offered me a weak smile, "I'm sorry I've burdened you with all of this. I will understand if you don't want to stay here anymore. I let your mum down, Luna and I'll never forgive myself."

"My dad told me once that regret is pointless. It is one of the worst emotions ever, along with shame, because we just can't change anything we've done, can we?"

"No, dear, we can't."

We both sat in silence for a few minutes. It was that time of quiet after a storm has passed when you kind of know that you've just survived and got over the worst.

"Tell you what, why don't I run you a nice hot bath, with plenty of bubbles?" Mrs Clarke asked. "Have a nice long soak and try to relax a little bit while I tidy up down here. If there's anything I've learned, it's that survivors keep going. If you're in the middle of a muddy swamp... you can't turn back because you've already come so far, so all you can do is keep going, and then you will get to the other side."

I gave a half smile back. "That's just the kind of thing my dad would have said, too." I replied.

As I soaked in the bath, with the hot water right up to my chin, I allowed myself the luxury of reflecting on life. So much had happened during my growing up years, and although I'd been through ordeals on The Omicron, I realised I probably came out of them emotionally stronger than Amy did. I'd had inspiring and spiritual people around me, helping to support and guide me and they had been a balm to my suffering. Amy had had no-one.

I always felt closer to Isayel when I was around water, so it was with some predictability that I found my thoughts turning to him whilst I was bathing. I thought back to the time when he'd saved me that day near the waterfall. He'd been so gentle with me and yet there had been such passion between us. His body had been close to mine, we were on the verge of lovemaking, and yet he had turned away from me then, holding himself in check. He did the honourable thing, I could see that now. Not like the man who had manipulated his way into Amy's bed. Isayel had been a gentleman, even if I hadn't understood his motives at the time. I wondered where he was now and what he was doing. Did he ever think of me? Could he see me? He was a Watcher, after all. As I thought about him, my thoughts delving into the essence of him, I allowed my senses to stretch out and flow with the water... it was Elisia's voice I could hear... it's all about the molecules, particles and atoms. "I love you Isayel," I whispered into the fluid lapping around my body, "I really, really love you."

The next couple of days went by in a blur. I felt as if I was on automatic pilot at work, present but not really concentrating. Mr Blake had commented on it too, asking if I was okay.

"Just some family stuff," I said, trying not to sound like a victim.

"I think it will perk you up if you have a bit of time out of the office. Would you like that?"

"Doing what?" I asked.

"Well, as you know, Ruth is off with one of her migraines

and then she's booked a couple of days leave. I'm a bit stretched at the moment too, so I just need someone to go take a look around a house that's just been placed in our hands to sell."

"I'm not experienced enough, am I?"

"Oh, it will be alright, I just want you to take some photos, you can use your own phone. Give me an idea of what the property is like, and take the laser measure, it will be easy enough to measure the rooms for me with that. I will do the proper survey later on."

I felt a flicker of interest, I would like to do that. It had always been my hope that I would be able to get out of the office more and maybe get trained up in a more specialised way and this seemed like a perfect first opportunity.

"Yes, I'd really love to," I said with enthusiasm.

"Fantastic, that's settled then. Polly can organise the paperwork in the morning for you. Take some gloves with you too, wear trousers and maybe take some elastic bands to put around the bottoms, you never know what you might find." He gave me a wink then, and I wasn't quite sure if he was being serious or pulling my leg.

That evening, as I made my way to the hospital, I felt brighter than I had for a little while, at least work was going in the right direction, and I'd decided that whatever life threw at me, I would cope with it. Sofia used to say perception was everything, and although she had been referring to art, I always thought the same thinking could be applied to life too.

James from the Job Centre had phoned me a couple of times during the week but I'd felt awkward chatting to him and when he'd asked me out for a drink I'd told him that I had a lot on my plate at the moment and maybe I would be able to sometime in the future. It wasn't an out-and-out no, but even considering dating someone else felt like I was being disloyal to Isayel. I guessed I needed to get over that and find a way to get on with my life without keeping referring to my past, but how could any mortal compare, when I'd been loved by an angel?

I knew, too, that once I'd spoken to Amy we would be able to clear up the whole sorry issue about the baby. Maybe I could even arrange for her to have some therapy or something too, so that she could move on and put it all behind her.

As for mum, I wasn't quite sure if she would ever recover properly. She'd really done some damage to her body with the heavy drinking but maybe even that situation could claw back from total disaster. I felt sure she just needed support and to be surrounded by people who loved her. I could do this, I thought. I would be strong enough for both of them.

I went to visit my mum first. She was in the intensive care unit and visiting had to be restricted, with only two visitors at a time at the bedside. Sadly, it wasn't likely that mum was going to have that problem.

Seeing her like that, so frail looking, the skin on her face like veined parchment, I felt a lump form in my throat and my previous positive mood dissolved. I'd promised myself that I wouldn't cry but it felt just as bad being here as it did when we had to visit dad at the hospice.

"Hey mum," I whispered. She was still attached to breathing apparatus and her eyes were softly closed. Even though the machine was helping her to breathe, it was hard to see her chest rising and falling. The curtains were drawn and there was a low murmur of machines in the background, reminding me of my first day on board the Omicron, when I'd been so afraid, and yet so wild at the same time.

I drew up the chair at the side of the bed and held one of her bird-like hands. "I've been thinking mum, now that I'm back… we can all be a family again. Would you like that?" I had no idea whether she could hear me, locked in that inner world, but I rather hoped that she could.

"You'd be really pleased with me, I'm getting on well at work and Mr Blake, my boss, is going to let me visit a property tomorrow, so that's much more responsibility than I've had before. I've started to save some money too. Maybe we can get a house together, you, me and Amy. We can start over." I studied mum's eyelids to see if there was any reaction, even a flicker of response, but there was nothing.

For the next thirty minutes I chatted away, under the watchful eye of the duty nurse, telling her about all the latest news and reminiscing about the past when things had been better for us. Eventually I stood and kissed her forehead, careful not to let my tears drip onto her face.

"I love you mum, and I'm sorry for everything I ever did to hurt you." It was all I could do not to race from the ward, but I needed some distance from the pain of seeing her so lifeless and still, beyond the world of men and madness.

By contrast, when I walked into Amy's ward she was sitting up in bed and drinking a warm drink through a straw.

"Thought you wasn't coming." She said, sullenly.

"Don't be silly, why wouldn't I?"

"I dunno," she replied. "That message you sent – how could you? That was so mean."

"Amy, I'm so sorry, I didn't know, it was just something that Tara said and I had no idea what happened back then."

"You know now?"

"Yes, Ann told me."

"And...?"

"And what?" I asked, wondering what she wanted from me.

"And what did you think?"

"Truth? I think you've been really brave and struggled

through some of the worst things I could ever imagine."

"Really?" Amy's eyes misted over and I went and sat on the edge of the bed, even though the nurses probably wouldn't have approved. Putting my arm around her I gave her a gentle squeeze.

"Yes Amy, truly, really. You are the bravest person I know and if we can just get you through this, you're going to grow up to be an amazing woman one day."

She shrugged. "I hate my life Luna. I can't stop thinking about all the awful things, and even though I love you and I'm glad you're back, it can't change what's happened, can it?"

Hearing these words, straight from my little sister's mouth, drove a stake right through the centre of my heart. Sometimes, there were no answers, and no words good enough to mend wounds as deep as hers and I had no real idea if anything I could say to her would make any difference.

"It's up to us where we spend our time Amy. If you dwell in the past then all that stuff will just continue to hurt you. I want to show you the future and let you really understand with the whole of your heart that it can be a better place. Don't let what happened back then ruin your whole life now."

"I just want to be dead." Her little shoulders shook with anguish and she looked so vulnerable and soft.

"You're just saying that because you're upset. I want you to promise me Amy, that you'll never try this again, do you promise?"

"I don't know if I can."

"Amy, please, this is so important to me... to us.... if you promise not to hurt yourself again, I promise I will never leave you. I'll always be here for you Amy but you have to promise me that you will do your bit to make your life better too."

"I'll do my best," she said at last and I hugged her to me, relief sweeping over me. I only hoped I could live up to my promise too.

CHAPTER 33

"If you feel you have to open a particular door, open it, other-wise all your life that door will haunt your mind!"

— MEHMET MURAT ILDAN

A s I walked to work the following morning the sun was already warming my skin. It should have been relaxing and made the walk a pleasant one, but I couldn't stop thinking about what a mess everything was. On one level, I really didn't understand mum or Amy. They both had a destructive streak and hadn't been strong enough to handle life without trying to commit suicide. I wondered if Amy had only tried it because mum had done it first and that meant it was somehow more acceptable? I couldn't imagine feeling like that myself. Even at the lowest point of my grovelling degradation under Keysha's control, I desperately wanted to live. I'd even eaten the grubs so that I would stay alive. I wished I could inject a little bit of that survivor streak into Amy.

As for mum, her body was so damaged from the heavy drinking and the stress, I really wasn't sure what would happen to her now. The doctors hadn't been very forthcoming when I'd asked yesterday and when I'd phoned the ward again this morning they said there'd been no change overnight but that I should make sure I was contactable throughout the day, should I be needed.

I was torn, I knew I should stay with her, be at her bedside in case she deteriorated further, but my mind was engulfed with images of my dad's passing. His body had been a shell, a breathing carcass of meat that didn't contain him anymore. How could I stand to go through that again? I wondered where her mind was and whether she'd try to fight for her life and come back to me. The sadness was that I didn't know how I could make a difference and so, instead of sitting at her bedside, I had decided to distract myself with work instead.

"Morning Polly," I put on a fake smile as I entered the offices and tried to sound more positive than I felt. It was Polly's job to open up and she was usually here quite a bit earlier than anyone else.

"Hi Luna. I've just printed off some info about the property you need to visit this morning, and the keys are labelled and on your desk."

"Wow, you're organised today. When you going to apply for a job co-ordinating for the Queen?"

"Ha, I think that's a bit more involved."

"Are you sure you're happy with me going instead of you? If I were you, I'd be itching to get out of the office for a bit"

"No, you go, I've got quite enough to do dealing with the paperwork and the customers who call in. Leaving the office for long periods is not really my thing."

I was relieved to hear Polly say that, as I didn't want her to think I was taking away any chance for her to escape from her desk.

I sat down and studied the information Polly had arranged for me, but as soon as I saw the address my heart sank. I couldn't possibly go into that house.

"Are you sure this is the right place?" I asked, feeling apprehensive.

"Yes, definitely, why?"

"It's that house... the one with the magnolia tree in the front garden."

"So? Lots of houses have magnolia trees."

I must have sounded a bit cryptic, so I tried to explain.

"It's not that, it's just... okay, promise not to think I'm too weird if I say it?"

"Hmm... well I already think you're too weird... what have you got to lose?" Polly threw me a somewhat exasperated look and I decided to tackle it head on.

"You might think I'm silly but, when I was younger, before... well, before I went away... I often passed this house and I really loved the pretty tree in the garden but, well, there was something weird too."

"What do you mean?"

"It's silly, and maybe it was just my imagination, but every time I walked by, I thought the net curtain moved. It used to feel very creepy."

"Maybe they had a fan near the window or something?" Polly was ever practical.

"I hadn't thought of that... I used to think it was a perv or a total nutcase... why else would someone just sit and stare out of the window all day long?"

"I don't know Luna. Some people are just nosey, or lonely. Maybe it was someone who didn't go out much or someone who was disabled?"

"That's true, I guess. I never did see who lived there."

"Well, it's empty now and we don't know who lived there either. The house was held in trust, which means that it was the trust that owned the property, not a particular person."

I chewed my bottom lip as I studied the address once more, "are you sure it will be empty?"

"It won't be occupied, if that's what you mean, but there's probably going to be some furniture around. We're not sure how far the removals have got with that yet. Don't touch anything personal and just take the measurements and photos as you go around. Make some notes too – look for things like how many plug sockets, how many rooms, whether there are radiators and stuff, state of décor, that sort of thing. It will just help Mr Blake until he has chance to do a proper survey. It's not a big deal Luna, I have to say I thought you'd be more grateful than this."

"Oh, I am grateful, please don't think that I'm not!" All of a sudden I felt awkward and embarrassed, hating the thought that she was judging me negatively for my comments.

"I'm really looking forward to it, don't worry about what I said earlier, just nerves I think."

"Shame you don't drive yet too," Polly added as she reclaimed her seat at her desk, "that's a real drawback for you at the moment. You live in the area too, don't you, so you'll know the bus route."

"Yes, I know the area well," I replied, gathering up all the equipment and information I would need for my visit.

It was an hour or so later that I got off the bus on the main road and started the walk towards my destination. What a familiar route, heading from the main road towards the house. It was a nice, quiet neighbourhood, particularly taking the back route through the church with its slightly overgrown lawns, worn flagstones and ancient gravestones. On the far side of the churchyard I approached the smaller intersecting road which cut across my route and headed into the village centre. It was only a single carriageway but quickly became congested with traffic. I managed to cross quickly at the new pedestrian crossing and then continued my walk through the narrow lane opposite, which was a partly pedestrianised area, not permitting vehicles to access from this side of the road.

My eyes were drawn to the crumbling stone walls of a separate section of church yard, partially covered in a thick entanglement of ivy. Beyond those walls ancient tombs and headstones nestled amongst the towering oak and yew trees. It looked gracefully neglected, with an olde-world charm about it and I felt the hustle and bustle of the city dropping away from me.

Within a few minutes I had passed the Black Horse pub, the double doors and gates closed at this time of day, but always a popular local hang out. I hadn't been old enough to drink before I went away but sometimes we would sit as a family in the pub gardens, enjoying the late afternoon sunshine and tucking into packets of crisps and pop after a long walk along the canal. The gnats used to bite my mum and she'd spend half her time swatting them away, waving a beer mat in front of her face to give her some relief, while me and Amy giggled over the slurpy noises our straws made as we played with our drinks. Dad was well then. He was always so chatty and friendly, making sure to speak to all the familiar faces around him. Faces that turned up at his funeral and wished him a speedy onward journey to wherever his soul was going and faces that I never remembered seeing since.

The road after the pub sloped round, linking into a wide leafy lane which was at the bottom of a forked piece of road that led to the address I was going to view. An assortment of houses lined the right-hand side of the street but on the left the outlook was more open. A large, faded, cream sign was displayed outside the farm, advertising potatoes and produce. People could also stable their horses here and arrange riding lessons and it brought back special memories of carefree days hanging over the field fences with dangly legs and arms, being nuzzled by a couple of my favourites as I tried to feed them with polo mints and sugar cubes.

My eyes wandered further along the road which curved underneath the railway bridge and then to the car parking spaces on the right. From there, there was only access by foot, across the packhorse bridge which spanned the canal, and also led straight over the River Soar and on towards the fields beyond.

I was so close, so very close, to the place where I'd been

abducted all those years ago. My heart started to quicken and random thoughts flashed into my mind... what if I threw down my briefcase with my notepads, colour coded pens and clipboards... what if I pulled off my very girlie shoes with the 3-inch heels, tore off my jacket and just raced back to Kings Lock, to the place where it had all begun? Would Isayel ever come back for me? Maybe he was already waiting there, just over the bridge, out of view. The temptation to try to find him was flowing through my veins like a wildfire and I could feel myself on the very edge of reason as I contemplated what would happen if I made such an impulsive gesture. I almost did it, I was so tempted, and the only thing that stopped me was the promise I'd made to Amy only yesterday, "I'll never leave you again." I could not take that back, not now.

I turned my attention back to the houses on the right-hand side of the lane and forced myself to concentrate on the project I'd been sent to do, realising that I would never know whether Isayel had been there or not and perhaps it was better that way.

There were four blocks of semi-detached houses, two each side of the large detached house that I'd been allocated to view. For a few moments I stood on the grassy verge outside, squared to the windows, scrutinising the net curtaining for the slightest bit of movement, but for the first time since I could remember, they were still. It was an intensely haunting feeling waiting there like that, watching for a sign that someone was inside, wondering if I was being watched and anticipating a menacing face jumping out at me from behind the nets at any second. I wondered whether the person who had lived in that house had intentionally moved the curtains way back then, just so that I would feel scared, but why would anybody do that?

"Because you were a special child Luna." I answered my own question in my head before taking a deep breath, seemingly putting my life in my hands, and walking down the path towards the dark wooden door. The front garden was wildly neglected, although rambling flowers were pushing their buds through the tangle of weeds that threatened to smother and take over. The magnolia tree that I'd loved as a child was still blossoming and I tried to remember whether I'd actually ever seen it dry and leafless.

I felt nervous standing on the doorstep and held my breath as I turned the key in the lock, fingers clumsy, dripping with fear. I was an intruder, stepping into someone else's private environment without invitation, and part of me was really scared about what I would find there. I thought back to what Mr Blake had said about tying up my trouser legs, half expecting to be wading through a moving carpet of slugs and rodents or, worse than that, tripping over a calcified dead body in the hallway, but nothing could have been further from the truth. It was actually very pretty in a mystical, charming sort of way. It was like stepping through the threshold into a wonderland of beautiful objects and mysterious looking artefacts. I could see quite clearly that the removal men couldn't have done much, if anything at all.

On the wall in the hallway was a large arched mirror with a chunky oak frame. Twists of engraved ivy and grapevine curled around it, together with an intricate pattern of swirls and symbols. There was also an antique looking church pew, beautifully restored and serving as a quaint looking seat, maybe a place someone would sit to remove or put on their shoes, I thought.

I allowed my fingers to linger over ornaments, careful not to displace anything. Whoever had lived here had the most amazing sense of creativity and style.

My mind wandered with the prospect of whether there would be an auction for all the items and, if so, whether I could possibly afford to buy anything. After all, I couldn't stay at Mrs Clarke's house forever, I reasoned, and I would need to think about furniture. I walked through the kitchen and into the lounge, taking notes, measurements and photos, as instructed. The fear that I'd felt on the doorstep had fallen away from me as soon as I'd crossed the threshold and now I was engulfed by an overwhelming urge to linger. There was such a vibrant, sunny aspect to the rooms, a gentle calming warmth that flowed all around me as I studied the space. It really did seem childishly silly to me now that I'd been so nervous about coming here.

From the lounge area I noticed a further room and beyond that there was an arched Gothic looking doorway with ornate cast iron fixtures and fittings. It was such a strange entrance and would have been more suited to a castle in a fairytale. I felt so drawn to this door that I stopped what I was doing and wandered over to it, placing the palm of my hand against the rich red wood. I could feel its heat and the slightly raised areas of grain that rippled through it. I knew it had a story and I ached to discover what tales it could tell and whether it would share its secrets with me. Above the lock there was a large circular looped handle and I gave it a sharp twist, but it was unyielding. I felt piqued, alive with curiosity, wanting more than anything to open the door to find out what lay beyond. I pressed my shoulder to it, but it was solidly resistant, and without a key I had little choice but to give up.

Turning away from the mysterious doorway, I headed up the stairs and the first room I came across was a beautiful bathroom, with a free-standing bath and walk-in shower. The trimmings were black and gold and there was a real sense of opulence. There was nothing to suggest anywhere that the owner of the property had been elderly or disabled in any way, as Polly had suggested.

There were five bedrooms in all, two of which had en-suites. Each one was curiously beautiful, some with an under-stated simplicity – perhaps guest rooms, I thought – and others were just magnificently mysterious looking. My whole brain was alive with interest and the glorious feeling of being useful and efficient, but as I walked into the master bedroom, I was about to witness something that I could not have anticipated in a million years.

There on the wall, in the centre spotlight, was the very picture that I'd sketched of Isayel back in Sofia's classroom. My whole body tensed in alarm and time fell away from me like rags as I remembered how I'd felt when I'd sketched that, even down to the weight of the pencils in my hand and the texture of the canvas. I'd worked so studiously to recreate the way he looked out from those blue eyes of his. The portrait was so lifelike it was like looking into the depths of his soul and just seeing it reminded me in every way of just how much I missed him.

"Oh Isayel, where are you?" I whispered into the empty room, my voice lingering in my ears and my heart. How had someone else managed to get their hands on this picture, which I'd left on the ship? Did it mean that The Omicron had returned? Had Isayel placed it there? Or Sofia? There were so many questions that my mind couldn't begin to comprehend what to do or think. Above all that, I felt the sense of a majestic force flowing through the universe, recognising that I'd been guided to be here today and that some omnipotent power had played a crucial part in lining up all the events of my life just to make this moment happen. The prospect of it just being chance seemed astronomically remote to me.

I slowly wandered around the room, not really heeding Polly's warning to not touch anything. I wanted to get to know who had lived here and what my picture of Isayel had meant to them. Walking slowly over to an antique dressing table, I admired the delicate trinkets lined up there. A small silver elephant, several crystals and... an envelope with my name written on it in a Copperplate style of writing.

"What the hell?" I cursed into the air and had to do a

double take. Had someone expected me to find it? Maybe there was another Luna, perhaps a relative of the owner? I doubted it somehow, because when I was born it had been an odd name to give to a child, straight out of science fiction itself. No one called their child Luna, except my mum, who'd always had her own eccentric streak. I was uncertain what to do but then got to thinking that maybe Mr Blake had left it for my attention. I pondered this, I had seen his handwriting at the office and it was more of an untidy scrawl, nothing like the writing on the note.

I crossed over to the bed, which was covered in a vast multi-coloured throw and scatter cushions, influencing the room towards an ethnic Bohemian kind of style, and sat down, carefully placing my bag to my side.

I knew that I needed to calm down and that if my head was in the right place then I'd be able to intuit more about my surroundings and what action to take next. I found that thinking back to my lessons with Elisia proved to be the easiest way to get my energy flowing and to have faith in some of the more mystical practices that I'd been taught, and so I brought her image, and the image of my old classroom, to the forefront of my mind.

After a few moments I knew then that I was connecting. I imagined it was probably similar to how a medium prepares themselves to embrace the voices of those who have passed over. It felt like a switch had been turned on inside and I felt alive in a way that I hadn't experienced in a while. Slowly images began to form beneath my eyelids as I breathed deeply, absorbing the molecules of this place into my body, potentially molecules of whoever had lived here before the fire. The fire? New information was pouring into my mind... there had been a fire. And yet there was no fire damage... it didn't make sense. After a while, I opened my eyes, shaking myself out of the stupor that I'd been in. I didn't really understand what any of it meant, but one thing I did know, was that I would open that envelope.

CHAPTER 34

"It isn't the mountains ahead to climb that wear you out; it's the pebble in your shoe."

- MUHAMMAD ALI

"Love is the Power" that was God's message. It is an absolute truth, because love is the beginning and end of all things. New mothers are suffused with the love hormone, oxytocin, nature's special gift that was designed to help them to bond with their offspring. In the fortunate life it guides and shapes us, so that we become the best that we can be, and learn how to be loving in return.

Love is also the catalyst of invention. Through the hands of the infant to the greatest artists, writers and craftspeople who ever lived, creations are made manifest in the world. It is the major force behind such creativity; giving us wings to soar to new heights, the great enabler. Most works of art are the incredible result of love. It trickles like a stream through the veins, flowing into the twin rivers of inspiration and originality, creating change and igniting the hearts of man. The universe pulses with this emotion, swelling into abundance as it creates and recreates, ever expanding as this endless process of manifestation continues into infinity, changing the mundane into something extraordinary.

But do not forget that love can also be the weapon, which can be wielded with brutal force and determination. It can be the most painful of all emotions, creating hurt and confusion, driving lovers to their premature deaths. It can be the sacrifice, the loss and the blindness. Love is a chameleon and, make no mistake, love can be as deadly and cruel as any other feeling in the heart of man. Both love and hate can conquer, but love will always be the strongest.

I sat alone in the First Heaven, contemplating the nature of love, aware that prior to loving others it is a necessity to first find love in oneself. Humanity alone exhibits its own self-loathing and criticism. A fox is just a fox and holds to its own nature, it does not judge itself for following its instincts. The fat house cat does not compare itself to the sleek panther and find itself lacking - man-made words like self-esteem and confidence do not enter into the conversation between them. Why then, do humans seek to destroy their own hearts with so many negative feelings?

In heaven I could contemplate nature more deeply, both the nature of man and angels. I was not above the spotlight of soul searching for I, too, had felt shame and remorse for actions done and things said. There were situations I could not change and acceptance was something that I had to hold closer to my heart.

As a Watcher each experience ultimately made me stronger and enhanced my empathy for others but I had to let the negativity fall away from me. With hammer and chisel I would sculpt myself anew, worthy of love in all its forms.

I had decided to remain in heaven for the purpose of restoring inner equilibrium. It would be easier here, without distraction or temptation. The darkness of the soul, once illuminated, works through its difficulties through observations of loving kindness and compassion. By working in the light and through the light, transformation occurs and the beast inside us is put to rest.

It was my intention to prepare for my next mission – it had been far too long since I had visited Zarnett-9 and my resident offspring. They were no longer children and did not need my guidance, but a father is a father not just in the laying of the seed but for the eternity of time and I took my responsibilities seriously.

As for Luna, she was like a pebble in my mind, that grain of sand in the oyster's shell that, through irritation, evolves into a pearl. I had been told the Karmic Wheel was at work, meting out justice, punishment and reward through the kaleidoscope of time. It was not my purpose nor my desire to upset the hand of fate so even though Luna's memory lingered with me, I would not change the course of events. I believed we had a destiny that would be fulfilled and that when the time was right we would be reunited.

CHAPTER 35

"It was true that the city could still throw shadows filled with mystifying figures from its past, whose grip on the present could be felt on certain strange days, when the streets were dark with rain and harmful ideas."

— CHRISTOPHER FOWLER

My fingers tried to prise open the envelope without causing damage to the edges. It was impossible, as the more I tried to be gentle, the more the little flakes of paper pulled away in my hands. Eventually I gave it a tug instead, pushing my thumb all the way inside and ripping apart the opening.

Inside was a note,

> *"Dear Luna, if you are reading this now, then you've done well. You've followed your instincts and your training and the world is turning just as it is meant to be, whether you like it or not. There is no need to question how, just know that all things are possible in an infinite universe.*
>
> *Enclosed are some instructions. I know you are curious about the door – I was too, the first time. Inside the dresser in the top right drawer is a wooden box, engraved with symbols on the lid – we like our symbols, don't we? Open the box to find what you need to do next."*

The note wasn't signed and for a moment I thought I should just leave and go back to work but I couldn't. This was like an open invitation back into the enchanted forest, and everything that I longed for in a life that had turned sour with bad news and situations that were really difficult for me to handle.

Opening the drawer, I found the box easily, nestled just inside. I let my fingers travel along the lines of the symbol. As I did so my fingertips began to tingle. There was a real energy there, I could feel it prickling at me and I wasn't sure what it meant, and whether it was a good energy or a bad energy. I drew my hand away sharply. The box was locked but there was a small key sellotaped to its side. It all seemed very surreal and time dragged as I held the box on my lap, wondering whether to open it or not. I was startled out of my ponderings by my mobile ringing. I jumped and quickly lifted the phone from my pocket. It was Polly.

"Hi"

"Hey, just checking you're okay. Are you still at the house?"

"Yes, almost finished." I replied, groaning inside. I wouldn't have time to do what I needed to do.

"That's good because Mr Blake is on his way back into the office and wanted a meeting with you."

"Oh. Have I done something wrong?" The worst thoughts went through my mind. Maybe there was CCTV in the house and they had staged all this to see how trustworthy I was. I looked around to see if I could notice any cameras, but knew they could be tiny and hidden anywhere. Maybe I was being paranoid.

"Mr Blake never said what the meeting will be about. I've no idea. Do you *think* you've done something wrong?"

"I hope not," was the only reply I could give her, as I disconnected the call and turned my attention back to the box. I would open it quickly and then I would know what to do next.

I peeled the key away from where it had been sellotaped to the side and carefully turned it in the lock, my hands feeling suddenly clammy. It felt dangerously exciting as I opened the lid. What if it was something gross, I thought, like a severed finger... I'd seen that film too, although I probably shouldn't have.

I took a deep breath. Adrenalin was pumping around my body as I examined the contents. It was a little bit of an anticlimax, but definitely a relief, to find there were no dismembered body parts. Instead there were several envelopes. The one on the top said, "read me now", the one underneath said, "do not read until told to do so," and the third one said the same thing. I felt like Alice in Wonderland as I opened the first one quickly. I'd need to get back to the office shortly and was starting to feel anxious about leaving.

I read it aloud,

> *"Well done Luna, you've done a good job so far. You need to leave now and come back tomorrow evening at 9.00pm. Enclosed is a front door key, this is yours to keep. On your return, you can open envelope number 2."*

I turned the envelopes around in my hand, to see that they were indeed numbered 1, 2 and 3. The second two envelopes were also heavier and contained something more than just a note. I placed the key in my pocket and carefully sealed the remaining envelopes inside the box, locking it up and putting it safely back where I'd found it. Life was just starting to become interesting again and little rockets of excited apprehension ran through me.

As well as that, I was more than relieved that the writer of the note had asked me to leave. I had the pressing feeling that if I didn't get back soon I would be in some kind of trouble and as time went by I'd felt more and more uncomfortable about being there.

The big question was whether I could return the following evening. It would be getting dark just after nine and there was no telling whether someone else might be at the house waiting to trap me. I'd been naive in the past when it came down to my own safety and I'd need to really think this one over. I had no friends to confide in or take with me and Amy was still in hospital. Even if she wasn't, it would break her curfew to leave the home so late at night.

Even so, my mind buzzed with curiosity as I thought over the events of the day on the bus ride back into work. In my hands I held the front door key, such a nondescript item, but it was my very own key to a mystery that was emerging as if from nowhere, filling my mind with something other than the difficulties of family life.

◆ ◆ ◆

I arrived back at the offices of Blake & Sharpe with some trepidation, not relishing the idea of a meeting with Mr Blake. There was no particular reason that I should feel so worried, as he'd been nothing but pleasant to me whenever I'd had any dealings with him. He did prefer working from his home-office though, and also spent lots of time visiting the properties on our books, so I hadn't spent too much time getting to know him better.

Polly was busy typing, looking up briefly when she heard the door open. "Glad you're back, feels like you've been gone ages."

"Well, I did have to wait for the buses." I found myself feeling defensive, there was an underlying accusation in her voice that I didn't like.

"Every twenty minutes this time of day." She carried on typing while I unbuttoned my coat and sat at my desk.

"Did you get the photos?"

"Yes, I'll send them over now."

I connected my phone to the computer and waited for the menu to appear, clicking onto the new drive option that had opened up, allowing me to see the contents of my phone's gallery. Several photos came into view, pictures of a kitchen, a dining area, a comfortable lounge, bathroom and bedrooms. All should have been fine except – these pictures were not the same as the ones I had taken earlier. A chill ran through me, there was no way I could explain this and I could only hope that Mr Blake hadn't already viewed the interior of the house himself. The photos showed a rather bland, almost empty house, with dull beige walls and was particularly boring in every aspect. Then, when I turned my attention to the final photograph in the series, I was shocked to see a room that was blackened with soot, the charred remains of a sofa and chairs still visible. I hadn't seen any evidence of a fire when I walked around and yet it had been the thing that had flashed into my mind when I'd got into my pranamios breathwork. I had no choice, I would have to send the pictures and just pretend I'd seen the room with the fire in it. I couldn't think of a rational alternative.

"Oh, by the way, I don't know if you know, but some of the house was fire damaged."

"Really? That's very surprising." Polly looked at me with a puzzled expression on her face, giving me a creepy feeling. I went and stood behind her desk, watching as she opened the photos I'd sent her, needing to validate with my own eyes that I wasn't going mad. I held my breath as the images slowly started to reveal themselves on her screen. One by one I saw the strange new photos appear and I had no explanation as to why they were not the same ones that I'd taken.

Polly threw me a strange look. "This can't be right. Wait here a minute while I find the file."

"You already have a file?"

"Yes, we marketed this property a few years ago, and I remember there'd been a fire then."

I drew back slightly from her desk, loitering in the central walkway, my hands clasped in front of me, and not really sure where this was all leading. A few minutes later Polly returned, holding a thin manilla wallet. "We didn't do a lot with this, but I remember a survey was done back then. We'd been instructed to put it up for sale but the seller backed out at the last moment." Polly carefully smoothed the contents of the wallet out onto her desk, showing in plain view a series of photographs which established that the house had looked exactly as my photos showed it.

"Maybe they haven't had any work done on it since then?" I asked, trying to prove my case.

"As I recall they had extensive building work done and that's why they took it off the market, they were going to renovate instead."

I stood silently, staring down at the printed version of the photographs that looked so like mine.

"Look at these... your photos are exactly the same, even down to the angle of the camera. You must have stolen these pictures and made copies, there's no other explanation. Mr Blake isn't going to be happy when he hears about this."

I gasped at the thought, "I'm not a thief. How could I have stolen the photos? You were here before me this morning. I can't get in by myself and you only gave me the address today."

"I don't know how you did it, but it's pretty obvious that you've not taken any new photos, the camera can't lie, can it? You've somehow cheated, maybe so that you didn't have to go into the house at all, I don't know."

"How can you say such horrible things about me? I thought we were friends and that we worked well together?"

Polly gave a non-committal shrug. "We get new people all the time. It's part of my job to try to get on with the new starters, but that's as far as it goes. If I'm honest, I always thought you were a little strange. I will be speaking to Mr Blake – he listens to me."

I was dumbstruck by the hostility in Polly's voice. This was a side of her I hadn't seen before and it now came as no surprise that Ruth had so much time off sick. Polly had been so nice to me before and I couldn't understand how she could change so quickly. She'd helped show me the ropes and seemed to have been patient with my initial blunders, and now she'd turned into the office psychopath, ready to stab me in the back as soon as I was in a vulnerable situation.

I went and sat back down at my desk, mortified that I'd somehow gotten myself into a real mess. Just then, Mr Blake wandered in from the street, looking somewhat stressed and a little agitated. His hair was sticking up in little tufts and it looked like he'd rushed to get there.

"Hello ladies," he said as he set his briefcase down. Cup of tea please Polly, and Luna, I need to see you in my office in five minutes."

I nodded. He was looking a bit grim and that was even before Polly had had time to convince him I was a liar and a cheat.

"Take a deep breath," I heard my dad's voice in my mind, "breathe in for the count of 5 and out for the count of 7. It will help to calm you."

"Thanks dad," I answered in my mind, but I knew that I needed a little bit more than a few deep breaths to get out of this one.

I gathered my few bits and pieces together off the desk, not wanting to leave anything personal around, and popped them into my handbag, then went to sit next to the yucca for a few minutes, feeding from its calming energies. Polly had made the tea and was just about to disappear into Mr Blake's office with it. I didn't want them to have a chance to chat before I'd had my meeting, so I got up quickly and headed over to the door.

"Let me help you, I can give Mr Blake his tea," I smiled brightly at her, and she glowered at me as she handed me the cup, realising that she'd been out-manoeuvred as I knocked on Mr Blake's door, ready for my meeting.

CHAPTER 36

"There is an alchemy in sorrow. It can be transmuted into wisdom, which, if it does not bring joy, can yet bring happiness."

- PEARL S BUCK

M r Blake looked up as I entered with his tea. He was definitely not in the best of moods.

"Please sit down, Luna. We seem to have a rather awkward situation on our hands." Carefully I placed his tea on the coaster so it didn't leave a mark on the polished surface of his desk and then gladly lowered myself into the chair that faced him.

"Something very strange has come to light."

"Yes," I said, nodding and twisting my hands in my lap while I waited for him to continue.

"Oh, so you already know do you?"

"Sorry? Know what?"

"About the Trust?"

"The Trust? No, I'm sorry, I don't know what you're talking about." It was my turn to look puzzled, I thought he was going to mention the photographs, but of course he wouldn't have discovered that little treat yet.

"I'm a man of the world Luna, a business man, and I've dealt with all sorts of situations during my life but, I have to say, there's something that's come to light that I find immensely puzzling."

"Oh?"

"Yes, and what I find particularly strange is that you've come to work here Luna, and in what.... how many weeks now? Three? Four? In just a very short time it would appear that you've landed on your feet in a very unusual way."

"What do you mean?"

Mr Blake put his curled-up fist against his mouth as he

coughed and then took a hearty gulp of tea, coughing again as he spluttered into the cup.

"I received a call earlier today from a friend of mine, who just happens to be a solicitor. We were chatting about some private matters and I mentioned to him that we had a new girl named Luna."

I nodded and waited for him to continue. I'd learned that sometimes it was better to just shut up and listen, especially when someone had a clear agenda about what they wanted to talk about.

"It was a very considerable surprise, both to myself and my friend, because he went on to impart some very strange news to myself."

I braced myself to hear him talk about my abduction. The one big secret that I avoided mentioning at all costs.

"Yes, very strange..." Mr Blake looked down to some notes he'd scribbled on a pad on his desk, my suspense ever increasing as he seemed to labour over how to carry this news forward.

"My friend advised that he had been trying to locate a Miss Luna May Mason for several months". He looked over at me, "I presume that is you? It's the name you gave me when you joined our company"

"Er, yes.. I guess so... that *is* my name."

"Exactly, so I confirmed that you were indeed my employee. Do you know why they have been trying to find you?"

"No sir," I shook my head, feeling mystified.

"It was to advise the beneficiary of an estate."

"An estate? What do you mean?"

"It seems Miss Mason, that an unknown person has placed the property at Sanville Lane in Trust for yourself. This means, in effect, that the house you visited today is technically your property."

"Mine?" I was dumbstruck.

"Yes. I find it very odd that this has transpired, very odd indeed. In retrospect, I'm not even sure why I let you view the property in the first place. What is even stranger is that the request to sell was revoked earlier today – I'd say at around the same time you were actually at the property. I find that rather unusual, don't you? Not only that, but it has lost me substantial revenue and I'm not one to take kindly to a loss of income."

He was doing his best to sound formal. He'd never called me Miss Mason before, always Luna. Now it seemed like a huge barrier had come up between us.

"The trustees of the estate will not divulge the settler's identity, which means it isn't known who has bequeathed you this property. Do you have any idea who might have done such a thing?"

"No, I don't really know anybody who would do that."

"That's what I thought you would say." Mr Blake cleared his throat before continuing, "in the circumstances, I think it's best if we terminate your employment. We can't have an employee making such gains whilst working here. It looks very fraudulent. I'm sure there may even be an enquiry."

"You're sacking me? But I've done nothing wrong!" I could feel the colour draining from my face, hardly believing he would do this.

"Wrong or not, it looks wrong and that's the end of it. It would be best if you leave now. We will pay you up until the end of the month as a gesture of good will and thank you for your services."

"But I really need this job." I cried, thinking of everything I'd planned for the future.

"I'm not sure you've understood what I've just told you

Miss Mason. Very soon you will become the owner of a sizeable property plus an undisclosed sum of money, which is also held in trust for you. In that situation, you almost certainly do not need this job."

Tears started to well up in my eyes. I'd never been fired before. "But I liked working here," I said, lamely.

"Unfortunate then, isn't it? No need to discuss this with Polly, I will talk to her separately. Please collect your things and see yourself out."

I stood up abruptly, feeling a surge of defiance slowly emerging from my sorry self. "I've misjudged you Mr Blake, and Polly too. I thought you were both nice, considerate, kind people. I was wrong. You have no thoughts for anyone but yourselves. You can stick your stupid job where the sun doesn't shine."

Mr Blake glared at me then, and as I turned to walk out of his office I could feel his eyes burning into my retreating back.

Luckily, I thought, I had already collected my things, so I held my head up high and tried my best to make a dignified exit from the building as I swept past Polly. She had a smug look on her face and I was very tempted to slap it off for her, but I recognised that it was not part of who I was anymore - I was not a thug. "Bye Barry, stay in touch," I addressed the Yucca on the way out. He was the most important thing left there, without a doubt.

With a bit of time on my hands before visiting times commenced at the hospital, I kicked around the shops for a bit of window shopping. If what Mr Blake had said was true, I expected the solicitors would contact me directly, assuming he had passed on my details. Mr Blake hadn't given me any further information about the solicitors so I had no way of contacting them.

What it also meant was that if I went back to the house this evening, as the note had requested, I wouldn't really be trespassing because somebody somewhere had decided that it should be mine anyway. A shiver ran down my spine as I thought of it. Growing up already had its fair share of problems and now this.

I arrived at the hospital carrying chocolates, some magazines and a fluffy teddy bear for Amy and although I'd walked past the florist's I knew that the hospital wouldn't allow them on the ward. Laden as I was, I decided to visit Amy first this time and mum after.

"Hey Pudding'... Santa's arrived." I thrust my gifts towards her and she took them from me with a small smile on her face. "Guess what? I've been given the all-clear to go back to the home tomorrow. Anne has arranged a taxi for me at eleven."

"That's good. And when you're nicely settled we can talk some more about the future. Our future together. Would you like that?"

Amy nodded and stuck a piece of chocolate into her mouth. My heart filled with love as I watched her enjoy the feast, gobbling it up as if she was on rations. I loved her so much and apart from mum, she was pretty much all I'd got. I decided that in the next couple of weeks I was going to tell Amy everything about my abduction. She had a right to know, and of all the people I could trust, she would be the one.

"Am I too old for a teddy bear? Amy asked at last, turning the soft white bear over as if it was doing a somersault on the bed.

"No one is ever too old for teddies." I smiled. She was so different to me at that age, but then I hadn't had chance to be a normal girl after the age of fifteen either. Perhaps we had more in common than I thought.

Our chat was light and fun, we teased each other and she seemed in much brighter spirits than the day before. There was no need to burden her with my recent dismissal. They could stuff their job.

Eventually our conversation turned to boys, and when I confessed to her that I was still a virgin, Amy laughed so much I thought she would roll off the bed. Her cheeks were flushed with pink as she gasped for breath. "Oh Luna, and I thought you were the one most likely to get laid first. All the boys fancied you, you know."

"No they didn't."

"Yes they did, you were dark and mysterious. Didn't you notice how they tried to get your attention?"

"Amy, you're making that up! How would you possibly know, you were only nine back then."

"Yeah, and I hung about with you and your friends a lot, remember? Of course I knew." She smiled and I smiled with her. The hour together passed quickly and, hugging her goodbye, I felt happier once more, everything would be alright, I would fix whatever I could. I felt smiley on the inside as I walked away and over to the ward my mum was in.

As I approached the ICU ward and got closer to mum's bed however, my high spirits quickly plummeted once more. I was tired of the way my emotions roller-coasted out of my control. I felt like a leaf in the breeze, constantly buffeted by the events that kept interrupting the normality of my life.

Mum's face had taken on a grey tinge and she looked lifeless and unresponsive. I sat at her bedside and read her a couple of short stories from my Kindle, stumbling over the words because my eyes kept misting over. The nurse on duty was watching over my mum vigilantly, ultimately responsible for any change. As I looked around the unit, I could count eight patients, all of whom looked seriously ill, just like my mum. There were other visitors at a couple of the other bedsides too and everyone looked gravely serious.

The nurse approached me shortly after I'd finished reading. "The consultant on duty would like to speak to you if at all possible."

"Thank you, that would be really helpful."

"He'll be along in a few minutes." I thanked the nurse again and continued to watch my mum breathing through the ventilator. She was wired up to so many drips and monitors I couldn't begin to imagine what they were all for.

There were so many things I wanted to tell her, things that should have been said a long time ago, but I'd been too immature and ungrateful to see it.

"I'm so sorry mum," I whispered, emotion welling up inside me. "I was mean and cruel and didn't understand what you were going through." I paused, gently holding the hand closest to me, avoiding where needles were inserted into her veins. Her skin looked so thin, as if it were tissue paper. "I know you didn't want us to talk about dad, and I didn't understand why back then, but I guess now I do. It's really hard to talk about people we won't see again, isn't it, mum?"

I wished she could answer me but there was just the sound of her breath through the ventilator. I carried on talking, needing to tell her how it was with me, because I'd never truly let her into my life once I'd become a teenager. I'd treated her darkly and when I thought of all the time we had lost through bickering and arguing, I could have wept with regret.

"I guess I felt lost and alone, but I was stupid, because I was never really alone. You were there for me, through everything, even when I was so horrible to you. I'm sorry I never thought more about you. I love you, and I really need you to know that."

I wanted to keep talking, to keep that thin thread of connection between us alive, but there was not a single sign that she could hear anything I said and I drifted into the silent darkness of my mind.

The consultant swept into the room, a concerned look upon his face. Seeing me at my mum's bed he acknowledged my presence with a professional smile and asked if I would like to step into a quiet room to discuss my mother's care. I quickly agreed and the nurse also followed us into a small space with three chairs. I looked up to the sound of his voice, "Miss Mason, I'm Dr Roberts, one of the consultants in charge of your mother's care here. Please have a seat." I did as he asked and waited for him to continue. "At present your mother isn't responding to the medication we're giving her. Her heart is very weak, but we are supporting her the best we can. We are also closely monitoring all her vital signs, including blood pressure, oxygen levels, urine and so on."

His voice was measured and slow, pausing often to give me chance to catch up with what he was saying, probably because he was so accustomed to giving out the kind of really bad news that people couldn't take in quickly.

"This is going to be very difficult to hear, but the next 24 to 48 hours is going to be crucial. Your mother is very weak and requiring an increasing amount of support to keep her alive. Because she is so weak, we will be treating her conservatively, which means that we are not considering surgery to be an option at this moment. Are you in agreement with that?"

I nodded, they would obviously know what was best.

"We are going to increase your mother's medication, but we do have a ceiling limit. If your mother is unresponsive once we reach that limit then unfortunately the outlook is not very favourable. Your mother's major organs are failing and I think it best you prepare for the worst and contact any family that may want to see her. I have to inform you that the prognosis is not looking good and it's unlikely your mum will recover."

"So, she's dying?"

"Yes, unfortunately that would seem to be the most likely outcome."

"Thank you, doctor." I scraped the chair away from beneath me and exited the room quickly, wiping my eyes on my sleeve.

I didn't want to stay there any longer. If felt like my mum had already left and all that remained was the broken shell that she'd lived in whilst alive.

As I walked away I had the overwhelming feeling that I would never see my mum alive again.

CHAPTER 37

"You may be deceived if you trust too much, but you will live in torment unless you trust enough."

— FRANK CRANE

The next morning, I stayed in bed until after ten. It was the latest I'd slept in for a long time, although several times in the night I'd startled awake, feeling uncomfortable and restless. I couldn't stop my thoughts from churning, going over and over all the recent events. If mum died Amy and I would technically be orphans, and I just couldn't imagine how that would feel, to have no-one to turn to, because even though I'd been away from mum for such a long time, I still had the knowledge that she was "there". There was a strong sense of irony in the fact that Mrs Clarke was now acting like a surrogate mum to me, considering how much she used to get on my nerves in the past.

I also wondered whether Amy would visit mum if she knew how seriously ill she was and I contemplated phoning her so that she could visit before leaving the hospital. I opted for texting instead, the coward's way out, but she'd made it very clear to me last time I'd spoken to her that she wanted nothing to do with mum ever again.

"Hi Puds, just to let you know, mum is very, very ill. I know you said you wanted nothing to do with her, but the doctors told me to tell family. If you did want to see her please do it now, before it's too late. Xxx." There was no reply and I hadn't expected one. This decision could only be Amy's.

Mrs Clarke fussed around me when I finally went downstairs, waiting on me with cornflakes, toast and tea. I'd told her how things were at the hospital and she listened with a sympathetic ear.

"I'll go spend some time with your mum today Luna, it's well overdue. You need to have a rest - all this is too much for you."

"Yes, that would be lovely, I think mum would like that and I am feeling pretty exhausted."

We both smiled at each other, a warm, open smile of friendship and I breathed a little easier. I hadn't told her about the house yet and wondered when I should. It was a huge secret to keep but until the solicitors got in touch with me, I wouldn't really be able to say it was mine.

The day dragged slowly, I decided not to go back to the hospital because it felt too intense and difficult. Mum's health was pretty much all I could think about and my fretting over it had overshadowed my thoughts about the house and my intention to return that evening. I knew Amy was busy back at the home, and that she was helping to organise their annual summer fete. Her last text to me had said she would see me the following day, which meant I had loads of free time on my hands. She hadn't mentioned whether she had visited mum or not and I decided not to press the matter.

There was really nothing I felt like doing and without a job to go to I was restless and bored. I'd also have to let the Job Centre know I'd been dismissed, and I couldn't imagine what James would think to that. He'd virtually stopped texting me now and had given up asking for a date. I knew he had liked me and I hadn't been sure what to do with that. I hadn't really even had a boyfriend, except for the very intense relationship with Isayel. That couldn't count, because we hadn't done stuff that normal people did. I wanted to be taken out to dinner and to go to the cinema, be bought flowers and chocolates and dance the night away in a club. I'd missed so much of my life and I couldn't help but feel different to everybody else and wonder if I would ever truly fit in with any of my old life again.

As the afternoon progressed, I became more and more agitated. It was a nervous excitement that filled me up, anticipating the thrill of going back inside the house and opening the envelopes inside the box, but it would be reckless to go on my own. I finally decided the matter by tossing a coin, whether to take someone with me or not... the silver ten pence flipped into the air and landed heads up, which I'd allocated to mean "yes". That settled it then, but the other bit was going to be extremely tricky to explain.

I wandered downstairs, where Mrs Clarke was standing up watching television and ironing at the same time.

"Mrs Clarke, do you have any plans tonight?" I still addressed her in this very formal way and she'd never asked me to call her by her first name.

"No dear, just the television and maybe a pizza for tea. What about you?" This was it, no turning back.

"I do actually have something to do, and it's a bit of a strange errand. I wondered if you'd like to come with me?"

"Come with you? Where to, love?" she looked up quickly but then carried on focusing on getting the creases out of her blouse.

"Do you remember me telling you about the house I had to visit at work?"

"Oh yes, it's lovely round there, isn't it? Nice and quiet."

"Er, yes... well, I need to go back."

"At this time of night? Whatever for? They shouldn't have you working evenings Luna."

"Actually, it's not connected with work, it's something personal I need to do."

"Is it legal?"

"Erm, yes... sort of...."

"Sort of? I don't like the sound of that. You're not in any trouble are you?"

"No, nothing like that. It's a very long story but I do have the key to get back into the house and I have had permission from the owner. In fact, it was a message from the owner that asked me to call back round. It's just that, well, just that I didn't want to go on my own."

"No, quite right dear. You mustn't go wandering off into strange houses on your own. I'll come with you, just let me know when you want to leave."

"That's really kind of you, thank you." There, that didn't seem as difficult as I'd expected, and there was a kind of subdued buzz around us as we left the house and set off in the direction of Sanville Lane.

We'd decided to walk and the lighter nights made it a pleasant evening stroll. To anybody looking at us from the outside, we might have been mother and daughter, or auntie and niece, which was a nice, comfortable feeling. It was a walk that took about half an hour and I was surprised to notice how easily Mrs Clarke kept up with me, briskly matching my pace and not seeming out of breath at all.

"I didn't realise you were so fit," I said, breaking the comfortable silence between us.

"Oh yes, don't let this extra bit of weight fool you. It's only recently that I've slowed down a bit."

Soon enough, we passed through the churchyard and crossed over, down the narrow lane, just minutes from our destination. Several cars were parked up at the roadside, thinning out as we passed the pub and approached the turning that led to the house. It didn't actually have a number but was named

"Healing Waters", unusually so, I thought, because although the canal was close by, it didn't look particularly healing and I doubted anyone would even want to put a toe in there.

Mrs Clarke looked inordinately pleased with the exterior of the place. "Oh. It's lovely, isn't it?" I agreed, it was lovely, even in its neglected state. The word "lovely" seemed to be the most over-used word in Mrs Clarke's dictionary and was added to almost everything she had an opinion about. I smiled at her positive outlook, it counted for a lot.

I took the key out of my pocket and turned it slowly, feeling the pressure on my fingers as the mechanism clicked and allowed us entry. It was a few minutes to nine o'clock, the time I'd been asked to return, and it was still light outside. I tested the lights in the house, knowing that it would soon be getting dark, and was surprised that they still worked.

"I need to go upstairs for a moment. Will you be alright down here on your own?"

"Oh yes dear, if you don't mind I'll just have a wander about."

"Yes, that should be fine, but please remember we're not allowed to touch anything."

Mrs Clarke smiled innocently, "but of course I won't." With that ambiguous reply ringing in my ears I bounded quickly up the stairs.

Everything was just as I remembered it, and I walked past the various bedrooms which led off the main landing and towards the particular room I was heading for, which was at the far end, where there was a small step, followed a gentle curve round. On entering the room, I smiled at the painting of Isayel. It wasn't such a shock to see it there now, and it made this room feel homely and safe to me – after all, it was my painting.

The box containing the envelopes was exactly where I'd left it and I carefully took it out and held envelope number

2 in my hands. It was nine o'clock exactly. Tearing it open I found another key. This one was large, black and ornately carved and I immediately knew what it was for, which was confirmed after reading the note:

"Dearest Luna, thank you for returning, it shows your spirit and your bravery. I know you may be wondering what you're doing here but all will become clear in the fullness of time.

Enclosed you will have found the second key. This is the key to the locked door downstairs. Prepare for your biggest surprise yet and take the third envelope with you – you will need it."

I took the envelopes and the key, carefully putting the box away again so that the room looked just as I had found it. Walking back into the lounge I found Mrs Clarke standing at the window, looking out into the street. She turned on my approach, letting her hand fall away from the curtaining, ruffling it slightly as she moved.

"Lovely view too," she said. "I'm glad you let me come with you Luna."

"Yes, I'm pleased you came too. I need to do a few more things before we leave, is that alright?"

"Oh, take your time, my lovely. This is much better than watching the television at home."

I gingerly placed the large black key into the Gothic lock, my heart pounding. I felt crazy, wondering what I'd got myself into. Having panicked about dismembered parts being in the small box upstairs and dead bodies behind the front door, I couldn't even begin to imagine what might be lurking behind this one. The key turned and I pushed the handle down with some effort. It seemed very stiff and as if nobody had entered for quite some time. The door swung open with a slow creak and I looked into the darkness, unable to see anything except the first few steps down into what looked to be a cellar.

I fumbled around the walls inside the door casing, brushing cobwebs which made me squeal and jump back. "There must be a light switch,"

"Perhaps a little lower dear?" Mrs Clarke suggested helpfully. I braced myself, expecting more cobwebby sensations but my hands contacted with a switch instead, lighting up the stairway and the first section of a corridor beyond.

"Wow, this is amazing. This must run all the way underneath the house."

"Would you like me to come with you?" Mrs Clarke raised a carefully thinned out eyebrow.

"Yes, I think so... it's a bit scary, isn't it?"

"Not scary Luna, an adventure... I'm sure you've been through worse." She was right, of course, I'd survived all sorts of things. There was a solid wooden handrail on the left-hand side, matching the thick wooden steps down. I held on firmly as I made my way down, with Mrs Clarke following behind me. Down and down we went, and just as the light was starting to dim again, I spied another switch on the wall ahead, which activated another series of lights.

"How can all this be under one house?"

"Intriguing, isn't it? I looked across at Mrs Clarke, she didn't look surprised or concerned at all and I was amazed at her calm composure.

The corridor opened up to a wide central space which was furnished with sofas and chairs and an open plan kitchen, complete with all the utensils and white goods needed to make it totally serviceable.

"Wow, this is amazing. I never expected this, it's like a whole self-contained apartment." I opened a door leading off and found another bathroom and two further bedrooms, all functional, with beds ready made-up. The ceilings were high too, towering above us, giving the impression of so much space.

"There must be ventilation somewhere, because we wouldn't be able to breathe down here else, would we?"

Mrs Clarke nodded. "I'm sure it's all taken care of, dear."

There was one more door that was very different to the rest, which was situated at the end of a further small corridor of no more than a few feet in length. This door was solid metal and had a sliding door at eye level.

"I don't like this," I looked at Mrs Clarke for reassurance.

"It will be alright. Why don't you take a peek? I'm here with you, don't worry." My hand trembled violently as I reached the sliding door and pushed it aside. A metal grill was exposed underneath and I stared through it into the darkened room beyond. My heart was pounding... boom... boom... boom... like a hammer, pushing the adrenalin around my body. There was someone or something lying huddled under a blanket on a large framed pallet which was pushed close to the far wall.

"What the hell is that?" I whispered.

Mrs Clarke came up behind me, "I think we should open the door, don't you?"

"No, I definitely don't! What if it's a dead body? Look, it's not moving! Or maybe it's someone pretending to be asleep who might leap out and attack us? Whatever is in there, there must be good reason why it's locked up!" My whole body had started to pour with sweat, and all I wanted to do was get as far away as I could.

"Open the door Luna." Mrs Clarke held out a key to me, one that I'd never seen before.

"Where did you get that?" I looked at her in alarm, starting to feel even more fearful than before.

"I've had this key for many years but, sadly, haven't been able to use it. You see, it takes a special person to open this door, it's what you might call rune-bound."

"What?"

"Yes, locked against me by forces even greater than my own." As she spoke Mrs Clarke's voice began to change, becoming deep and throaty. "Don't look so surprised, it's not all bad."

As I continued to look across at her, her appearance began to change too. I watched in fascinated horror as the rolls of tubby middle-aged fat disappeared, together with the frumpy old-fashioned clothes that I'd always seen her wear, to be replaced by her customary black flowing robes. Her hair, in the guise of Mrs Clarke, was a nondescript ash brown, now transformed into an abundance of dark, bouncy curls that nestled round her attractive, but unmistakable face. Green eyes stared at me from dark lashes and a secret smile played upon her lips.

"Keysha!"

"Indeed. I imagine this is a little surprising for you."

"You... are... Mrs Clarke?"

"Yes... always... and I've always been in your life Luna, although often disguised. My special talent is shapeshifting, you see, and it's been a wonderful experience to see how you've changed over the years."

I shook my head, this could truly not be happening to me.

"I've tried to guide you through the years, to encourage your behaviour but... well, you were always a precocious child and when your father died it was easy to see how problematic that would be for you."

"You nearly killed me," I turned an accusing stare in her direction.

"No, my job has never been to kill you. Do you not think that I could have done that a thousand times over, if I'd wanted to? I kept you safe and I kept you out of danger."

"You beat me, starved me and made me eat bugs."

"All for your own good Luna. We don't learn to be strong unless we are challenged. We learn through adversity, failure and hardship. I kept you alive and made you tough - tougher than you even know yourself yet. All I've ever done has always been for your own protection and future resilience."

"Does that include stealing my chance at happiness with Isayel?"

"Ah that.. yes… it was a little diversion.. I needed a little something for myself, you see. But not to worry, I have no long-term interest in him. As far as I'm concerned you can keep your little love interest for yourself."

I was rendered speechless, truly shocked. Under the guise of Mrs Clarke she had been a total life saver, giving me the shelter of her home, feeding me and looking after me without complaint for the last few months. As Keysha she had cruelly snatched away my one chance at happiness with Isayel and the opportunity for me to be the mother of his child.

Keysha looked directly at me, "our friends do not always deserve us, and we do not always deserve our enemies, but you will come to trust me Luna, because you will see that, despite all appearances to the contrary, you and I are on the same side."

"How can I trust you after what you did to me?"

"You will."

"What's in the dungeon?" I turned my attention back to the grated door, fearful in case she had any thoughts about throwing me in there too.

"That, dear, sweet Luna, is my child or, to be precise, mine and Isayel's child. I named him Isaké, after the both of us."

"The Nephilim?" My eyes widened, I'd heard the tales about the murderous Nephilim, who destroyed everything they came into contact with.

"Yes, Nephilim, but this one is different. You see, I'm not just an ordinary human woman, as you know. I have... certain powers... certain skills. My offspring will not be a monster."

"Yet it's locked up?"

"Merely a safeguard, a precaution."

"And unable to move?"

Keysha studied me as a full dawning came into my mind,

"you've put symbols on him, haven't you?"

"Yes Luna, it has to be that way for now, for his own protection too."

"How could you do that to your own child?"

"He's not a child as you would think it, and he is perfectly safe in the mindscape where he is."

"I know what's in that mindscape."

"Yes, you do... it's something you both have in common now, and perhaps it will forge an unlikely connection between you both in the future."

I didn't want to listen to her any further, "I want to go home..." as I said it, I realised that I no longer even had a place to call home now, because Mrs Clarke was not even a real person and there was no way I could sleep in her house ever again.

"I'm never going to open the dungeon for you. Your child will have to stay in there forever."

"I thought you might be a little reluctant, which is why I kept hold of this." Keysha waved the third envelope at me.

"You will be very interested to know what this envelope contains."

"How did you get that?"

"You left it on the counter top, and I'm just looking after it for you."

"It's mine, meant for me, give it back." I went to snatch the envelope but Keysha lifted it gracefully out of the way. "It's as much mine as it is yours Luna, for I am the author of these little notes."

Once more she shocked me. Keysha wrote the notes!

"Don't you see? The clue is in my name really, named by an ancient tribe in a distant place. I am Keysha, Keeper of the Keys. No lock can keep me out, no door can bar my way – except this one, and this is the most important door of all, at least to me."

"Who locked the door so you couldn't open it?"

"That I cannot tell you but, know that this is my house, which I have bequeathed to you... a generous gift, don't you think? But not a free one, because in order to claim it as your own you will need to open the dungeon door for me."

"So that I can share my house with a monster?" I shouted, anguished and upset at the whole turn of events.

"How dare you call my child a monster. Isaké is no monster." She looked wounded and for a moment I felt sorry for her. Maybe she *was* trustworthy, it was true that she could have done away with me at any time, even back on the Omicron.

"I will make a promise to you Luna. Isaké will sleep on, whether the door is opened or not, but as a mother I have a right to care for and love my own child. I kept you safe and I would do the same for him."

"How do I know you will keep him in the mindscape?"

"Because to prevent him from being afflicted by his bloodline and genetic make-up, I need to perform a very powerful alchemical spell working which will take many years to put together. To start with, I need to travel to Zarnett-9 to find herbs and minerals that are only available there, and then to other settlements on other planets for different components. Before I can even perform such a spell, I need certain lunar and solar alignments, a west wind, rainwater from a storm filled sky, not to mention raw spun silk from the spirits of 6,000 silk worms not of this world, in order to make Isaké a shroud. And believe me, when I have completed my magic, Isaké will be everything he needs to be."

She sounded convincing, but Keysha had tricked me before.

"I'm not sure..."

"Luna, it was myself that created this place. It was I who created the dungeon and I who placed Isaké in there. Me, his own mother. Why would I do that unless I was responsible? Do you not think I know more than anybody about what my son needs?"

I sighed, she was beating me down with her arguments. If she had put him in the dungeon in the first place, then maybe it would be alright to unlock the door.

"Unlock the door for me Luna and I will give you this third envelope – and trust me, when I say that whatever is contained in here will entirely change your life."

CHAPTER 38

"I know the hard ground and the taste of the salt water I'm made of and the way even getting out of bed feels impossible some days. I know how some moments there's not even enough air.

I know the desperate and the bargains you want to make with the universe and every last prayer you've prayed to gods you don't even believe in.

But stupid? No, love.

Not stupid. Not you. You are infinitely, impossibly, beautifully human."

— JEANETTE LEBLANC

I felt torn between my new-found friendship with Mrs Clarke and my old hatred of Keysha. The fact that they were one and the same person confused the hell out of me and I really wasn't sure whether I should place any trust in her at all. But she hadn't let me die back on The Omicron and she'd looked after me so nicely recently in the guise of Mrs Clarke, so maybe there was some good in her?

My own life was such a shambles it was difficult to think on a more global scale. If Keysha released that abomination that was locked in the dungeon, and if he went on the rampage and hurt people, would it matter? It wouldn't matter to me, would it? Except I couldn't help but think of those faceless, nameless people who might suffer because of him.

"Let me open the envelope first and then I will unlock the door." I agreed finally, trying to gain some control over my thoughts.

"That's a good girl, you've made the right choice. Here…" Keysha held out the envelope and I took it carefully from her outstretched fingers.

Opening it slowly, I read the beautiful Copperplate writing out loud,

> "*my dearest Luna, chances are that, as you read this, we are now in the same room together. This means I will have had chance to explain a little more about this whole situation. Inside this envelope you will find not a key, but a crystal. This is a very special artefact which will be of great benefit to you one day, guard it carefully. Your next instruction is to enter the garden at the rear of the house.*

*Sit down there and use your training to con-
nect you to the earth's treasures. If you are
worthy, you will be guided."*

I turned the paper over but the back of it was blank.

"Is that it?" Keysha nodded and I thrust my hand into the envelope, bringing out a perfectly round stone that shimmered with a milky whiteness.

"And you want me to go outside and leave you here with... with Isaké, trusting you to not do anything dangerous?"

"That's right."

I stood for a moment, perfectly still but with my mind racing, as I studied the emerald green of her eyes and the cool way she was surveying me. She could break me at any moment, I knew this. If I opened the door, she might have no further use for me and kill me anyway, but... I had made a promise.

I took the proffered key from her hand and walked over to the dungeon door. The form on the pallet hadn't moved and that, at least, gave me a small measure of comfort. The key was a smooth fit and it turned easily for me, allowing the door to swing open. As soon as it did so, Keysha pushed past me and rushed ahead into the small room, "Isaké, my love," she crooned, bending over the huddle.

I watched as she lifted the blanket from around him, and gasped in shock when I saw his face. A distorted, twisted looking being, eyes closed, heavy jaw hanging open and congested with foaming spittle and drool, which had pooled around the soiled mattress that he was resting on. His body looked misshapen and deformed, about the size of a small pony or a very large dog. Would a child of mine turn out like that?

"Oh, my sweet angel," she cried, oblivious to my presence

and cradling his head to her bosom. She rocked him then, his heavy head supported against her as she crooned a lullaby and whispered of her love whilst he slept on, oblivious.

As I watched Keysha fawn over her freakish offspring I was driven by pure instinct, knowing exactly what I had to do. Very quickly I closed the door on them both and turned the key in the lock. Keysha had been totally absorbed in her ministrations with Isaké but as soon as she heard the slam of the door she dropped his head back onto the pillow, turned and leapt towards me, her eyes glowing like green coals burning two holes in her face. A wall of anger flowed all around her.

"What are you doing you stupid girl? Let me out! Open the door!"

"I'm doing exactly what you did to me. You left me in that terrible place, an inch from death, locked away with no chance to escape. Perhaps it's karma that I get the chance to repay the favour."

"You don't know what you're doing. You will be sorry you ever crossed me," she spat, her whole face contorted with rage. "Open this door!"

I was truly scared then, knowing what a terrible adversary I'd made, but there was no way on earth that I could change what I'd just done.

"I'm sorry, truly I am, but I had to do it. I can't trust you."

She clasped the bars with her hands, knuckles whitening under the pressure of her grip as she pushed and pulled at the grill, almost with an expectation that they would just lift out of their casings, but they proved to be solid and unyielding.

I avoided looking into her eyes as I placed the key safely in my pocket and made my retreat back up the stairwell, turning off the lights as I went and ensuring that the door at the top of the stairs was also locked tightly shut. All the while Keysha's shouts followed me as she screeched her profanities into the space between us. As soon as the second door was sealed I breathed a sigh of relief, no sound could penetrate through this barrier and in the silence I could almost pretend that nothing had happened.

I couldn't escape into the garden quick enough and as the coolness of the night washed over me I took a great big gulp of air and leaned forward, hands on knees. I could hardly believe what I'd just done, but Keysha seemed too much of a threat to leave wandering around. Isaké was a truly monstrous looking creature that would never be able to exist in the modern world on Earth and it made me sick to think that Isayel had fathered such a beast. It took me several minutes to calm my mind and, listening to the natural night sounds of insects and nocturnal creatures scurrying through the wild parts of the garden, I felt reassured that I could hear no screams or shouts coming from inside the house.

My eyes slowly adjusted to the darkness and I could just make out the soft outline of an old arbour placed on the lawn area. I wandered over to it, wading through the long grasses that dampened my shoes and the lower parts of my trousers. Sitting down on the firm wooden surface I tried to focus on my breath and ignore the cold damp that was penetrating through the wooden planking into my rear end and lower back.

Tendrils of honeysuckle and clematis climbed around the trellis and I breathed in their perfume, slow and steady, calming my mind, reaching out, connecting with this natural world. I was part of nature, and nature was part of me. I kicked off my shoes and allowed my bare feet to sink into the earth, connecting with the subterranean energies beneath its surface. It was like wading through many layers in my mind, and beneath my closed eyelids a kaleidoscope of soft, muted colours started to emerge. I swam into the centre of those colours, pushing through the layers, deeper and deeper into the depths of my being, until language fell away and symbols and impressions began to imprint themselves on the screen in my mind.

Illumination pierced through me, and I had what can only be described as "a knowing" about what to do next. I opened my eyes and stood up, walking with certainty across the garden until I stood in the east, symbolic of new beginnings.

The dark pushed in on me but I wasn't scared. I knew spirits stirred amongst the trees, guardians of the land, spirits of this place, and other life forms which were concealed from mankind's ordinary sight. As my eyes stared out into the darkness, I felt my vision begin to change, adjusting and transforming, enabling me to process my environment with clarity even through the twilight. I'd never experienced this before although Elishia had spoken of it often. It was a sign of great attunement to my surroundings and I felt graced by a magical awe which streamed through me.

Directly in front of me, my gaze fell to a tropical looking plant around three feet tall with an abundance of pink and white flowers protruding from a trunk like, bulbous base. It was unusually situated in an English country garden and looked totally unsuited to a British climate. There was a small stake in the ground by its side, labelled "Desert Rose" and I knelt down in the sodden grasses to study it more closely.

Kneeling there, fingers touching the thickened trunk of the plant, I felt the urge to dig at its base. With clumsy fingers I tried to claw back the soil but it was obstinate against my endeavours. Mud pushed its way beneath my fingernails but as soon as I displaced a section it collapsed back in on itself, making the work futile. I stood up, looking around for any kind of implement, and was pleased to notice a small trowel, perfect for the job, laying at the side of the path. Armed with my new tool I bent once more to the task. The soil was crumbly and soft and I carefully scooped the layers away, not wanting to hurt the plant's root system. It wasn't long before my trowel scraped against something hard and solid. I dug around it, revealing a small silver box. With grubby fingers I lifted the box out of the soil and studied it for a moment. I recognised it as being a trinket box that belonged to Cassiel; I'd seen him with it back on the ship although I'd never witnessed him open it. I wondered how it had found its way here but was beginning to realise that nothing was straightforward anymore. Slowly I wiped the surface soil away from the lid and prised it open. There, nestled inside on a bed of blue velvet, was the necklace that Isayel had given to me on my eighteenth birthday, the gift which I had so thoughtlessly rejected.

Seeing that discarded treasure lying there brought back a flood of difficult memories. The night Isayel had given it to me I'd been swamped by feelings of jealousy. I'd wanted a gift of two hearts entwined as a symbol of our togetherness, wanting to believe that I was the only important person in his life. Instead, the necklace he gave me was a circle of several hearts and I'd thought it cruel at the time, almost a rejection of my singular love for him. Back then I'd been filled with fairy tale thoughts about love and romance, idealistic notions of happy-ever-after and one soaring love that would be to the exclusion of all others.

I'd been crushingly jealous of his friendships with Elisia, Sofia and the other Mothers, even though I knew those relationships were platonic. I'd recognised he had a deep love for these women and I'd hated it, despite recognising what beautiful and graceful souls they were. I could never be equal to any one of them, for they were unconditional in their caring, even down to supporting me in the mindscape where I'd lingered on the fringes of death. They always put other people first and I'd never had that level of kindness in me. I'd been the brat that wanted Isayel all to herself.

Isayel had tried to teach me that love did not diminish in the sharing, but that there was enough love inside him for all the people he cared about. When he spent time with the Mothers he was simply enjoying their company, just as I did when I spent time with Cassiel. I could see the similarities now because I loved Cassiel too, as I might love a brother or close friend, and having that relationship did not lessen my feelings for Isayel.

In a world where we lose connection to others, where objects start to become more valuable than people, it is love that can save us and bring us back from the brink of emotional infertility. It is love that gives the soul a voice and a purpose and love that becomes the light of the world.

I sat all that night through, listening to the night sounds around me and watching the shadows as they oscillated under the moon's soft light. It was a time of just reflecting on the many things that were relevant in my life. I clasped that silver box to me, feeling that I was still somehow connected to those that I loved out there and that maybe I still had a purpose even though I'd been put back onto the earth.

I resolved right there and then to start living my life in a much kinder, more heartfelt way, showing mercy, love and compassion to all that might need it, because we could never know the impact of a smile or a kind word.

For the first time that I could remember I felt that I'd come to terms with all the parts of my life up to that point. My shoulders were broad and I would survive and that gave me a sense of empowerment that I'd never known before.

When the first light of dawn began to soak through the darkness, lifting the stain of night away, my phone rang and I received the heart-breaking news that my mother had passed away.

CHAPTER 39

"We all deserve second chances, but not for the same mistake."

- THABISO OWETHU XABANISA

My hands were numb as I stuffed my phone back into my bag. Mum's death had been expected but, even so, I didn't feel ready for it. So, it was just me and Amy now and a house that could hardly be safely lived in when a monster and a powerful sorceress languished in the dungeons below.

My previous resolve and strength of spirit waivered as I tried to make sense of everything. I could have cried, but I didn't. Nor did I want to re-enter the house. Instead I dragged myself up from the arbour bench, feeling cold and stiff, and walked over to the middle of the lawn, noticing for the first time a perfect circle of decorative paving stones that seemed to be laid out for a special purpose. It was easy to see that this area had been recently maintained because the grass around the circular edge had been trimmed back a foot or so all round. Some of the stones were inscribed with glyphs and there were pointers to show the directions of North, East, South and West. I could feel a powerful undercurrent beneath my feet as I stood in the centre of the circle.

There, in that place, I took my necklace from its box and prised the clasp apart with my soiled fingernails, carefully placing it around my neck. As soon as it connected with my skin images began to flash into my mind. I closed my eyes as this inner reality of times past replayed like a film on an inner screen. Times when I'd made wrong choices or just been downright nasty. That day when I'd seen mum reach for a bottle of wine because I'd told her that I hated her. Other times, when I'd walked off or disappeared, leaving her upset and distressed... it was like I could see what was happening from her perspective back then. She'd started drinking because she couldn't handle dad's death and, on top of that, she couldn't handle me. When I'd been abducted it became so much worse and then mum couldn't handle Amy or even herself. I saw the threads that were woven through that awful, sad story, how there could be no happy ending, only the ruptured fragments of our lives.

From a higher vantage point I witnessed how one event trickled into another, forming a pool of grief, betrayal and misery. Poor Amy's abuse and then disintegration, the hopeless and despondent way she viewed herself and her life, mum's alcoholism, and dad's death - a storybook of tragedy that turned all of our lives upside down.

I could have been the one to make the difference in mum's life. She'd relied on my dad so much that when he died, she'd been broken by it. If I'd changed my behaviour, even by just doing one small thing differently each day, everything else would have changed too. I knew it now, but couldn't see it before when I was so wrapped up in my own selfish problems.

What if... what if instead of insulting her and walking away I had held her hand, or told her that I loved her? What if I had chatted to her about my days at school or made plans for us to have family time together at the weekends? I could have helped her with the housework, washed my own dirty clothes or helped to prepare dinner. There was so much more I could have done for her than what I did. I could have been a proper daughter and allowed her to be my one true mother. Countless 'what ifs' poured through my mind, each one stabbing me with painful regret. It was all too late.

Inside me I could feel a hollow brittleness, like a wall of paper-thin crystal that was disintegrating with every second that passed. I was losing it, and when the tears came they poured from me like a swollen river of pain. I hadn't realised that I'd dropped to my knees until I felt the cold dampness penetrating through my clothing and, as I lay down on the stones, it seemed as if the sobbing no longer came from inside me, but instead it sounded like the distant keening from a wild thing. My cheek scratched against the hard, uncaring surface. This earth. My world.

Above me the skies were blue and clear but my face was turned away from the heavens and towards the womb of the earth, where all of life begins and ends. Beneath me the worms turned the soil, where rot and decay issued forth vitality and new life in a never-ending cycle, the rhythm of all that ever was, still in existence in a different form. I don't know how long I lay there, lost in thought and confusion, but somewhere in the midst of all that, it felt as if I could feel the heartbeat of the earth. It rose up through those stones and pulled me down into a trance-like state of mind. Elisia had called it the Schumann resonance and I felt it pour through my whole being, as if I was an empty vessel that needed to be filled. Then I did something that I had never done in my entire life before, something I had never expected to do. I prayed.

I prayed to God from the tortured depths of my soul. I begged for forgiveness and mercy, throwing myself upon God's benevolence and asking to be absolved of my sins. For the first time in my life I felt a faith that had never been there before and that I could never have imagined feeling. I truly believed in this magnificent, omnipotent entity, in the same way that Isayel and the others believed in him, no longer a figment or an imaginary character in an ancient book, but a truly dynamic living force that transcended all my previous understanding. I felt that he or she, or whomever God truly was, could hear me and that if Isayel was anywhere in the whole of the universe, he would hear me too.

My eyes were still swollen with tears when I prised them open and my blood felt like a crimson whisper flowing through my veins. I allowed my consciousness to settle on the deep throbbing pulse at the base of my throat as I surveyed my surroundings.

Everything looked exactly the same, except – over there, in the North quarter of the circle was a small round indent, like a half cup that could cradle an acorn, except this one had a dark golden metallic veneer. I wondered why I hadn't noticed this before. *"Because it wasn't there before,"* I thought.

Fumbling in my pocket to find the crystal that Keysha had given me earlier, I instinctively knew I needed to use it. I rolled the stone beneath my fingertips, liking the way it felt so smooth and warm against my skin.

I made my way unsteadily to the North quarter, overcome with tiredness, hunger and cold, but determined to see this through. I carefully placed the stone into the indentation, letting it slide into place. It was a perfect fit.

As soon as it dropped into place, a sharp jolt of energy burst through my body and the white heat of it pulsed through me like a throbbing super-charged venom. Within moments I found myself once more on the ground, my neck jarring against the hard surface as a series of mini convulsions ripped through me. I curled myself into a tight ball, defensively trying to protect myself from this charge, burying my head in my hands and squeezing my eyes tightly shut. It would stop soon, it would stop soon. Ragged breath, pain beneath my eyelids, the world spinning away from me. I was nothing, a mere dot in the cosmos, less than a grain of sand or a drop of water in the ocean. I felt I was in the throes of death and at that moment it really didn't matter to me whether I lived or died.

When I next opened my eyes, I was filled with confusion. I looked down at my hands, to see that I was holding my mobile and I slowly scanned the message that lit up the screen.

"Hey, save me from boredom, where are you?"

Disorientated, I looked up and realised I was no longer lying on the ground in the garden at Healing Waters, but instead was standing on the street outside Tara's house. Looking down at my clothes, I realised that they were the same ones I'd been wearing the day I'd been abducted. My heart was pounding as I checked the date on my phone, it was impossible but it read 7th August 2010. The slow realisation dawned on me that I hadn't been taken yet, even though I still had all the memories of my time away etched clearly in my mind. If I hadn't been taken yet... that meant... I stuffed my phone quickly into my pocket and headed towards the canal, breaking into a run. The Omicron would be there and I could be reunited with Isayel, I would have the future with him that I wanted... be able to have his child, become a mother... a burst of joy danced inside me as I sped along in anticipation of seeing my one true love again, only slowing as I approached the house on Sanville Lane. I didn't want to, but couldn't resist glancing up at the window and when I saw the net curtain flutter in that old familiar way a massive feeling of Deja-vu swept over me.

My God, was I stupid? what was I doing?

I stopped still in my tracks outside the house, panting heavily from the run. Hadn't I just had an epiphany of sorts, back in that garden? Hadn't I begged to be released from my sins, prayed for mercy? It dawned on me that my prayers had been answered and that I'd been given a second chance for a reason.

Mum would still be alive now and Amy would be nine years old, an innocent, playing with her dolls. This was a time before the abuse, before the alcoholism and the drugs, before the abduction and the general decline of our family. We could be together again, as a real family that loved and cared for each other.

I could make changes, and grow up to be the woman that I wanted to be. I could support mum, pulling her through the hard times, and be a real sister to Amy too, nurturing her in the same way that The Mothers had nurtured me.

I felt Elisia's spirit smiling down at me in kindness and the radiance of God flicker inside me, like a small rose-coloured flame within my heart. My hand reached up to my neck and I was reassured by the comforting circle of hearts that nestled there. I wasn't alone and I knew that one day the future would open up to me once more but, right now, there were things I needed to sort out.

With a strength of spirit and self-control I never knew I possessed, I dropped my gaze from the window, allowing a slow smile to illuminate my face. With carefully measured steps I turned around, pulled my shoulders back, held my head high and retraced my steps. I would do the right thing. I would go home, with the knowledge held deep inside me that my family came first, and that Isayel and the Omicron could wait for another day.

Printed in Poland
by Amazon Fulfillment
Poland Sp. z o.o., Wrocław

51564775R00230